Dick Francis was one of the most successful post-war National Hunt jockeys. The winner of over 350 races, he was champion jockey in 1953/1954 and rode for HM Queen Elizabeth, the Queen Mother, most famously on Devon Loch in the 1956 Grand National. On his retirement from the saddle, he published his autobiography, *The Sport of Queens*, before going on to write forty-three bestselling novels, a volume of short stories (*Field of 13*), and the biography of Lester Piggott.

During his lifetime Dick Francis received many awards, amongst them the prestigious Crime Writers' Association's Cartier Diamond Dagger for his outstanding contribution to the genre, and three 'best novel' Edgar Allan Poe awards from The Mystery Writers of America. In 1996 he was named by them as Grand Master for a lifetime's achievement. In 1998 he was elected a fellow of the Royal Society of Literature, and was awarded a CBE in the Queen's Birthday Honours List of 2000.

Dick Francis died in February 2010, at the age of eighty-nine, but he remains one of the greatest thriller writers of all time.

Books by Dick Francis

10-LB PENALTY

Dick Francis

PENGUIN BOOKS

PENGUIN BOOKS

Published by the Penguin Group
Penguin Books Ltd, 80 Strand, London WC2R 0RL, England
Penguin Group (USA) Inc., 375 Hudson Street, New York, New York 10014, USA
Penguin Group (Canada), 90 Eglinton Avenue East, Suite 700, Toronto, Ontario, Canada M4P 2Y3
(a division of Pearson Penguin Canada Inc.)
Penguin Ireland, 25 St Stephen's Green, Dublin 2, Ireland (a division of Penguin Books Ltd)
Penguin Group (Australia), 707 Collins Street, Melbourne, Victoria 3008, Australia
(a division of Pearson Australia Group Pty Ltd)
Penguin Books India Pvt Ltd, 11 Community Centre, Panchsheel Park, New Delhi – 110 017, India
Penguin Group (NZ), 67 Apollo Drive, Rosedale, Auckland 0632, New Zealand
(a division of Pearson New Zealand Ltd)
Penguin Books (South Africa) (Pty) Ltd, Block D, Rosebank Office Park,
181 Jan Smuts Avenue, Parktown North, Gauteng 2193, South Africa

Penguin Books Ltd, Registered Offices: 80 Strand, London WC2R 0RL, England

www.penguin.com

First published by Michael Joseph Ltd 1997
Reissued in Penguin Books 2014
001

Typeset by Jouve (UK), Milton Keynes
Printed in Great Britain by Clays Ltd, St Ives plc

ISBN: 978–1–405–91685–1

www.greenpenguin.co.uk

CHAPTER ONE

Glue-sniffing jockeys don't win the Derby.

I'd never sniffed glue in my life.

All the same, I stood before the man whose horses I rode and listened to him telling me he had no further use for my services. He sat behind his large antique paper-covered desk fidgeting with his clean fingernails. His hands were a yellowish white, very smooth.

'I have it on good authority,' he said.

'But I don't!' I protested in bewilderment. 'I've never sniffed glue or anything else. Certainly not cocaine. I've never even smoked pot. It's not true.'

He looked at me coldly with the knowing eyes of a rich, powerful, assured and physically bulky man who had inherited a good brain and a chunk of merchant bank, and trained racehorses prestigiously out of obsession.

I was not yet eighteen at that point and, I now know, immature for my age, though of course I wasn't aware of it at the time. I felt helpless, though, in the face of his inaccurate certainty, and had no idea how to deal with it.

'Sir Vivian...' I began with desperation, but he effortlessly cut me off with his heavier authoritative voice.

'You can clear off at once, Benedict,' he said. 'I'll not have my stable contaminated by rumours of a drug-taking jockey, even if he is an amateur and not much good.' He saw me flinch but went on relentlessly. 'You'll never be a top race rider. You're too big, for one thing, or at least you will be in a year or two and, frankly, you look clumsy on a horse. All arms and legs. In your hands, the most collected jumper turns in a sprawling performance. With that and an unsatisfactory reputation ... well, I no longer want you associated with my stable.'

I stared at him numbly, hurt more deeply by his fairly brutal assessment of my lack of riding ability, which could perhaps be substantiated, rather than by the accusations of drug-taking, which couldn't.

Around me the familiar walls of his stable office seemed to recede, leaving me isolated with a thumping heart and no feeling below the ankles. All the framed photographs of past winners, all the bookshelves and the olive-green wallpaper faded away. I saw only the stony faces spelling out the effective end of my long-held dream of winning all races from the Grand National down.

I expect seventeen is a better age than most to be

chopped off at the ambitious knees. It just didn't feel like it at that moment of the slice of the axe.

'Outside that window,' said Sir Vivian Durridge, pointing, 'a car is waiting for you. The driver says he has a message for you. He's been waiting a good hour or more, while you've been out at riding exercise.'

I followed the direction of his finger, and saw, some way across the raked gravel of the imposing entrance driveway to his porticoed domain, a large black car inhabited solely by a chauffeur in a peaked cap.

'Who is it?' I asked blankly.

Vivian Durridge either didn't know or wasn't telling. He said merely, 'On your way out, you can ask him.'

'But, sir . . .' I began again, and dried to fresh silence in the continuing negation of his distrust.

'I advise you to clean up your act,' he said, making a gesture that directed me to leave. 'And now, I have work to do.'

He looked steadfastly down at his desk and ignored me, and after a few seconds I walked unsteadily over to the high polished door with its gilded knob and let myself out.

It was unfair. I had not cried much in my life but I felt weak then and near to weeping. No one before had pitilessly accused me of something I hadn't done. No one had so ruthlessly despised my riding. I still had a thin skin.

No other good trainer would let me into his stable if Vivian Durridge had kicked me out of his.

In a mist of bewildered misery I crossed the wide Durridge entrance hall, made my way through the heavy front door and crunched across the gravel to where the car and chauffeur waited.

I knew neither of them. The August morning sun gleamed on black spotless bodywork, and the chauffeur with the shiny black peak to his cap let down the window beside him and stretched out a black uniformed arm, silently offering me a white unaddressed envelope.

I took it. The flap was only lightly glued. I peeled it open, drew out a single white card from inside, and read the brief message.

'*Get in the car.*'

Underneath an afterthought had been added.

'*Please.*'

I looked back towards the big house from which I'd been so roughly banned and saw Vivian Durridge standing by his window, watching me. He made no movement: no reconsidering action, no farewell.

I understood none of it.

The handwriting on the card was my father's.

I sat on the back seat of the car for almost an hour while the chauffeur drove at a slow pace through

Sussex, south of London, approaching finally the seaside spread of Brighton.

He would answer none of my questions except to say that he was following instructions, and after a while I stopped asking. Short of jumping out and running free at any of the few traffic-light stops, it seemed I was going to go wherever my father had ordained, and as I had no fear of him I would, from long conditioned habit, do what he asked.

I thought chiefly – and in a mixture of rage and unhappiness – of the scene in Durridge's study, his words circling endlessly in memory and not getting more bearable as time went by.

The black car drifted past Regency town houses and open-fronted souvenir shops, past old grandeur and new-world commercialism, and sighed to a stop on the sea front outside the main door of a large hotel of ancient French architectural pedigree with bright beach towels drying on its decorative wrought-iron balconies.

Porters appeared solicitously. The chauffeur climbed out of his seat and ceremoniously opened the door beside me and, thus prompted, I stood up into the sea air, hearing gulls crying and voices in the distance calling on the wet ebb-tide strand, smelling the salt on the wind and unexpectedly feeling the lift of spirits of the sandcastle holidays of childhood.

The chauffeur made me a small sketch of a bow and pointed at the hotel's main door, and then, still without explaining, he returned to his driving seat and at a convenient moment inserted himself into the flow of traffic and smoothly slid away.

'Luggage, sir?' one of the porters suggested. He was barely older than myself.

I shook my head. For luggage I wore the clothes suitable for first-lot August morning exercise with the Durridge string: jodhpurs, jodhpur boots, short-sleeved sports shirt and harlequin-printed lightweight zipped jacket (unzipped). I carried by its chin-strap my shiny blue helmet. With a conscious effort I walked these inappropriate garments into the grand hotel, but I needn't have worried: the once-formal lobby buzzed like a beehive with people looking normal in cut-off shorts, flip-flop sandals and message-laden T-shirts. The composed woman at the reception desk gave my riding clothes an incurious but definite assessment like a click on an identification parade and answered my slightly hoarse enquiry.

'Mr George Juliard?' she repeated. 'Who shall I say is asking for him?'

'His son.'

She picked up a telephone receiver, pressed buttons, spoke, listened, gave me the news.

'Please go up. Room four-twelve. The lift is to your left.'

My father was standing in an open doorway as I walked down a passage to locate four-twelve. I stopped as I approached him and watched him inspect me, as he customarily did, from my dark curly hair (impervious to straightening by water), to my brown eyes, thin face, lean frame, five foot eleven (or thereabouts) of long legs to unpolished boots: not in any way an impressive experience for an ambitious parent.

'Ben,' he said. He breathed down his nose as if accepting a burden. 'Come in.'

He tried hard always to be a good father, but gave no weight to my infrequent assurances that he succeeded. I was a child he hadn't wanted, the accidental consequence of his teenage infatuation with a woman biologically just old enough to be his own mother. On the day I went to Brighton I was almost as old as he had been when he fathered me.

Over the years I'd gleaned the details. There had been a hullabaloo in both extended families when they were told of the pregnancy, an even worse fuss (product of the times) when my mother refused an abortion, and a frosty turning of backs at the hasty (and happy) wedding.

The marriage-day photograph was the only record I had of my mother, who ironically died of pre-eclampsia at my birth, leaving her very young husband literally holding the baby with his envisaged bright future in ruins, so it was said.

George Juliard, however, who wasn't considered bright for nothing, promptly rearranged his whole life, jettisoning the intended Oxford degree and career in law, persuading his dead wife's sister to add me to her already large family of four sons, and setting forth into the City to learn how to make money. He had paid from the beginning for my keep and later for my education and had further fulfilled his duties by turning up at parent–teacher meetings and punctiliously sending me cards and gifts at Christmas and birthdays. A year ago for my birthday he'd given me an air ticket to America so that I could spend the summer holidays on a horse farm in Virginia owned by the family of a school friend. Many fathers had done less.

I followed him into four-twelve and found without surprise that I was in the sitting-room of a suite directly facing the sea, the English Channel stretching blue-grey to the horizon. When George Juliard had set out with the goal of making money, he had spectacularly hit his target.

'Have you had breakfast?' he asked.

'I'm not hungry.'

He ignored the untruth. 'What did Vivian Durridge say to you?'

'He sacked me.'

'Yes, but what did he *say*?'

'He said I couldn't ride and that I sniffed glue and also cocaine.'

My father stared. 'He said *what*?'

'He said what you asked him to, didn't he? He said he had it on good authority that I took drugs.'

'Did you ask him who his "good authority" was?'

'No.' I hadn't thought of it until too late, in the car.

'You've a lot to learn,' my father said.

'It was no coincidence that you sent a car to wait for me.'

He smiled marginally, light gleaming in his eyes. He was taller than I, with wider shoulders, and in many ways inhabited an intenser, more powerful version of the body I had been growing into during the past five years. His hair was darker than mine, and curlier, a close rug on his Grecian-like head. The firmness in his face, now that he was approaching his late thirties, had already been apparent in his wedding photograph, when the gap in age had showed not at all, where the bridegroom had looked the dominant partner and the bride, smiling in her blue silk dress outside the registry office, had shone with youthful beauty.

'Why did you do it?' I asked, trying to sound more adult than bitter, and not managing it.

'Do what?'

'Get me kicked out.'

'Ah.'

He walked over to a pair of glass doors leading to a balcony and opened them, letting in the vivid coastal air and the high voices from the beach. He stood there silently for a while, breathing deeply, and then, as if making up his mind, he closed the windows purposefully and turned towards me.

'I have a proposition for you,' he said.

'What proposition?'

'It will take a good while to explain.' He lifted a telephone receiver and told the room service that whether or not breakfast had been officially over an hour ago, they were to send up immediately a tray of cereal, milk, hot toast, grilled bacon with tomatoes and mushrooms, an apple, a banana and a pot of tea. 'And don't argue,' he said to me, disconnecting, 'you look as if you haven't eaten for a week.'

I said, 'Did *you* tell Sir Vivian that I take drugs?'

'No, I didn't. Do you?'

'No.'

We looked at each other, virtual strangers though as closely tied as genetically possible. I had lived according to his edicts, had been to his choice of schools, had learned to ride, to ski and to shoot because he had distantly funded my preference for those pursuits, and I had not received tickets for Beyreuth, Covent Garden or La Scala because he didn't enthuse over time spent that way.

I was his product, as most teenage sons were of their fathers. I was also aware of his strict sense of honour, his clear vision of right and wrong and his insistence that shameful acts be acknowledged and paid for, not lied about and covered up. He was, as my four older cousins/brothers told me pityingly, a hard act to follow.

'Sit down,' he said.

The room was warm. I took off my jazzy zipped

jacket and laid it on the floor with my helmet and sat in a light armchair, where he pointed.

'I have been selected,' he said, 'as a candidate in the Hoopwestern by-election, in place of the sitting MP who has died.'

'Er...' I blinked, not quickly taking it in.

'Did you hear what I said?'

'Do you mean... you are running for office?'

'Your American friend Chuck would say I'm running for office, but as this is England, I am standing for Parliament.'

I didn't know what I should say. *Great? How awful? Why?* I said blunderingly, 'Will you get in?'

'It's a marginal seat. A toss up.'

I looked vaguely round the impersonal room. He waited with a shade of impatience.

'What is the proposition?' I asked.

'Well, now...' Somewhere within him he relaxed. 'Vivian Durridge treated you harshly.'

'Yes, he did.'

'Accusing you of taking drugs... That was his own invention.'

'But what *for*?' I asked, bewildered. 'If he didn't want me around, why didn't he just say so?'

'He told me you would never be more than an average-standard amateur. Never a top professional jockey. What you were doing was a waste of time.'

I didn't want to believe it. I couldn't face believing it. I protested vehemently, 'But I enjoy it.'

11

'Yes, and if you look honestly inside yourself, you'll admit that a pleasant waste of time isn't enough for you at this stage.'

'I'm not you,' I said. 'I don't have your . . . your . . .'

'Drive?' he suggested.

I thought it over weakly, and nodded.

'I am satisfied, though,' he said, 'that you have sufficient intelligence and . . . well . . . *courage* . . . for what I have in mind.'

If he intended to flatter me, of course he succeeded. Few young boys could throw overboard such an assessment.

'Father – ' I began.

'I thought we agreed you should call me Dad.'

He had insisted at parent-teacher-schoolboy meetings I should refer to him as 'Dad', and I had done so, but in my mind he was always Father, my formal and controlling authority.

'What do you want me to do?' I said.

He still wouldn't answer straightaway. He looked absent-mindedly out of the window and at my jacket on the floor. He fiddled with his fingers in a way that reminded me of Sir Vivian, and finally he said, 'I want you to take up the place you've been offered at Exeter University.'

'Oh.' I tried not to appear either astonished or annoyed, though I felt both. He went on, however, as if I'd launched into a long audible harangue.

'You've promised yourself a gap year, is that it?'

12

A gap year, so-called, was the currently fashionable pause between school and university, much praised and prized in terms of growing up in worldly experience before graduating academically. A lot to be said for it . . . little against.

'You agreed I should have a gap year,' I protested.

'I didn't prohibit it. That's different.'

'But . . . *can* you prohibit it? And why do you want to?'

'Until you are eighteen I can legally do almost anything that's for your own good or, rather, that I consider is for your own good. You're no fool, Ben. You know that's a fact. For the next three weeks, until your birthday on August thirty-first, I am still in charge of your life.'

I did know it. I also knew that though by right I would receive basic university tuition fees from the state, I would not qualify for living expenses or other grants because of my father's wealth. Working one's way through college, although just possible in some countries, was hardly an option in Britain. Realistically, if my father wouldn't pay for my keep, I wouldn't be going to university, whether Exeter or anywhere else.

I said neutrally, 'When I asked you, ages ago, you said you thought a gap year was a good idea.'

'I didn't know that you intended your gap year to be spent on a racecourse.'

'It's a growing-up experience!'

'It's a minefield of moral traps.'

'You don't trust me!' Even I could hear the out-raged self-regard in my voice. Too near a whine. I said more frostily, 'Because of your example, I would keep out of trouble.'

'No bribes, do you mean?' He was unimpressed by my own shot at flattery. 'You'd throw no races? Everyone would believe in your incorruptibility? Is that it? What about a rumour that you take drugs? Rumours destroy reputations quicker than truth.'

I was silenced. An unproven accusation had that morning rent apart my comfortable illusion that inno-cence could shield one from defamation. My father would no doubt categorise the revelation as 'growing up'.

A knock on the door punctuated my bitter thoughts with the arrival of a breakfast designed to give me a practically guilt-free release from chronic hunger. The necessity of keeping down to a low racing weight had occasionally made me giddy from deprivation. Even as I fell on the food ravenously I marvelled at my father's understanding of what I would actually eat and what I would reject.

'While you eat, you can listen,' he said. 'If you were going to be the world's greatest steeplechase jockey, I wouldn't ask ... what I'm going to ask of you. If you were going to be, say, Isaac Newton, or Mozart, or some other genius, it would be pointless to ask that you should give it up. And I'm not asking you to give up riding altogether, just to give up trying to make it your life.'

Cornflakes and milk were wonderful.

'I have a suspicion,' he said, 'that you intended your gap year to go on for ever.'

I paused in mid munch. Couldn't deny he was right.

'So go to Exeter, Ben. Do your growing up *there*. I don't expect you to get a First. A Second would be fine; a Third is OK, though I guess you'll manage good results, as you always have done, in spite of the disadvantage of your birth date.'

I zoomed through the bacon, tomatoes and mushrooms and accompanied them with toast. Because of the rigid education system that graded schoolchildren by age and not ability, and because I'd been born on the last day of the age-grading year (September 1st would have given me an extra twelve months), I had always been the youngest in the class, always faced with the task of keeping up. A gap year would have levelled things nicely. And he was telling me, of course, that he understood all that, and was forgiving a poor outcome in the degree stakes before I'd even started.

'Before Exeter,' he said, 'I'd like you to work for *me*. I'd like you to come with me to Hoopwestern and help me get elected.'

I stared at him, chewing slowly but no longer tasting the mouthful.

'But,' I said, swallowing, 'I don't know anything about politics.'

'You don't have to. I don't want you to make speeches or any policy statements. I just want you to be with me, to be part of my scene.'

'I don't ... I mean,' I more or less stuttered, 'I don't understand what I could do.'

'Eat your apple,' he said calmly, 'and I'll explain.'

He sat in one of the armchairs and crossed his legs with deliberation, as if he had rehearsed the next bit, and I thought that probably he had indeed gone over it repeatedly in his mind.

'The selection committee who chose me as their candidate,' he said, 'would frankly have preferred me to be married. They said so. They saw my bachelor state as a drawback. I told them therefore that I *had* been married, that my wife had died, and that I had a son. That cheered them up no end. What I'm asking you to do is to be a sort of substitute wife. To come with me in public. To be terribly *nice* to people.'

I said absentmindedly, 'To kiss babies?'

'*I'll* kiss the babies.' He was amused. '*You* can chat up the old ladies, and talk football, cricket and racing to the men.'

I thought of the wild thrill of riding in races. I thought of the intoxication of risking my neck, of pitting such skill as I had against fate and disaster, of completing the bucketing journeys without disgrace. A far cry from chatting up babies.

I yearned for the simple life of carefree reckless speed; the gift given by horses, the gift of skis; and I

16

was beginning to learn, as everyone has to in the end, that all of life's pleasures have strings attached.

I said, 'How could anyone think I would bother with drugs when race-riding itself gives you the biggest high on earth?'

My father said, 'If Vivian said he would take you back, would you go?'

'No.' My answer came instinctively, without thought. Things couldn't be the same. I had gone a long way down reality's road in those few hours of an August Wednesday. I could acknowledge grimly that I would never be my dream jockey. I would never win my Grand National. But patting babies instead? Good grief!

'Polling day,' he said, 'is more than three weeks before term starts at Exeter. You will be eighteen by then...'

'And,' I said, without either joy or regret, 'I wrote to Exeter to say I wouldn't be taking up the place they'd offered me. Even if you instruct me to go, I can't.'

'I overruled your decision,' he told me flatly. 'I thought you might do that. I've observed you, you know, throughout your young life, even if we've never been particularly close. I got in touch with Exeter and reversed your cancellation. They are now expecting your registration. They have arranged lodging for you on campus. Unless you totally rebel and run away, you'll go ahead with your degree.'

I felt a lurching and familiar recognition of this man's power as a force that far outweighed any ordinary family relationship. Even Exeter University had done his bidding.

'But, Father . . .' I said feebly.

'Dad.'

'Dad . . .' The word was wholly inappropriate both for the image of him as the conventionally supportive parent of a schoolboy and for my perception of him as something far different from an average man in a business suit.

The Grand National, for him, I saw, was the road to Downing Street. Winning the race was the Prime Ministership in Number Ten. He was asking me to abandon my own unobtainable dream to help him have a chance of achieving his own.

I looked at the untouched apple and banana and had no more appetite.

I said, 'You don't need me.'

'I need to win votes. You can help with that. If I weren't totally convinced of your value as a constituent-pleaser you wouldn't be sitting here now.'

'Well . . .' I hesitated, 'to be honest, I wish I wasn't.'

I would have been pottering about happily in Vivian Durridge's stable yard, untroubled in my illusions. And I would have been drifting towards a less abrupt, less brutal awakening. I would also, I supposed, have been going to be cumulatively depressed. The alternative future thrust at me now was at least challenging, not a slow slide to nowhere.

'Ben,' he said briskly, almost as if he could read my thoughts, 'give it a try. Enjoy it.'

He gave me an envelope full of money and told me to go out and buy clothes. 'Get anything you need. We're going to Hoopwestern from here.'

'But my stuff – ' I began.

'Your stuff, as you call it, is being packed into a box by Mrs Wells.' Mrs Wells had rented me a room in her house along the road from the Durridge stable. 'I'm paying her until the end of the month,' my father said. 'She's quite pleased about that, though she said, you'd like to know, that you were a nice quiet boy, a pleasure to have around.' He smiled. 'I've arranged for your things to be collected. You'll be reunited with them soon, perhaps tomorrow.'

It was a bit, I thought, like being hit by a tidal wave, and it wasn't the first time he had yanked me out of one easy way of life and set me down on a different path. My dead mother's sister, Aunt Susan (and her husband Harry) who had reluctantly agreed to bring me up, had felt affronted, and said so bitterly and often, when my father plucked me out of the comprehensive school that had been 'good enough' for her four sons, and insisted that I take diction lessons and extra tuition in maths, my best subject, and had by one way or another seen to it that I spent five years of intensive learning in a top fee-paying school, Malvern College.

My cousins/brothers had both envied and sneered, so that effectively I had become the 'only' child that I actually was, not the petted last addition to a big family.

The father who had planned my life to the point of my unsought arrival in Brighton took it for granted that in the last three weeks of his legal guardianship I would still act as he directed.

I suppose, looking back, that many boys of seventeen would have complained and rebelled. All I can say is that they weren't dealing with a trusted and proven benevolent tyranny: and since I knew he meant me the opposite of harm, I took the envelope of money and spent it in the Brighton shops on clothes I thought his constituents would have voted for if they'd been judging a candidate by his teenage son's appearance.

We left Brighton soon after three in the afternoon, and not in the morning's overpowering black car with the unnervingly silent chauffeur (obeying my father's 'no explanation' instructions, it seemed) but in a cheerful metallic coffee-coloured Range Rover with silver and gold garlands of daisy-like flowers in metal paint shining along the sides.

'I'm new in the constituency,' my father said, grinning. 'I need to get myself noticed and recognised.'

He could hardly be missed, I thought. Heads turned

to watch us all along the south coast. Even so, I was unprepared for Hoopwestern (in Dorset), where it seemed that every suitable pole and tree bore a placard saying simply 'VOTE JULIARD'. No one in the town could avoid the message.

He had driven the advertisement-on-wheels from Brighton, with me sitting beside him on the front seat, and on the way he gave me non-stop instruction on what I should say and not say, do and not do, in my new role.

'Politicians,' he said, 'should seldom tell the whole truth.'

'But – '

'And politicians,' he went on, 'should *never* lie.'

'But you told me always to tell the truth.'

He smiled sideways at my simplicity. 'You better damn well tell *me* the truth. But people as a rule believe only what they *want* to believe, and if you tell them anything else they'll call you a trouble-maker and get rid of you and never give you your job back, even if what you said is proved spot on right by time.'

I said slowly, 'I suppose I do know that.'

'On the other hand, to be caught out in a lie is political death, so I don't do it.'

'But what do you say if you're asked a direct question and you can't tell the truth and you can't tell a lie?'

'You say "how very interesting" and change the subject.'

21

He drove the Range Rover with both speed and caution, the way he lived his whole life.

'During the next weeks,' he said, 'people will ask you what I think about this and that. Always say you don't know, they'd better ask me themselves. *Never* repeat to anyone anything I've said, even if I've said it in public. OK?'

'If you say so.'

'Remember this election is a contest. I have political enemies. Not every smiling face is a friend.'

'Do you mean . . . don't trust anyone?'

'That's exactly what I mean. People always kill Caesar. Don't trust *anyone*.'

'But that's cynical!'

'It's the first law of self-preservation.'

I said, 'I'd rather be a jockey.'

He shook his head in sorrow. 'I'm afraid you'll find that every world has its share of villains and cheats, jockeys not excepted.'

He drove into the centre of Hoopwestern, which proved to be one of those old indigenous market towns whose ancient heart had been petrified into a quaint cobbled pedestrian precinct, with the raw pulse of modern commerce springing up in huge office buildings and shopping malls on three sides around a ring road.

'This used to be a farming community,' my father said neutrally. 'Farming is now an industry like the factory here that makes light bulbs and employs more people. I need the light-bulb votes.'

His campaign headquarters, I found, were in a remarkable back-to-back hybrid house with an old bay-windowed frontage facing the cobbled square and a box-like featureless shop behind, one of a row looking out over a half-acre of car park. The house, with basic living accommodation for him (and me) upstairs, had once been a shoe store (now bankrupt because of an aggressive local mall) and was the twin of the place next door to it, a charity gift shop.

The political headquarters bustled with earnest endeavour, brightly coloured telephones, a click-clacking floor-standing photocopier, constant cups of tea, desks, computers, maps on the walls with coloured pins in, directories in heaps, envelopes by the carton-load and three middle-aged women enjoying the fuss.

We had parked in the car park and walked to the unmistakable glass-fronted premises where it not only said VOTE JULIARD in huge letters but displayed three large pictures of my father, all of them projecting a good-natured, intelligent, forward-looking person who would do an excellent job at Westminster.

The three women greeted him with merry cries of pleasure and a stack of problems.

'This is my son,' he said.

The merry smiles were bent my way. They looked me up and down. Three witches, I thought.

'Come in, dear,' one of them said. 'Cup of tea?'

CHAPTER TWO

The double shop, I found, was the regular constituency office of the party to which my father belonged. It was where Dennis Nagle, the previous Member, had lately held his Saturday 'surgeries', being present himself to listen to local problems and do his best to sort them out. Still in his fifties, he had died, poor fellow, of pancreatic cancer. His ambitious wife, Orinda, was reportedly steaming with vitriolic anger since the selection committee had passed her over in favour of my parent to fight to retain the vacant seat at the behest of the central party.

I learned about Orinda by sitting on an inconspicuous stool in a corner and listening to the three helpers describe to my father a visit the dispossessed lady had paid that day to the office.

The thinnest, least motherly help, who was also the most malicious, said with lip-curling glee, 'You'd think she'd be grieving for Dennis, but she just seems furious with him for dying. She talks about "*our* constituents", like she always did. She says she wrote his speeches and formed his opinions. She said it was understood from when Dennis was first ill that she would take his place. She says we three are traitors to be working for you, George. She was absolutely stuttering with rage. She says if you think she'll meekly go away, you have another think coming. And she says she is going to tonight's dinner!'

My father grimaced.

I thought that the selection committee had probably acted with good sense.

From my stool I also learned that the main opposition party was fielding 'a fat slob with zero sex appeal' against my father. His – Paul Bethune's – party had recently picked up a couple of marginal seats in by-elections and were confident of taking Hoopwestern since 'the need for change' was in the air.

In the days that followed I saw his picture everywhere: a grin above the slogan '*Bethune is better. Give him your X.*'

It made me laugh. Was he collecting divorcées?

On that first evening, though, all I learned of him was that he was a local councillor and losing his hair. Incipient baldness might in fact lose him the election, it seemed (never mind his mental suitability). America hadn't elected a bald president since the soldier-hero Eisenhower, and few people nowadays named their babies Dwight.

I learned that votes were won by laughter and lost by dogma. I learned that the virility of George Juliard acted like a friction rub on the pink faces of his helpers.

'My son will come with me to the dinner tonight,' he said. 'He can have Mervyn's place.' Mervyn Teck, he explained was the agent, his chief of staff, who was unavoidably detained in the Midlands.

The three aroused ladies looked me over again, nodding.

'The dinner,' he explained to me briefly, 'is being held at the Sleeping Dragon, the hotel straight across the square from here.' He pointed through the bow-fronted windows, showing me a multi-gabled façade, adorned with endless geraniums in hanging baskets, barely a hundred yards away. 'We'll walk over there at seven-thirty. Short reception. Dinner. Public meeting in the hall to the rear of the hotel. If we get some good hecklers, it may last until midnight.'

'You *want* hecklers?' I said, surprised.

'Of course. They set fire to things. Very dull otherwise.'

I asked weakly, 'What do I wear?'

'Just look tidy. There's a Front Bench bigwig coming. They wheel out the big guns to support a by-election as marginal as this. I'll wear a dinner jacket to start with, but I'll strip off my black tie later. Maybe unbutton my shirt a bit. See how it goes.' He smiled almost calmly, but I could sense excitement running in him deeply. He's a *fighter*, I thought. He's my father, this extraordinary man. He's kicked my dreams away and shown me a different world that I don't like very much, but I'll go with him, as he wants, for a month, and I'll do my best for him, and then we'll see. See how it goes ... as he'd said.

We walked across the square at seven-thirty, I in grey trousers and navy blazer (new from the Brighton shops), he in black tailoring that was in itself a step forward in my education.

He was received with acclaim and clapping. I smiled and smiled at his shoulder and was terribly *nice* to everyone, and shook hand after hand as required. No babies in sight.

'My son,' he gestured. 'This is my son.'

Some of the perhaps eighty people at the reception and dinner were dressed formally like my father, others made political-equality statements like open-necked shirts and gingham with studs.

The Front Bench bigwig came with black bow sharply tied, his wife discreetly diamonded. I watched her being unpretentiously and endlessly charming to strangers, and when I in my turn was introduced to her she clasped my hand warmly and grinned into my eyes as if meeting me was a highlight of her evening. I had a long way to go, I thought, before I could put that amount of genuine and spontaneous friendliness into every greeting. I saw also that Mrs Bigwig's smile was worth a ballot-box full of Xs.

I realised slowly, as the room filled up, that the dinner was a ticket affair; that, except for the Bigwigs and my father, everyone had paid for their presence. My father, it appeared, had paid for me. One of the evening's organising committee was telling him he didn't have to.

'Never accept gifts,' he had warned me on the drive from Brighton. 'Gifts may look harmless, but they can come back to haunt you. Say no. Pay for yourself, understand?'

'Yes, I think so.'

'Never put yourself into the position of having to return a heavy favour when you know what you're being asked to do is wrong.'

'Don't take sweets from strangers?'

'Exactly so.'

The organising lady informed my father that if he had had a wife, her ticket would have been free.

He said with gentle, smiling finality, 'I will pay for my son. Dearest Polly, don't argue.'

Dearest Polly turned to me with mock exasperation. 'Your father. What a man!' Her gaze slid past me and her face and voice changed from blue skies to storm. '*Bugger*,' she said.

I looked, of course, to see the cause of the almost comic disapproval and found it was an earnest-eyed thin woman of forty or so sun-baked summers, whose tan glowed spectacularly against a sleeveless white dress. Blonde streaked hair. Vitality plus.

Dearest Polly said, 'Orinda!' under her breath.

Orinda, the passed-over candidate, was doing her

best to eclipse the chosen rival by wafting round the room embracing everyone extravagantly while saying loudly, 'Daaarling, we must all do our best for the party even if the selectors have made this *ghastly* mistake . . .'

'Damn her,' said Dearest Polly who had been, she told me, a selector herself.

Everyone knew Orinda, of course. She managed to get the cameraman from the local television company to follow her around, so that her white slenderness would hog whatever footage reached the screen.

Dearest Polly quietly fumed, throwing out sizzling news snippets my way as if she would explode if she kept them in.

'Dennis was a cuddly precious, you know. Can't think why he married that *harpy*.'

Dearest Polly, herself on the angular side of cuddly, had one of those long-jawed faces from which condensed kindness and goodwill flowed forth unmistakably. She wore dark red lipstick as if she didn't usually: it was the wrong colour for her yellowish skin.

'Dennis told us he wanted us to select Orinda. She *made* him say it. He knew he was dying.'

Orinda flashed her white teeth at a second cameraman.

'That man's from the *Hoopwestern Gazette*,' Dearest Polly said disgustedly. 'She'll make the front page.'

'But she won't get to Parliament,' I said.

Polly's eyes focused on me with awakening

29

amusement. 'Your father's son, aren't you, then! It was George's ability to identify the essential points that swayed us in his favour. There were seventeen of us on the selection panel, and to begin with most people thought Orinda the obvious choice. I know she took it for granted . . .'

And she'd reckoned without Dearest Polly, I thought. Polly and others of like mind.

Polly said, 'I don't know how she has the nerve to bring her lover!'

'Er . . .' I said. 'What?'

'That man just behind her. He was Dennis's best friend.'

I didn't see how being Dennis's best friend made anyone automatically Orinda's lover, but before I could ask, Polly was claimed away. Dennis's best friend, a person who managed to look unremarkable even in a dinner jacket, seemed abstracted more than attentive, but he did stick faithfully to Orinda's back: rather like a bodyguard, I thought.

I realised in consequence that Mr Bigwig himself had a genuinely serious bodyguard, a young muscular-looking shadow whose attention was directed to the crowd, not his master.

I wondered if my father accepted that bodyguards would be the price of success as he went up his chosen ladder.

He began circling the room and gestured for me to

join him, and I practised being Mrs Bigwig but fell far short of her standard. I could act, but she was real.

There was a general movement into the dining-room next door, where too many tables laid for ten people each were crowded into too small a space. Places were allocated to everyone by name and, my father and I entering almost last, I found that not only were we not expected at the same table – he was put naturally with the Bigwigs and the Constituency Association's chairman – but I was squeezed against a distant wall between a Mrs Leonard Kitchens and Orinda herself.

When she discovered her ignominious location Orinda flamed with fury like a white-hot torch. She stood and quivered and tried to get general attention by tapping a glass with a knife, but the noise was lost in the general bustle of eighty people chattering and clattering into their places. Orinda's angry outburst barely reached further than her knives and forks.

'This is an insult! I always sit at the top table! I *demand*...'

No one listened.

Through the throng I saw Dearest Polly busily settling my father into a place of honour and guessed with irony that Orinda's quandary was Polly's mischief.

Orinda glared at me as I hovered politely waiting for her to sit. She had green eyes, black lashed. Stage grease-paint skin.

'And who are *you*?' she demanded; then bent down

and snatched up the name card in front of my place. My identity left her speechless with her red mouth open.

'I'm his son,' I said lamely. 'Can I help you with your chair?'

She turned her back on me and spoke to her body-guard (lover?) best friend of her dead husband, a characterless-seeming entity with a passive face.

'Do something!' Orinda instructed him.

He glanced past her in my direction and with flat expressionless eyes dismissed me as of no consequence. He silently held Orinda's chair for her to sit down and to my surprise she folded away most of her aggression and sat stonily and with a stiff back, enduring what she couldn't get changed.

At school one learned a good deal about power: who had it and who didn't. (I didn't.) Orinda's under-stated companion had power that easily eclipsed her own, all the more effective for being quiet.

Mrs Leonard Kitchens, on my right, patted my chair with invitation and told me to occupy it. Mrs Leonard Kitchens, large, comfortable in a loose floral dress and with the lilt of a Dorset accent on her tongue, told me that my father looked too young to have a son my size.

'Yes, doesn't he,' I said.

Leonard himself, on her other side, bristled with a bad-tempered moustache and tried unsuccessfully to talk to Orinda across his wife and me. I offered to change places with him: his wife said sharply, 'No.'

Mrs Leonard Kitchens' gift for small talk took us cosily through dinner (egg salad, chicken, strawberries), and I learned that 'my Leonard', her husband, was a nurseryman by trade with fanatical political beliefs and a loathing for Manchester United.

With the chicken Mrs Kitchens, to my surprise, mentioned that Dennis Nagle had been an Under-Secretary of State in the Department of Trade and Industry, not a simple backbencher, as I had somehow surmised. If my father won the seat, he would be a long way behind Dennis in career terms.

Mrs Leonard Kitchens spoke conspiratorily into my right ear. 'Perhaps I shouldn't tell you, dear, but Polly very naughtily changed the name cards over, so as to put Orinda next to you. I saw her. She just laughed. She's never *liked* Orinda.' The semi-whispering voice grew even quieter, so as not to reach the ears on my left. 'Orinda made a great constituency wife, very good at opening fêtes and that sort of thing, but one has to admit she did tend to boss Dennis sometimes. My Leonard was on the selection panel and he voted for her, of course. Men always fall for her, you know.' She drew back and looked at me with her big head on one side. 'You're too young, of course.'

To my dismay I could feel myself going red. Mrs Kitchens laughed her worldly laugh and shovelled her strawberries. Orinda Nagle ignored me throughout, while pouring out non-stop complaints to her companion, who mostly replied with grunts. I thought I would rather be almost anywhere else.

Dinner finally over, the talkative throng rose to its collective feet and transferred down a passage into the large room lit by chandeliers which made the Sleeping Dragon the area's popular magnet for dances, weddings and – as now – political free-for-alls.

Orinda's companion left his name card on the table, and out of not-very-strong curiosity I picked it up.

Mr A.L. Wyvern, it said.

I let 'Mr A.L. Wyvern' fall back among the debris of napkins and coffee cups and, without enthusiasm, drifted along with everyone else to the rows of folding chairs set up for the meeting. I'd read somewhere that affairs like this could draw tiny crowds unworthy of the name, but perhaps because my father was new to the district, almost double the number of the diners had turned up, and the whole place buzzed with the expectation of enjoyment.

It was the first political meeting I'd attended and at that point I would have been happy if it had been my last.

There were speeches from the small row of people up on a platform. The chairman of the Constituency Association rambled on a bit. Mr Bigwig was on his feet for twenty minutes. Mrs Bigwig smiled approvingly throughout.

My father stood up and lightened the proceedings

by making everyone laugh. I could feel my face arranging itself into Mrs Bigwig-type soppiness and knew that in my case anyway it had a lot to do with relief. I had been anxious that he wouldn't grab his audience, that he would embarrass me into squirming agony by being boring.

I suppose I should have known better. He told them what was right with the country, and why. He told them what was wrong with the country, and how to fix it. He gave them a palatable recipe. He told them what they wanted to believe, and he had them stamping their feet and roaring their applause.

The local TV station cameraman filmed the cheers.

Predictably, Orinda hated it. She sat rigidly, her neck as stiff as if she had an unbending rod there instead of vertebrae. I could see the sharp line of her jaw and the grim tight muscles round her mouth. She shouldn't have come, I thought: but perhaps she truly had believed that the selectors had made a ghastly mistake.

Dearest Polly, chief de-selector of Dennis's widow, regarded my father euphorically, as if she had invented him herself; and, indeed, without her he might not have been there to seize the first rung of his destiny.

Eyes alight with the triumph of his reception he asked for questions and, true to his intention, he stripped off his tie. He flung it on the table in front of him, and then he rounded the table so that there was nothing between him on the platform and the crowd below. He opened his arms wide, embracing them. He invited them to join him in a political adventure, to build for a better world and in particular for a better world for the constituents of Hoopwestern.

He held them in his hands. He had them laughing. His timing could have been learned from stand-up comics. He generated excitement, belief, purpose; and I, in my inconspicuous end-of-row seat, I swelled with a mixture of amazement, understanding and finally pride that my parent was publicly delivering the goods.

'I'm here for you,' he said. 'Come to my office across the square. Tell me your concerns, tell me what's troubling you here in Hoopwestern. Tell me who to see, who to listen to. Tell me your history . . . and I'll tell you your future. If you elect me I'll work for you, I'll take your wishes to Westminster, I'll be your voice where it matters. I'll light a bulb or two in the House of Commons . . .'

Laughter drowned him. The light-bulb factory fuelled the town's economy, and he wanted the light-bulb votes.

To do good one needed power, he said. Light bulbs were so much wire and glass without power. In humans, power came from inside, not delivered and metered. Power gave light and warmth. 'If you give me power, I'll light your lamps.'

My father's own electricity galvanised the crowd. They shouted questions, he shouted answers. He was serious where it mattered and funny everywhere else.

He had horror for genocide and sympathy for cats. He dodged cornering demands and promised never to put his name to anything whose consequences he didn't understand.

'Legislation,' he said jokingly, 'often achieves exactly what it is designed to avoid. We all know it. We moan about the results. I promise not to jump into emotional deep ends on your behalf. I beg the brains and common sense of Hoopwesterners to foresee disaster and warn me. I'll raise your voices in whispers, not shouts, because shouts annoy but whispers go round persuasively and travel sweetly to the heart of things, and lead to sensible action.'

Whether they understood him or not, they loved him.

The most dedicated hecklers of the evening proved not to be the Paul Bethune opposition supporters, several of whom had bought tickets to the dinner and who had afterwards formed an aggressive bunch on the flip-up chairs, but my father's presumed political allies (but in fact personal enemies), Orinda Nagle and Leonard Kitchens.

Both of them demanded firm commitments to policies they both approved. Both shouted and pointed fingers. My father answered with unfailing good humour and stuck to the party's overall stated position: he needed also to keep the die-hard backbone votes safely in his bag.

Orinda was professional enough to see she was

outgunned, but she didn't give up trying. Mr A.L. Wyvern narrowed his eyes and sank his ears down into his collar. Mr A.L. Wyvern's influence over Dennis and Orinda waned before my eyes.

My father paid tribute to Dennis Nagle. Orinda, far from placated, said that no way could an inexperienced novice like George Juliard replace her husband, however Hollywood-handsome he might be, however manly his hairy chest, however witty, quick-tongued, charismatic. None of that made up for political know-how.

Someone at the back of the hall booed. There was general laughter, a nervous release of the tension Orinda had begun to build up. The impetus swung back to my father, who sincerely thanked Orinda for her years of service to the party cause and deftly led an appreciation to her by clapping in her direction and encouraging everyone else to copy him. The clapping grew. The crowd gave generous but unaffectionate acclaim.

Orinda, to her impotent fury, was silenced and defeated by this vote of thanks. Leonard Kitchens bounced to his feet to defend her, but was shouted down. Leonard's moustache quivered with frustration, his thick glasses flashing in the light as he swung from side to side like a wounded bull. His cosy wife looked as if she would deliver the *coup de grâce* when she got him home.

My father courteously admired Leonard for his

faithfulness and told him and everyone that if elected he would aim always for Dennis Nagle's high and honest standard. Nothing less was worthy of the people of Hoopwestern.

He had them cheering. He exhorted them again to talk to him personally and the crowd stood and surged forward round the seats to take him at his word.

Dearest Polly chatted happily with the Bigwigs and beckoned me up onto the platform, and Mr Bigwig, regarding the clamorous excited throng, told me that my father already had all the skills that would propel him into high office. 'All he needs is luck – and to keep out of trouble,' he said.

'Trouble like Paul Bethune,' Polly said, nodding.

'What trouble?' asked Bigwig.

'Oh dear!' Polly looked flustered. 'George forbids us to attack Paul Bethune's character. George says negative campaigning can rebound on you. Paul Bethune has a mistress with an illegitimate daughter by him which he's tried hard to hush up and George won't attack him for it.'

Mrs Bigwig looked at me assessingly. 'I suppose there's no shadow over *your* birth, is there, young Ben?'

Polly assured her vehemently. 'No, of course not,' and I wondered if my father, all those years ago, could possibly have reckoned that my legitimacy would one day be important to him. After what I'd learned of him that day I saw that anything was possible, but in fact I stayed as convinced as I'd always been that his marriage to my mother had been an act of natural characteristic honour. I still believed, as I always had, that he would never shirk responsibility for his actions. I knew my birth had been a mistake and, as I'd often said, I had no quarrel at all with the quality of life he'd given me since.

It was indeed midnight by the time most of the crowd left to go home. Mr and Mrs Bigwig had long gone, with chauffeur and bodyguard in attendance. Polly yawned with well-earned fatigue. Orinda and Mr A.L. Wyvern were nowhere to be seen and Mrs Leonard Kitchens had hauled her Leonard away with the rough edge of her energetic tongue.

I waited for my father to the end, not only because I had no key to get into my bedroom above the campaign headquarters but also because he would need someone to unwind on after the cheers had died away. Even at not quite eighteen I knew that triumph needed human company afterwards. I'd gone back to an empty room in Mrs Wells's house after three (infrequent) wins in steeplechases and had had no one to bounce round the place with, no one to hug and yell with, no one to share the uncontainable joy. That night my father needed me. A wife would have been better; but he certainly would need *someone*. So I stayed.

He put his arm round my shoulders.

'*God*,' he said.

'You'll be Prime Minister,' I told him. 'Mr Bigwig fears it.'

He looked at me vaguely, his eyes shining. 'Why should he or anyone fear it?'

'They always kill Caesar. You said so.'

'What?'

'You were brilliant.'

'I can do without your sarcasm, Ben.'

'No, seriously, Father . . .'

'Dad.'

'Dad . . .' I was tongue-tied. I couldn't talk to him as Dad. Dads were people who drove you to school and threw snowballs and ticked you off for coming home late. Dads didn't send you a ticket to ski school in a Christmas card. Dads didn't send an impersonal fax to a hotel saying 'well done' when one won a teenage downhill ski race. Dads were there to watch. Fathers weren't.

Remnants of the meeting came up with shining faces to add congratulations. He took his arm off my shoulder and shook their hands, friendly and positive to all; and I had a vision of them going around for the next four weeks saying, 'Juliard, a very good man, just what we need . . . Vote Juliard, couldn't do better.' The ripple from that night would reach the Hoopwestern boundaries and eddy along its roads.

My father slowly came down a little from his high and decided he'd done enough for one day. We left the hall, returned to the hotel and eventually through

41

a harmony of 'Good Nights' made our way out into the warm August night to walk across to the dimly lit bow-front opposite.

There were street lights round the square and the hotel lights at our back, but underfoot the decorative cobbles were dark and lumpy. In icy winters, I learned later, elderly people tended to skid on them and fall and crunch their bones; and on that euphoric night my father tripped on the uneven surface and went down forward on one knee, trying not to topple entirely and not managing it.

At exactly the same moment there was a loud bang and a sharp zzing and a scrunch of glass breaking.

I bent down over my father and saw in the light that his eyes were stretched wide with anxiety and his mouth grim and urgent with pain.

'Run,' he said. 'Run for cover. God dammit, *run*.'

I stayed where I was, however.

'Ben,' he said, 'for God's sake. That was a gunshot.'

'Yes, I know.'

We were halfway across the square, easy immobile targets. He struggled to get to his feet and told me again to run: and for once in my life I made a judgement and disobeyed him.

He couldn't put his weight on his left ankle. He half rose and fell down again and beseeched me to run.

'Stay down,' I told him.

'You don't understand . . .' His voice was anguished.

'Are you bleeding?'

'What? I don't think so. I twisted my ankle.'

People ran out of the hotel, drawn by the bang that had re-echoed round the buildings fringing the square. People came over to my father and me and stood around us, curious and unsettled, noncomprehension wrinkling their foreheads.

There was confusion and people saying, 'What happened, what happened?' and hands stretching down to my father to help him up, cushioning him with a lot of well-meaning concern and kindness.

When he was well surrounded he did finally take my arm and lean on other people and pull himself to his feet: or rather, to his right foot, because putting his left foot down caused him to exclaim with strong discomfort. He began to be embarrassed rather than frightened and told the crowding well-wishers that he felt stupid, losing his footing so carelessly. He apologised. He said he was fine. He smiled to prove it. He cursed mildly, to crowd approval.

'But that *noise*,' a woman said.

Heads nodded. 'It sounded like . . .'

'Not here in Hoopwestern . . .'

'Was it . . . a *gun*?'

An important-looking man said impatiently, 'A rifle shot. I'd know it anywhere. Some madman . . .'

'But where? There's no one here with a gun.'

Everyone looked round, but it was far too late to see the rifle, let alone the person taking pot-shots.

My father put his arm round my shoulders again,

but this time for a different, more practical sort of support, and cheerfully indicated to everyone that we should set off again to finish the crossing of the square.

The important-looking man literally shoved me out of the way, taking my place as crutch and saying in his loud authoritative way, 'Let me do this. I'm stronger than the lad. I'll have you over to your office in a jiffy, Mr Juliard. You just lean on *me*.'

My father looked over his shoulder to where I now stood behind him and would have protested on my behalf, I could see, but the change suited me fine and I simply waved for him to go on. The important-looking man efficiently half-carried my hopping father over the remaining stretch of square, the bunch of onlookers crowding round with murmurs of sympathy and helpful suggestions.

I walked behind my father. It came naturally, to do that. There was a high voice calling then, and I turned to find Polly running towards us, stumbling on the cobbles in strappy sandals and sounding very distressed.

'Ben . . . Ben . . . has George been shot?'

'No, Polly.' I tried to reassure her. 'No.'

'Someone said George had been shot.' She was out of breath and full of disbelief.

'Look, there he is.' I took her arm and pointed. 'There. Hopping. And hopping mad with himself for twisting his ankle and needing someone to help him along.'

Polly's arm was vibrating with the inner shakes, which only slowly abated when she could see that indeed George was alive and healthily swearing.

'But . . . the shot . . .'

I said, 'It seems someone did fire a gun at the same moment that he tripped on the cobbles, but I promise you he wasn't hit. No blood.'

'But you're so young, Ben.' Her doubts still showed.

'Even a tiny kid could tell you there's no blood.' I said it teasingly, but I guess it was my own relief that finally convinced her. She walked beside me and followed the pied-piper-like procession to the head-quarters' door, where my father produced a key and let everyone in.

He hopped across to his swivel chair behind his accustomed desk and, consulting a list, telephoned the local police.

'They've had several complaints already,' he told everyone, putting down the receiver. 'They're on their way here. Letting off a firearm . . . disturbing the peace . . . that sort of thing.'

Someone said, 'What you need is a doctor . . .' and someone else arranged for one to come.

'So kind. You're all so bloody kind,' my father said.

I left the hubbub and went to the open door, looking across the square to the Sleeping Dragon, who perversely had every eye wide open, with people leaning out of upstairs windows and people standing in brightly lit doorways below.

I remembered the '*zzing*' of the passing bullet and thought of ricochets. My father and I had been steering a straight line from hotel to headquarters; and *if* the bullet had been aimed at *him*, and *if* he'd stumbled at the exact second that the trigger was squeezed, and *if* the bullet's trajectory had been from upstairs somewhere in the Sleeping Dragon (and not from downstairs because there were still too many people about), and *if* the bullet had smashed some glass so that I heard the tinkle, then why was every pane of the window in the bow-fronted headquarters intact?

Because, I told myself, the whole thing had been a coincidence. The bullet had not been intended to stop George Juliard's political career before it started. Of course not. Dramatics were childish.

I turned to go back inside, and saw for an instant a flash of light on broken glass down on the ground.

It was a window of the charity shop next door that had been hit.

Zzing. Ricochet. Smash. The straight trajectory could have been deflected by the curve of a cobble. A rifle bullet travelling straight and true would very likely have gone right through glass without breaking it, but a wobbling bullet... that might set up glass-smashing vibrations.

The police arrived at the car-park side of the head-quarters, and the doctor also. Everyone talked at once.

The doctor, bandaging, said he thought the injury a strain, not a break. Ice and elevation, he prescribed.

The police listened to the self-important man's view on gunshots.

I stood to one side and at one point found my father looking at me through the throng, his expression both surprised and questioning. I smiled at him a bit, and the window of line of sight closed again as people moved.

I did tell a junior-looking uniformed policeman that the glass of the charity shop's bow-front was broken, and he did come outside to look. But when I tentatively mentioned ricochets he looked quizzical and asked how old I was. I had done a bit of rifle shooting at school, I said. He nodded, unimpressed, and made a note. I followed when he returned to join his colleagues.

Dearest Polly stood at my father's side and listened to everything worriedly. A man with a camera flashed several pictures. Considering that no one had actually been shot the fuss went on for a long time and it was nearly two o'clock when I finally closed and bolted the doors, front and back, and switched off a few of the lights.

My father decided to go upstairs backwards, sitting down. He would accept only minimal help and winced himself in and out of the bathroom and into one of the single beds in the bedroom. I was to sleep on the pull-out sofa-bed in the small sitting-room, but I ended up lying on the second single bed, next to my father, half dressed and not at all sleepy.

I had in the past twenty hours hummed along from Mrs Wells's house on my bicycle and ridden a canter on grassy sunlit Downs. I'd had my life torn apart and entered a new world, and for long minutes I'd wondered if I would collect a bullet in the back. How could I sleep?

I switched off the bedside light.

In the dark, my father said, 'Ben, why didn't you run?'

After a pause I answered. 'Why did you tell me to?'

'I didn't want you to get shot.'

'Mm. Well, that's why I didn't run. I didn't want you to get shot.'

'So you stood in the way . . .?'

'More fun than patting babies.'

'*Ben!*'

After a while, I said, 'I'd say it was a .22 rifle, the sort used for target shooting. I'd say it was a high-velocity bullet. I know that noise well. If a .22 bullet hits you in the body, it quite likely won't kill you. You need to hit the head or the neck to be most probably lethal. All I did was shield your head.'

There was a silence from the other bed. Then he said, 'I'd forgotten you could shoot.'

'I was in the school team. We were taught by one of the country's best marksmen.' I smiled in the dark. 'You paid for it, you know.'

CHAPTER THREE

Before nine the next morning I went downstairs and unbolted the door to the car park at the shrill summons of a man who was standing there with his finger on the bell button. He was short, black-haired, softly plump, held a bunch of keys in his hand and was very annoyed.

'Who are *you*?' he demanded. 'What are you doing in here? Why is the door bolted?'

'Benedict – ' I began.

'What?'

'Juliard.'

He stared at me for a moment, then brushed past and began bad-temperedly setting to rights the untidiness left all over both front and back offices by the events of the night.

'You're the son, I suppose,' he said, picking up scattered envelopes. 'George wasted all of yesterday going to collect you. As you're here, do something useful.' He gestured to the mess. 'Where is George, anyway? The radio is red hot. What did happen last night?'

'Upstairs. He sprained his ankle. And . . . er . . . who are *you*?'

'Mervyn Teck, of course.' He looked impatiently at my blank face. 'I'm the agent. Don't you know *anything*?'

'Not much.'

'I'm running this election. I'm here to get George Juliard into Parliament. The radio says someone shot at him. Is that true?' He seemed unconcerned and went on straightening papers.

'Possibly,' I said.

'Good.'

I said, 'Er . . .?'

'Free publicity. We can't afford to buy air time.'

'Oh.'

'It will get rid of Titmuss and Whistle.'

'Who are they?' I asked.

'Fringe candidates. We don't need to worry about them.'

My father hobbled downstairs saying, 'Morning, Mervyn. I see you've met my son.'

Mervyn gave me an unenthusiastic glance.

'Lucky he's here,' my father said. 'He can drive me around.'

I'd told him on the way from Brighton that I'd done errands to earn money for driving lessons and had held a full licence by then for nearly five weeks.

'Good,' he'd said.

'But I haven't driven since the test.'

'All in good time.' His bland expression now forbade me to reveal my inexperience. There was tolerance between the candidate and the agent, I saw, but no warmth.

A sharp-boned young woman arrived with disciplined hair and a power-dressing grey suit with a bright 'Juliard' rosette pinned to one shoulder. She was introduced as Crystal Harley, Mervyn Teck's secretary, and, as I learned during the morning, she was the only person, besides Mervyn himself, who received pay for running the by-election. Everyone else was a volunteer.

The three volunteer witches from the day before arrived one by one and smothered my father with cooing solicitude and endless coffee.

I had forgotten their names: Faith, Marge and Lavender, Faith chided me gently.

'Sorry.'

'A good politician remembers names,' Lavender told me severely. 'You won't be much use to your father if you forget who people are.' The thin lady with the sweet-smelling name was the one who had disapproved of Orinda Nagle. Difficult to please her, I thought.

Mervyn Teck and my father discussed streets and leaflet distributions. Crystal Harley entered endless details into a computer. Motherly Faith went round with a duster and Marge set the photocopier humming.

I sat on my stool and simply listened, and learned many surprising (to me) facts of electoral life, chief among which was the tiny amount of money allowed to be spent. No one could buy themselves into Parliament: every candidate had to rely on an army of unpaid helpers for door-to-door persuasions and the nailing of 'Vote for Me' posters to suitable trees.

There were Representation of the People Acts, Crystal told me crisply, her fingers busy on the keyboard, her eyes unwaveringly turned to the screen. The Acts severely limited what one could spend.

'There are about seventy thousand voters in this constituency,' she said. 'You couldn't buy seventy thousand half-pints of beer with what we're allowed to spend. It's impossible to *bribe* the British voters. You have to *persuade* them. That's your father's job.'

'Don't buy a stamp, dear, for a local letter,' Faith said, smiling. 'Get on a bicycle and deliver it by hand.'

'Do you mean you can't buy *stamps*?'

'You have to write down every cent you spend,' Crystal nodded. 'You have to make an itemised return after the election to show where the money went, and you can bet your sweet life Paul Bethune's people will be hoping like hell they'll find we've gone over the limit, just like we'll be scrutinising his return with a magnifying glass looking for any twopenny wickedness.'

'Then last night's dinner ...' I began.

'Last night's dinner was paid for by the people who ate it, and cost the local Constituency Association nothing,' Crystal said. She paused, then went on with my education. 'Mervyn and I are employed by the local Constituency Association of this party, not directly by Westminster. The local association pays for these offices here, and the whole caboodle relies on gifts and fundraising.'

She approved of the way things were set up, and I wondered vaguely why, with everything carefully regulated to ensure the election of the fittest, there were still so many nutcases in the House.

The relative peace of just seven bodies in the offices lasted only until an influx of the previous night's social mix trooped in through both doors and asked endless questions to which there seemed no answers.

Mervyn Teck loved it. The police, the media people, the party enthusiasts and the merely curious, he expansively welcomed them all. His candidate was not only alive but being perfectly charming to every enquirer. The TV cameraman shone his bright spotlight on my father's face and taped the sincerity of his smile. Local newspapermen had been augmented by several from the major dailies. Cameras flashed. Microphones were offered to catch anything worth saying, and I, doing my bit, simply smiled and smiled and was terribly nice to everyone and referred every question to my parent.

Crystal, trying to continue working but having to cling physically to her desk to avoid being swept round the place like flotsam, remarked to me tartly that there would hardly have been more fuss if George Juliard had been killed.

'Lucky he wasn't,' I said, wedging my stool next to her to keep us both anchored.

'Did the noise of the gunshot make him trip?' she asked.

'No. He tripped first.'

'Why are you so sure?'

'Because the bang of a high-velocity bullet reaches you after the bullet itself.'

She looked disbelieving.

'I learned it in physics lessons,' I said.

She glanced at my beardless face. 'How old are you?' she asked.

'Seventeen.'

'You can't even vote!'

'I don't actually want to.'

She looked across to where my father was winning media allies with modesty and grace.

'I've met a fair number of politicians,' she said. 'Your father's different.'

'In what way?'

'Can't you feel his power? Perhaps you can't, as you're his son. You're too close to him.'

'I do sometimes feel it.' It stunned me, I should have said.

'Look at last night,' Crystal went on without pausing. 'I was there in the hall, sitting at the back. He set that place alight. He's a natural speaker. I mean, I *work* here, and he had my pulse racing. Poor old Dennis Nagle, he was a nice worthy man, pretty capable in a quiet way, but he could never have got a crowd cheering and stamping their feet like last night.'

'Could Orinda?' I asked.

Crystal was startled. 'No, she can't make people laugh. But don't judge her by last night. She's done devoted work in the constituency. She was always at Dennis's side. She's feeling very hurt that she wasn't selected to follow Dennis, because until your father galvanised the selection panel she was unopposed.'

'In fact,' I said, 'if *anyone* had a motive for bumping off my father, it would be her.'

'Oh, but she wouldn't!' Crystal was honestly dismayed. 'She can sometimes be a darling, you know. Mervyn *loves* her. He's quite put out that he's not working to get *her* elected. He was looking forward to it.'

My first impression of Crystal's sharp spikiness had been right only as regarded her outward appearance. She was kinder and more patient than she looked. I wondered if at one time she had been anorexic: I had known anorexic girls at school. The teeth of one of them had fallen out.

Crystal's teeth were straight and white, though seldom visible, owing to an overall serious view of life. I thought she was probably twenty-five or -six and hadn't had enough in life to smile about.

Mervyn Teck zig-zagged to my elbow through the busy crowd and said it was time to think about driving my father to his day's engagements in the outlying

55

town of Quindle. The constituency was large in area with separate pockets of concentrated inhabitation: Mervyn gave me a map with roads and destinations marked, but looked at me doubtfully.

'Are you sure you're competent enough?'

I said, 'Yes,' with more confidence than I felt.

'One incident like last night's is a godsend,' he said. 'A car crash on top would be too much. We don't want any whiff of accident-prone.'

'No,' I said.

Across the room my father was dangling the Range Rover's keys in my direction. I went over to him and took them and he, with the help of a walking stick, detached himself from the chattering well-wishers (the police and media had long gone) and limped through the office and out to the car park.

Crowds beget crowds. There was a bunch of people outside the rear door who clapped and smiled at my father and gave him thumbs-up signs. I looked across the car park to where we had left the Range Rover on our arrival from Brighton the previous afternoon and my father asked me to fetch it over so that he wouldn't need to hobble that far.

I walked across to the conspicuous vehicle and stopped beside it, the keys in my hand. The sun shone again that day, gleaming on the gold-and-silver-painted garlands; and after a moment I turned away and went back to my father.

'What's the matter?' he said, half annoyed. 'Can't you drive it?'

'Is it insured for someone my age?'

'Yes, of course. I wouldn't suggest it otherwise. Go and fetch it, Ben.'

I frowned and went back into the offices, ignoring his displeasure.

'It's time you went,' Mervyn said, equally impatient. 'You said you could drive George's car.'

I nodded. 'But I'd be better in a smaller car. Like you said, we don't want an accident. Do you have a smaller one? Could I borrow yours?'

Mervyn said with obvious aggravation, 'My car isn't insured for drivers under twenty-one.'

'Mine is, though,' Crystal said. 'My nineteen-year-old brother drives it. But it's not very glamorous. Not like the Range Rover.'

She dug the keys out of her handbag and said that Mervyn (to his impatience) would give her a lift home if we were not back by five-thirty, and would pick her up again in the morning. I thanked her with an awkward kiss on the cheek, and with Mervyn Teck repeating his disapproval, went out to rejoin my father.

'I'm disappointed in you, Ben,' he said, when Mervyn Teck explained. 'You'd better practise in the Range Rover tomorrow.'

'OK. But today, now, before we go, would you arrange for some mechanics to come here and make sure there's nothing wrong with it?'

'Of course there's nothing wrong with it. I drove it to Brighton and back yesterday and it was running perfectly.'

'Yes, but it's been standing out in the car park all night. Last night it's possible someone tried to shoot you. Suppose someone's hammered a nail or two into the Range Rover's tyres? Or anything.' I finished self-deprecatingly, as if I thought sabotage a childish fantasy; but after a brief thoughtful silence my father said to Mervyn, 'I'll go in Crystal's car. Ben can practise on the Range Rover tomorrow. Meanwhile, Mervyn, get the Range Rover overhauled, would you?'

Mervyn gave me a sour look, but it was he, after all, who had most wanted to avoid the accident-prone label: or so he'd said.

In Crystal's small work-a-day box on wheels I therefore drove the candidate safely to his far-flung appointments, and again I saw and heard him shake awake the apathetic voting public, progressively attracting more and more people as his voice raised laughter and applause. His audience approved with their eyes and shouted questions, some friendly, some hostile, all of them getting thoughtful answers, lightly phrased.

I didn't know how much of the day's flashing enthusiasm would actually carry the feet to the polling booths, but it was enough, my father assured me, if they didn't walk into the opposition camp and write their X for Bethune.

We had squeezed into Crystal's car an invention of my father's that was basically two wooden boxes, each a foot high, one larger than the other, that would bolt together, one on top of the other, to form an impromptu stepped platform to raise a speaker above his listeners: just enough for him to be comfortably heard, not high enough to be psychologically threatening. 'My soapbox' my father called it, though it was many years since such crowd-pulling structures had contained soap.

I assembled the 'soapbox' in three places in the town's scattered focal points, and at each place a crowd gathered, curious, or anti, or uncommitted, and at each place, as I unbolted, or assembled or packed away the stepped platform, people would crowd round me with (mostly) friendly enquiries.

'Are you his chauffeur?'

'Yes.'

'Is he as knowledgeable as he seems?'

'More so.'

'What does he think about education?'

I smiled. 'He's in favour of it.'

'Yes, but – '

'I can't answer for him. Please ask him yourself.'

They turned away and asked him, and got politically correct and truthful answers that would never be implemented without a huge increase in taxes: I was learning the economic facts as rapidly as I'd ever assimilated quadratic equations.

My father's appearance in Quindle had been well publicised in advance by posters all over the town. Volunteers had distributed them and volunteers met and escorted us everywhere, their faces shining with commitment. My own commitment, I had already found, was to my father himself, not to his party nor his beliefs. My private views, if I had any, were that good ideas were scattered around, not solely the property of any shade of rosette: and of course what were to me good ideas were hateful errors to others. I didn't embrace any single whole agenda package, and it was always those who didn't care passionately, those who changed their minds and swung with the wind, those who felt vaguely dissatisfied, they it was who swayed one side in or another side out. The 'floating voters', who washed back and forth with the tide, those were my father's target.

Quindle, like Hoopwestern, had grown in response to industries planted in the surrounding fields; not light bulbs this time, but furniture and paint. There had then been a long policy of 'infilling' – the building of large numbers of small houses on every patch of vacant grass. The resulting town strained against its green belt and suffered from interior traffic snarl-ups on a standstill scale. It worked well for soapbox orators: in the summer heat cars crept past with their windows down, getting the message.

Among the blizzard of VOTE JULIARD posters there were some for TITMUSS and WHISTLE and, of course, many for BETHUNE IS BETTER. GIVE HIM YOUR X. Bethune's notices on the whole looked tattered, and I found it wasn't merely because it was three days since he'd stomped inner Quindle on his own soapbox tour, but because the local weekly paper, the *Quindle Diary*, had hit the newsagents with 'Bethune for Sleaze' as its headline.

One of the volunteers having tucked the *Quindle Diary* under my elbow, I read the front page, as who wouldn't.

'As our representative in Westminster, do we want an adulterer who says he upholds the family values to which this newspaper in this young town is dedicated? Do we believe the promises of one who can't keep a solemn vow?'

I read to the end and thought the whole tone insufferably pompous, but I didn't suppose it would do the Bethune camp much good.

At each of his three ascents of the soapbox, my father was bombarded with demands that he should at least deplore the Bethune hypocrisy, and at each place, carefully side-stepping the loaded come-ons, he attacked Bethune and his party only for their political aims and methods.

His restraint didn't altogether please his own army of volunteers.

'George could *demolish* Bethune if he would only take a hatchet to his character,' one of them complained. 'Why won't he do it?'

'He doesn't believe in it,' I said.

'You have to play the aces you're given.'

'Not five aces,' I said.

'What?'

'He would think it cheating.'

The volunteer raised his eyes to heaven but changed his approach. 'You see that thin man standing near your father, writing in a notebook?'

'Do you mean the one in a pink jogging suit and a baseball hat on backwards?'

'I do indeed. He's called Usher Rudd. He writes for the *Hoopwestern Gazette* and his column is also syndicated to the *Quindle Diary*. It's he who wrote the personal attacks on Paul Bethune. He's been following Bethune around ever since his party chose him as their candidate. Rudd's a highly professional siever of mud. Never, *never* trust him.'

I said in apprehension, 'Does my father know who he is?'

'I told George that Usher Rudd would be bound to turn up again, but he doesn't always look the same. The pink overalls and baseball cap are new.'

'Usher Rudd's an unusual name.'

The volunteer laughed. 'He's really young Bobby Rudd, always a menace. His mother was Gracie Usher before she married a Rudd. The Rudd family have a string of repair garages, for anything from bicycles to combine harvesters, but fixing cars isn't to young

Bobby's taste. He calls himself an investigative journalist. More like a muck-raker, I'd say.'

I said tentatively, 'Was he at the dinner last night?'

'That big do at the Sleeping Dragon? He would have been for a certainty. He'll be furious that the gunshot and all that happened was too late for today's *Gazette*. The *Gazette* is only twenty-four pages long, mostly advertisements, sports results, local news and re-hashed world events. Everyone buys it for the dirt Rudd digs up. He was a rotten peeping tom as a little boy, always had his snotty nose glued to people's windows, and he hasn't got better with time. If you want to have sex with the vicar, don't do it in Quindle.'

I said dryly, 'Thanks for the advice.'

He laughed. 'Beware of Bobby Rudd, that's all.'

With the present crowd listening to my galvanic father with devouring eyes as much as persuadable ears, I slowly strolled round to guard his back; I was some poor sort of guardian to my parent, I thought with self-condemnation, if I left him wide open to repeat bullets or other jokers.

I did my best to look purposeless, but clearly failed with that message as Usher Rudd, also as if guileless, came to stand casually beside me. His baseball cap advertised vigorous sports goods, as did his footwear, and he wore between, from neck to ankle, a soft rose-pink loose exercise suit of nylon-like fabric which, instead of hiding the thinness of his body inside, gave an impression that the arms and legs functioned on a system of articulated rods. I, in my jeans and T-shirt, looked almost invisibly ordinary.

'Hello,' he said. 'Where is the Juliard battle-wagon?'

Puzzled, I answered, 'We came in a different car.'

'I'm Usher Rudd.'

His accent was unreconstructed Dorset, his manner confident to arrogant. He had unexcited blue eyes, sandy lashes and dry freckled skin: the small-boy menace who had peeped through windows still lived close to the surface and made me for once feel older than my years.

'What's your name?' he demanded, as I made no response.

'Benedict,' I said.

'Ben,' he asserted, nodding his recognition, 'Ben Juliard.'

'That's right.'

'How old are you?' He was abrupt, as if he had a right to the information.

'Seventeen,' I said without offence. 'How old are *you*?'

'That's none of your business.'

I gazed at him with a perplexity that was at least half genuine. Why should he think he could ask questions that he himself would not answer? I had a lot to learn, as my father had said; but I instinctively didn't like him.

Close behind my back my father was answering the sort of questions it was proper he should be asked:

where did he stand on education, foreign policy, taxes, the dis-united kingdom and the inability of bishops to uphold the ten commandments? 'Shouldn't sins be modernised?' someone shouted. Moses was out of date.

My father, who certainly lived by 'thou shalt not' rather than by 'what can I get away with?' replied with humour, 'By all means pension off Moses if you would like your neighbour to covet your ox and your ass and carry off your wife and your lawn mower...'

The end of his sentence drowned in laughter and cheers, and for fifteen more minutes he had them spellbound, feeding them political nuggets in nourishing soup, producing a performance without microphone or footlights that they would never forget. All my life people would say to me, 'I heard your father speak in Quindle,' as if it had been a revelation in their existence: and it wasn't altogether *what* he said that mattered, I reckoned, but his whole, honest, joyous, vigorous presentation.

Against the final applause, Usher Rudd said to me, 'Birthday?'

'What?'

'Your birthday?'

'Yes,' I said.

'Yes, what?'

'Yes, I do have a birthday.'

He thought me dim. 'What's your mother's name?' he said.

'Sarah.'

'Her last name?'

'Yes. She's dead.'

His expression changed. His gaze grew thoughtful and flicked downward to the *Quindle Diary* that I held rolled in my hand. I saw him understand the obtuseness of my answers.

'Bethune deserves it,' he said sharply.

'I don't know anything about him,' I said.

'Then read my column.'

'Even then...'

'Everyone has secrets,' he declared with relish. 'I just find them out. I enjoy doing it. They deserve it.'

'The public has a right to know?' I asked.

'Of course they do. If someone is setting themselves up to make our laws and rule our lives they shouldn't sleaze it off with dirty sex on the side, should they?'

'I haven't thought about it.'

'If old George is hiding dirty secrets, I'll find them out. What's your mother's name?'

'Sarah. She's dead.'

He gave me a bitter antagonistic glare.

'I'm sure you do a good detective job,' I said mildly. 'My mother's name was Sarah Juliard. Married. Dead. Sorry about that.'

'I'll find out,' he threatened.

'Be my guest.'

My father disengaged himself from eager clutching

66

voters and turned to say he was ready for his lunch engagement: a volunteers' gathering in a pub.

'This,' I said, indicating the inhabitant of the pink tracksuit and the energetic shoes and baseball hat, 'is Usher Rudd.'

'Nice to know you,' my father said, automatically ready to shake hands. 'Do you work for the party, er . . . Usher?'

'He writes for newspapers,' I said. I unrolled the *Quindle Diary* so he could see the front page. 'He wrote this. He wants me to tell him my mother's name.'

I was getting to know my father. Twenty-four hours earlier I wouldn't have been aware that a tiny tensing of muscles and a beat of silence meant a fizzingly fast assessment of unwelcome facts. Not only powerful but dauntingly rapid: not only analytical but an instant calculator of down-the-line consequences. Some brain.

He smiled politely at Usher Rudd. 'My wife's name was Sarah. Unfortunately she died.'

'What of?' Usher Rudd, disconcerted by my father's pleasant frankness, sounded aggressively rude.

'It was a long time ago.' My father remained civil. 'Come on, Ben, or we'll be late.'

We turned away and walked three paces; and Bobby Usher Rudd, darting round and wheeling in the running shoes, came to a halt facing us, standing in our way.

His voice was thin, malicious and triumphant. 'I'll get you de-selected. Orinda Nagle will have her rights.'

'Ah.' My father packed all the understanding in the world into one syllable. 'So you rubbished Paul Bethune to give her a clear run, is that it?'

Usher Rudd was furious. 'She's worth ten of you.'

'She's a lucky woman to have so many fans.'

'You'll lose.' Usher Rudd almost danced with rage. 'She would have won.'

'Well . . .' My father detoured past him with me at his heels, and Usher Rudd behind us yelled the question I would never have asked but wanted like crazy to know the answer to. 'If your wife died long ago, what do you do for sex?'

My father certainly heard but there wasn't a falter in his step. I risked a flick of a glance at his face but learned nothing: he showed no embarrassment or anxiety, only, if anything, *amusement*.

The lunch in the pub was up-beat, the volunteers all intoxicated with the speech stops of the morning. In the afternoon we toured a furniture factory and then a paint factory, where the candidate (leaning on his walking stick) listened intently to local problems and promised remedies if he were elected. He shook countless hands and signed countless autographs, and left behind an atmosphere of hope.

When Mervyn Teck had made his plans he had expected it to be Orinda who charmed the wood-workers and the colour mixers, and there had been resistance in parts of the factories to the one seen as a usurper. My father defused criticism by praising

Orinda steadfastly without apologising for having been chosen to take her place.

'A natural-born politician,' one of the lady volunteers said in my ear. 'The way the country's leaning, we'd lose this marginal seat with Orinda, though she doesn't believe that, of course. With your father we've a better chance, but voters are unpredictable and can often be downright vindictive, and they mostly vote for party, not for individuals, and the sleaze accusations won't hurt Paul Bethune much, especially with male voters who privately don't think a spot of adultery too much of a big deal, and will think "good luck to him". And you'd fancy women wouldn't vote for adulterers, but they do.'

'Doesn't Usher Rudd shift the Xs from one slot to another?'

'Not as much as he believes, the little weasel. It's not the locals that pay attention to him as much as the big noises in Westminster. They're all shit-scared of him digging into their pasts, and the higher they climb the more they hate him. Haven't you noticed that when an MP screws up his or her reputation, it's their own party that dumps them quickest?'

The correct answer was no, I hadn't noticed, because I hadn't been looking.

On our way back to Hoopwestern I asked my father what he thought of Usher Rudd but he yawned, said he was flaked out and his ankle hurt, and promptly went to sleep. I drove carefully, still not instinctive in traffic, and woke the candidate by a jerking halt at a red light at a crossroads.

'Usher Rudd,' he said without preamble, as if twenty minutes hadn't passed between question and answer, 'will burn his fingers on privacy laws.'

I said, 'I didn't know there were any privacy laws.'

'There will be.'

'Oh.'

'Usher Rudd has red hair under that baseball cap.'

'How do you know?'

'He came to the meeting after last night's dinner. Polly pointed him out to me. He wore a black tracksuit and black trainers. Didn't you see him?'

'I don't remember him.'

'Find out if he can shoot.'

I opened my mouth to say 'Wow' or 'How?' and thought better of both. My father glanced at me sideways, and I felt him smile.

'I don't think it was him,' I said.

'Why not?'

'His bullets of choice are acid ink.'

'Are you sure you want to be a mathematician? Why don't you try writing?'

'I want to be a jockey.' Might as well walk on the moon.

'Exeter University required to know where you would spend your gap year before they offered you a deferred entry: that is to say, you're going there not this October, but next year. They weren't enthusiastic about racecourses.'

'There's an Exeter racecourse.'

'You know damned well what they mean.'

'I don't like politics.' Change the subject.

'Politics are the oil of the world.'

'You mean . . . the world doesn't run without oil?'

He nodded. 'When politics jam solid, you get wars.'

'Father – ' I said.

'Dad.'

'No. Father. Why do you want to be a politician?'

After a pause he said, 'I am one. I can't help it.'

'But you've never . . . I mean . . .'

'I've never made a move before? Don't think I haven't considered it. I've known since I was your age or younger that one day I would try for Parliament. But I needed a solid base. I needed to prove to myself that I could make money. I needed to understand economics. And then there came a time not long ago when I said to myself "now or never". So it's now.'

It was the longest statement about himself that he'd ever made in my hearing; and he had simplified for my sake, I thought, an urge that had taken time to ripen and had burst out fully grown at the Sleeping Dragon. The Juliard dragon was awake now and roaring and prowling up broad Whitehall towards Number 10.

Thinking about him, I lost the way home. He made no sarcastic comment when I stopped, consulted the

71

map, worked out where I'd gone wrong and finally arrived in the car park from an unexpected direction; and for that forbearance alone I would have served him as an esquire to a knight. How old-fashioned could one get?

It was well after six o'clock when we reached the car park which, in consequence, was almost empty. All the bordering shops had closed for the day. The late afternoon sunshine weakened to soft gold as I pulled up and applied Crystal's brakes.

There were dim lights in the office, but no people. I unlocked the door and we found a large note laid out prominently on Mervyn Teck's desk.

'The Range Rover is in Rudd's Repair Garage. They thoroughly overhauled it, and found nothing wrong.'

CHAPTER FOUR

I would have expected the nervous energy of the day-long performance in Quindle to have earned my father an evening's rest, but I had barely begun to wake up to the stamina demanded of would-be public servants. It seemed that far from a quiet top-up of batteries, he was committed to another marathon shake-hands-and-smile, not this time in the chandeliered magnificence of the Sleeping Dragon's all-purpose hall, but in much more basic space normally used as a schooling ground for five-year-olds in Hoopwestern's outer regions.

There were kids' attempts at pictures pinned to cork boards all round the walls, mostly thin figures with big heads and spiky hair sticking straight out like Medusa's snakes. There were simple notices – 'do not run' and 'raise your hand' – all written in self-conscious lower case letters.

Primary colours everywhere bombarded the eyesight to saturation point, and I couldn't believe that this sort of thing had been my own educational springboard; but it had. Another world, long left behind.

There were several rows of the temporary flip-up seats that grew more and more familiar to me as the days passed, and a makeshift speaker's platform, this time with a microphone that squeaked whenever tested, and on several other occasions when switched on or off.

The lighting was of unflattering greenish-white fluorescent strips, and there weren't enough of them to raise spirits above depression. Limbo must look like this, I thought: and the unenticing room had in fact drawn the sort of audience you could count on fingers and toes and still have enough left over for an abacus.

Mervyn Teck met us on the doorstep looking at his watch and checking, but by good luck and asking the way (less pride on my part than shame of arriving late) we had turned up at the exact minute advertised by a scatter of leaflets.

On the table on the platform, beside the temperamental microphone, there was a gavel for calling the meeting to order and two large plates of sandwiches secured by cling film.

Two or three earnest lady volunteers crowded round the candidate with goodwill, but it was plain, ten minutes after start time, that apathy, and not enthusiasm, had won the evening.

I expected my father to be embarrassed by the small turn-out and to hurry through the unsatisfactory proceedings, but he made a joke of it, abandoning the microphone and sitting on the edge of the platform, beckoning the sparse and scattered congregation to come forward into the first few rows, to make the meeting more coherent.

His magic worked. Everyone moved forward. He spoke to them familiarly, as if addressing a roomful of friends, and I watched him turn a disaster into a useful exercise in public relations. By the time the sandwiches had been liberated from the cling film even the few who had come to heckle had been tamed to silence.

Mervyn Teck looked both thoughtful and displeased.

'Something the matter?' I asked.

He said sourly, 'Orinda would have drawn a much better house. She'd have packed the hall. They love her here: she presents prizes to the children here every term. She buys them herself.'

'I'm sure she'll go on doing it.'

I meant it without irony, but Mervyn Teck gave me a glance of dislike and moved away. One of the lady volunteers sweetly told me that the time of the meeting had clashed with the current rave series on the television, and that even the pubs were suffering from it on Thursday nights. Tomorrow would be different, she said. Tomorrow the Town Hall would be packed.

'Er . . .' I said, 'what's happening in the Town Hall?'

'But you're his son, aren't you?'

'Yes, but . . .'

'But you don't know that tomorrow night your

father goes face to face in a debate with Paul Bethune?'

I shook my head.

'Fireworks,' she said happily. 'I wouldn't miss it for the world.'

My father, when I asked him about it on the short drive back to the centre of Hoopwestern, seemed full of equal relish.

'I suppose,' I said, 'there'll be more point to it than the sort of fiasco tonight could have been.'

'Every vote counts,' he corrected me. 'If I won only a few tonight, that's fine. You have to win the floaters over to your side, and they have to be persuaded one by one.'

'I'm hungry,' I said as we passed a brightly lit take-away, so we backtracked and bought chicken wings with banana and bacon, and even there my father, recognised, fell into political chat with the man deep-frying chips.

In the morning early I went out and bought a copy of the *Gazette*. Sleaze and Paul Bethune filled pages four and five (with photographs) but the front-page topic of concern was headlined 'JULIARD SHOT?'

Columns underneath said Yes (eyewitnesses) and No (he wasn't hurt). Statements from the police said nothing much (they couldn't find a gun). Statements from onlookers, like the self-important gunshot expert, said Juliard had definitely been the object of an assassination attempt. He thought so and he was always right.

The consensus theory of the reporters (including Usher Rudd) was that resentment against Juliard was running high in the Orinda Nagle camp. The editor's leader column didn't believe that political assassination ever took place at so low a level. World leaders, perhaps. Unelected local candidates, never.

I walked through the town to the ring road looking for Rudd's Repair Garage and found the staff unlocking their premises for the day. They had a large covered workshop and an even larger wire-fenced compound where jobs done or waiting stood in haphazard rows. The Range Rover was parked in that compound, sunlight already gleaming on its metallic paint.

I asked for, and reached, the manager, whose name was Basil Rudd. Thin, red-haired, freckled and energetic, his likeness to Usher Rudd made twins a possibility.

'Don't ask,' he said, eyeing my newspaper. 'He's my cousin. I disown him, and if you're out to be busy with your fists, you've reached the wrong man.'

'Well, I really came to collect that Range Rover. It's my father's.'

'Oh?' He blinked. 'I'll need proof of identity.'

I showed him a letter of authorisation signed by my parent and also my driving licence.

'Fair enough.' He opened a drawer, picked out a labelled ring bearing two keys and held them out for me to take. 'Don't forget to switch off the alarms. I'll send the bill to Mr Juliard's party headquarters. OK?'

'Yes. Thank you. Was there anything wrong?'

He shrugged. 'If there was, there isn't now.' He consulted a spiked worksheet. 'Oil change. General check. That's all.'

'Do you think I could talk to whoever did the job?'

'Whatever for?'

'Er... I've got to drive my father round in that vehicle and I've never driven it before... and I thought I might get some tips about engine management ... so I don't overheat it by crawling along the roads canvassing door to door.'

Basil Rudd shrugged. 'Ask for Terry. He did the work.'

I thanked him and sought out Terry who gave three instant physical impressions: big; bald; belly. Brown overalls, grease-stained from his job.

He too eyed my newspaper. He spoke with venom in a powerful Dorset voice.

'Don't mention Bobby bloody Rudd round here.'

I hadn't been going to, but I said, 'Why not?'

'He'll listen to you and your missus in bed with one of them window-vibrating bugging contraptions and before you know it, never mind the sex, he'll be printing what you said about the boss having his hand up a customer's skirt when she brings her car in for the twentieth time to be overhauled, though there's bugger all wrong with it in the first place. Got me sacked, Bobby did.'

'But,' I suggested, 'you're still here.'

'Yeah, see, Basil took me on because he loathes Bobby, who's his cousin, see. It was over in Quindle I got sacked by Bobby's dad, that's Basil's uncle, drunk half the time . . .' He broke off. 'If it's not to complain about Bobby Usher bleeding Rudd, what is it you want, lad?'

'I . . . er . . . you serviced my father's Range Rover. What was wrong with it?'

'Apart from the fancy paintwork?' He scratched his shiny head. 'Foreign body in the oil sump. I suppose you might say that. Nothing else. I gave it a good clean-out.'

'What sort of foreign body?'

He looked at me dubiously. 'I don't rightly know.'

'Well, um . . . how do you know it was there?'

He took his time in answering by starting at the beginning of his involvement. 'A man in your party's headquarters – said his name was Teck or some such – he phones Basil saying there might be something dicey about a fancy Range Rover they'd got there and to send someone over pronto to take a decko, so I went over there and this Mr Teck gave me the keys and the Range Rover started at first touch, sweet as anything.'

I looked at him without comment.

'Yeah, well,' he said, scratching his bald head again. 'This Teck guy said something about maybe someone took a pot shot at your old man and to check that the Range Rover's brakes hadn't been mucked about with or anything, so I looked it all over and could see nothing wrong. No bombs, nothing like that, but anyway this Teck guy said to bring it here and do a thorough service, so I did.'

He stopped for effect. I said obligingly, 'What did you find?'

'See, it was what I *didn't* find.'

'I wish you'd explain.'

'No plug on the sump.'

'What?'

'Oil change. Routine service. I run the Range Rover over the inspection pit and I take a spanner to unscrew the sump-plug to drain out the old oil, and there you are, no plug. *No plug*, I ask you. But there's oil there, according to the dipstick. Normal. Full. So I run the engine a bit and the oil pressure gauge reads normal, like it did on my way round here, so there has to be oil circulating round the engine, see, so why, if the sump-plug is missing, why hasn't the oil all emptied out?'

'Well, why?'

'Because there's something else plugging up the hole, that's why.'

'A rag?' I suggested. 'A wad of tissues?'

'Nothing like that, I don't think. Something harder.

Anyway, I poked a bit of wire into the hole and freed whatever was there and the oil poured out like it always does. Not filthy oil, mind you. It hadn't been long since the last oil change.'

'So the plug, whatever it is, is still in the sump?'

He shrugged. 'I dare say so. It won't do much harm there. The sump drain-hole's not much bigger than a little finger.' He held up his own grimy hand. 'It wasn't a *big* plug, see.'

'Mm.' I hesitated. 'Did you tell Basil Rudd about it?'

He shook his big head. 'He'd gone home for the day when I put the work-done sheets in his office, and I didn't think much of it. I found a new plug that fits the Range Rover and screwed it up tight. Then I filled up with clean oil, same as usual, and put the Range Rover out in the yard, where it is now. It's all hunky-dory. You'll have no trouble with it.'

'I'll take it in a minute,' I said. 'I'll just go back into the office to see about settling up.'

I went into the office and asked Basil Rudd if I could telephone my father in the party headquarters and he obligingly held out the receiver to me with a be-my-guest invitation.

I said to my father, 'Please could you ask whoever it was who worked on your Range Rover last if there was a normal plug on the oil-sump drain.' I relayed Terry's finding and his solution to the problem.

Basil Rudd looked up sharply from a sheet of paper

he was writing on and began to protest, but I smiled, said it was an unimportant enquiry, and waited for my father's answer. He told me to stay right where I was and five minutes later was back on the line.

'My mechanic is very annoyed at any suggestion that there was any irregularity at all with any part of the Range Rover. He did a complete overhaul on Monday. So what is going on?'

'I don't exactly know. It's probably nothing.'

'Bring the Range Rover back. We need it today.'

'Yes,' I said.

I gave the receiver back to Basil Rudd and thanked him for the call.

'Just what is this all about?' he said.

'I don't know enough,' I replied. 'I haven't been driving long. But I am concerned with keeping my father safe since the episode with the gun . . .' I waved the newspaper, 'so I'm probably being fussy over nothing. But on its last overhaul there was an ordinary plug screwed into the sump drain, and yesterday there wasn't.'

Basil Rudd showed first of all impatience and then anxiety, and finally stood up and came with me back to talk to Terry.

Terry, for a change, was scratching his brown-overalled belly.

I said, 'I'm not complaining about anything here, and please don't think I am. I do want to know what was plugging the sump, though, because I'm frankly scared of mysteries concerning anything to do with my father. So, please, how would you put a substitute plug in the drain-hole, and most of all, why?'

The two motor men stood in silence, not knowing the answers.

'The oil was quite clean,' Terry said.

Another silence.

Basil Rudd said, 'If you drain the new oil out again, and take the engine apart, you'll find whatever the stopper was that Terry pushed through the sump, but that's a very expensive procedure and not justified, I don't think.'

Another silence.

'I'll ask my father,' I said.

We trooped back to the office and I reported the last-resort expensive solution of dismantling the engine.

'Do nothing. Stay where you are,' my father commanded. 'Just do nothing, and wait. Let me speak to Basil Rudd.'

The chit-chat went on for several minutes. Basil Rudd said he thought the boy – meaning me – was making a hullabaloo over nothing much, but in the end he shrugged and said, 'Yes, yes, all right.' He put down the receiver and said to me, 'Your father is sending someone for the Range Rover. He wants you to stay here for now.'

Terry muttered that he had done a proper service on the Range Rover and no one could tell him different. Basil Rudd gave me a look of disfavour and said he couldn't waste any more time, he had mountains of paperwork to see to. I didn't exactly apologise, but I said I would wait outside in the Range Rover and walked peacefully across to where it stood in the wire-fenced compound. I disarmed the alarms, opened the door and sat behind the driving wheel, going through the systems and reading the instruction book.

I waited for over an hour until Basil Rudd appeared at the window beside me. I opened the door, stepped down to the ground and met the man accompanying the garage owner, who announced with a glint of irony that he had come to solve the mystery of the missing sump-plug. His name, he said, was Foster Fordham. He looked more like a lawyer than a mechanic: no blue collar to his grey and white pinstriped shirt or his neat dark suit. He had straight, dark, well-brushed hair, light-framed glasses and polished black shoes.

Basil Rudd, turning away, asked Foster Fordham to report to him in the office before leaving and, watching Rudd's departing back, Fordham, apparently bored to inertia, informed me that he was here to do my father a big favour, as normally he was a consultant engineer, not a hands-on minion.

I began to explain about the gunshot, but he interrupted that he knew all about it, and all about the missing plug.

'I work in car-racing circles,' he said. 'My field is sabotage.'

I no doubt looked as inadequate as I felt in the face of his quiet assurance.

He said, 'I understand that yesterday you were going to drive this vehicle from here to Quindle. How far is that?'

'About twelve miles.'

'Dual carriageway? Flat straight roads?'

'Mostly single lane, a lot of sharp corners, and some of it uphill.'

He nodded. He said we would now take the road to Quindle and he would drive.

Perplexed but trusting I climbed into the passenger seat beside him and listened to the healthy purr of the engine as he started up and drove off out of the garage compound onto the ring road round Hoopwestern, bound for Quindle. He drove fast in silence, watching the instrument panel as intently as the road, and said nothing until we had reached the top of the long steep incline halfway to what I thought was our destination. He stopped up there, however, and, still without explaining, did a U-turn and drove straight back to Rudd's garage.

Cars flashed past, appearing fast towards us from blind corners, as they had the day before. Fordham drove faster than I'd felt safe doing in Crystal's car, but if his field was racing, that was hardly surprising.

At the garage he told Terry to drain the engine oil into a clean container. Terry said the oil was too hot to handle. Fordham agreed to wait a little, but insisted that the oil should still be hot when it was drained.

'Why?' Terry asked. 'It's clean. I did the oil change yesterday.'

Fordham didn't answer. Eventually, wearing heavy gloves, Terry unscrewed the sump-plug and let the hot oil drain out as requested into a clean plastic five-gallon container. Fordham had him put the container into the luggage space at the back of the Range Rover and then suggested he should screw the sump-plug back into place and refill the engine with fresh cool oil.

Terry signalled exasperation with his eyebrows but did as he was asked. Mr Fordham, calm throughout, then told me that he had finished his investigation and suggested we say farewell to Basil Rudd and return in the Range Rover to my father's headquarters. Basil Rudd, of course, wanted to know reasons. Fordham told him with great politeness that he would receive a written report, and meanwhile not to worry, all was well.

Fordham drove composedly to the car park outside my father's headquarters and, with me faithfully following, walked into the offices where my father was sitting with Mervyn Teck discussing tactics.

My father stood at the sight of us and limped outside with Fordham to the Range Rover. Through the window I watched them talking earnestly, then Fordham took the plastic container of oil out of the

Range Rover, put it into the boot of a Mercedes standing nearby, climbed into the driver's seat, and neatly departed.

My father, returning, told Mervyn cheerfully that there was now nothing wrong with the Range Rover and it could safely be driven all round the town.

We finally set off. I drove, feeling my way cautiously through the gears, learning the positive message of the four-wheel drive. My father sat beside me, accompanied by his walking stick. Mervyn Teck, carrying a megaphone, sat in the rear seat, squeezing his lumpy knees together to allow more space for two volunteer helpers, thin bittersweet Lavender and motherly Faith.

The rear-seaters knew their drill from much past practice, and I with eye-opening wonderment became acquainted with the hardest graft in politics, the door-to-door begging for a 'yes' vote.

The first chosen residential street consisted of identical semi-detached houses with clipped garden-defining hedges and short concrete drives up to firmly closed garage doors. Some of the front windows were adorned with stickers simply announcing 'BETHUNE': he had worked this land before us.

'This road is awash with floaters,' Mervyn said with rare amusement. 'Let's see what we can do about turning the tide our way.'

Directing me to stop the vehicle, he untucked himself from his seatbelt and, standing in the open air, began to exhort the invisible residents through the reverberating megaphone, to vote JULIARD, JULIARD, JULIARD.

I found it odd to have my name bouncing off the house fronts, but the candidate himself nodded with smiling approval.

Lavender and Faith followed Mervyn out of the car, each of them carrying a bundle of stickers printed JULIARD in slightly larger letters than BETHUNE. Taking one side of the road each they began ringing front door bells and knocking knockers and, where they got no response, tucking a sticker through the letter-box.

If a door was opened to them they smiled and pointed to the Range Rover from where my father would limp bravely up the garden path to put on his act, at which he was clearly terrific. I crawled up the road in low gear, my father limped uncomplainingly, Mervyn activated his megaphone and Lavender and Faith wasted not a leaflet. In our slow wake we left friendly waves and a few JULIARDS in windows. By the end of the street I was bored to death, but it seemed Lavender and Faith both revelled in persuasion tactics and were counting the road a victory for their side.

After two more long sweeps through suburbia (in which at least one baby got kissed) we respited for a late sandwich lunch in a pub.

'If ever you get invited into someone's home,' my father said (as he had been invited five or six times that morning), 'you go into the sitting-room and you

say, "Oh, what an attractive room!" even if you think
it's hideous.'

Lavender, Faith and Mervyn all nodded, and I said,
'That's cynical.'

'You've a lot to learn.'

We were sitting by a window. I looked through it
to the Range Rover parked outside in plain view and
reckoned that one way or another I actually had
learned a lot that morning, and that what I'd learned
had probably saved a good many votes.

My father, as if following my thoughts, said lightly,
'We'll talk about it later,' but it wasn't until we were
changing before going to the Town Hall debate that
he would discuss Foster Fordham.

By then I'd persuaded Mervyn to arrange a securely
locked overnight garage for the Range Rover, backed
by my casual parent who said mildly, 'The boy's got a
point, Mervyn. It might be more satisfactory for us all.
No harm, anyway, in keeping it safe from thieves,' and
as the car belonged to my father himself and not to
the party, he had his way.

'Foster Fordham wasn't sure how much you understood,' he said, combing through his tightly curled dark
hair and leaving it much as it had been before. 'He
was surprised you didn't ask him questions.'

'Terry – the mechanic – did ask. Fordham wouldn't
answer.'

'So what do you conclude it was all about?'

'Well ... if you or I or anyone else had driven the

Range Rover yesterday towards Quindle, it would quite likely have crashed. Or, at least, I think so.'

My father put down his comb and with stillness said, 'Go on.'

I said, 'I do think the bullet that came so near us was deliberately aimed at you, and even if it hadn't killed you, it would have stopped your campaign if you'd been badly injured. But all the town could see that all you'd done was twist your ankle. So if anyone was looking around for another way to put a stopper on you, there was the Range Rover, just standing there unguarded all night in the car park, conspicuously yours and painted with silver and gold to attract attention.'

'Yes.'

'When I was taking driving lessons, which was mostly in the Easter holidays, I read a lot of motoring magazines – '

'I thought you were supposed to be revising for your A levels, your university entrance exams.'

'Um ... I was riding for Sir Vivian, too. I mean, I can *think* in algebra. I just had to make sure I understood all the exam questions that have been set before, set in the past. I don't mean to sound big-headed, really I don't, but I had sort of a lot of spare mental time, so I read the motor magazines. I didn't know you had a Range Rover – but I read about them. I read about their anti-thief devices. So when your Range Rover had stood quiet in the car park all night, and you had the only keys to disarm the screech alarms, then if anyone had done any harm it had to have been from outside ... or underneath ...' I tapered off, feeling silly, but he waved for me to go on.

'I thought the brake fluid might have been drained so that the brakes wouldn't work,' I said. 'I thought the tyres might have been slashed so that you'd have a blow-out when you were going fast. Things come whizzing round corners on that road to Quindle ... you wouldn't have much chance in a car out of control, but a Range Rover is pretty well built like a tank – so *you* might be unhurt in a crash, but you might kill the people you crashed *into* ... or at least injure them badly ... and that would stop you being elected, wouldn't it?'

My father took his time in moving, and in answering. 'It wasn't the brakes or the tyres,' he said.

'It was the engine oil.'

He nodded. 'Tell me what you think.'

I said, 'I think Fordham knew what was wrong before he came. He said he was an expert in sabotage in motor racing, and nothing about the Range Rover surprised him. It must have seemed pretty elementary to him.'

My father, smiling, said, 'I've known him a long time. So, what did he tell me?'

This is some sort of test, I thought. I could only guess at answers; but anyhow, I guessed. 'Someone unscrewed the sump-plug and removed it, and stuffed up the hole so that the oil couldn't all run out.'

'Go on.'

'The stopper was something that would fall out later, so the oil would all drain out of the engine when it was going along, and the engine would seize up solid, and as it's a four-wheel drive you wouldn't be able to steer and you would be like a block of stone in the middle of the road.'

'Not bad.'

'But Terry – the mechanic – pushed the substitute plug right through into the sump like a cork in a bottle, which I honestly don't think he should have done, and screwed in a new plug before he refilled with clean oil . . . like I told you on the phone.'

'Mm. So what was the substitute plug made of?'

I'd been thinking about it while we drove round the suburbs. I said hesitantly, 'To begin with I thought it would be something chemical that could react with the oil and make it like jelly, or something, so that it couldn't be pumped round the pistons and they would seize up in the cylinders, but that can't have been right as the plug was in the sump when Foster Fordham drove fast towards Quindle and deliberately made the engine very hot, and he insisted on Terry draining out the clean oil again when it was still hot, so I thought that perhaps the temporary stopper had *melted*, and Fordham has taken the oil away to see what was in it.'

'Yes,' my father said.

'Because if it had melted away in the sump drainhole when we were on our way to Quindle yesterday, it would have taken only about a minute for all the oil to drain out and ruin the engine. When the oil was hot this morning, when Terry drained it, it ran out as thin as water.'

'Fordham says it's an old trick. So old, it's never attempted now in motor racing.'

'Well ... what was the plug made of?'

'What would you think?'

I hesitated. 'It had to be pretty simple. I mean, almost spur-of-the-moment, after the bullet had missed.'

'So?'

'So how about shoving a candle up the spout, and cutting it off? How about *wax*?'

My father peacefully tied his unexuberantly striped tie. 'Foster Fordham,' he said, 'will let us know.'

It was extraordinary, I thought, as we entered the Town Hall for the Bethune face-to-face confrontation, how many people I'd come to recognise in only two days.

Orinda was there, torturing herself, wearing a very short gold dress with a black feather boa that twisted round her neck and arms like the snake it was named for, and demanded admiring attention. Her green eyes flashed. An emerald and diamond bracelet sparkled on her wrist. No one could be unaware of her vibrant attendance.

A pace behind her, as ever, stood her shadow, whose name I remembered with an effort was A.L. Wyvern. 'A.L.', I thought, 'Anonymous Lover' Wyvern. He had looked uninteresting in a dinner jacket at the Sleeping Dragon dinner: in the Town Hall, in a grey suit and a blue shirt, he filled space without making an impression.

Large Mrs Kitchens, eagle-eyed, in navy blue with purple frills, held tight to 'my Leonard's' arm and succeeded in preventing him from beaming his sickly moustache into Orinda's airspace. Mrs Kitchens gave me a cheery wave and a leer -- and I would *not* let her embarrass me.

Mervyn, of course, had arrived with Crystal at his side to take notes. The three witches were helping to seat people, and Dearest Polly, at the sight of us, made an enthusiastic little run in our direction, and bore off my father like a trophy to show him the lectern behind which he was to stand on the platform. Dearest Polly, it seemed, was stage-managing the evening.

As if with a flourish of trumpets the Bethune camp arrived. There was a stir and a rustle in the hall and a sprinkle of clapping. Hooray for adultery, I thought.

Paul Bethune, seen for the first time, was a portly and portentous-looking fifty or so with a double chin and the thinning hair that might in the end confound his chances more thoroughly than a love-child. He was accompanied by a busy Mervyn Teck lookalike, who was indeed his agent, and by a nervous woman who looked at the world in general in upward glances from under her eyebrows. She was shown to a seat in the front row of spectators and Dearest Polly, beckoning to me strongly, introduced me to Paul Bethune's wife, Isobel.

Isobel emitted severe discomfort at having me to sit beside her, but I gave her my best harmless grin and told her she couldn't want to avoid being there more than I did myself.

'I've only just left school,' I said. 'I don't know anything about politics. I understand this is the third campaign for you and Mr Bethune, so you probably don't find it as confusing as I do.'

'Oh dear,' she said. 'You're such a child, you can't possibly know . . .'

'I'm nearly eighteen.'

She smiled weakly, then suddenly stiffened to immobility, her face pale with a worse disaster than my proximity.

I said, 'What's the matter, Mrs Bethune?'

'That man,' she murmured. 'Oh God.'

I looked where she was looking, and saw Basil Rudd.

'That's not Usher Rudd, the newspaperman,' I said, understanding. 'That's his cousin. That's Basil Rudd. He mends cars.'

'It's *him*. That beastly writer.'

95

'No, Mrs Bethune. It's his cousin. They look alike, but that's Basil.'

To my absolute horror, she began to cry. I looked around urgently for help but Polly was elbow-deep in wires to microphones and television cameras, and Paul Bethune, eyeing his wife's distress, turned away deliberately with a sharply displeased grimace.

Unkind bastard, I thought. Stupid, too. A show of fondness might have earned him votes.

Isobel Bethune stumbled to her feet, searching unsuccessfully in her well-worn black handbag for something to mop up tears, and I, clumsily but with pity, offered her an arm to hold on to while I cleared a path towards the door.

She talked all the way in broken half-intelligible explanations. 'Paul insisted I came ... I didn't want to, but he said I might as well stab him in the back if I didn't ... and now he'll be so *furious*, but what does he expect me to do after all those pictures in the paper of him and that girl ... and she had nothing on, well, next to nothing. He wants me to smile and pretend I don't mind, but he makes me look a fool and I suppose I am, but I didn't know about that girl until it was in the paper, and he doesn't deny it. He says what did I expect ...'

We went through the entrance hall and out into the fresh air with everyone arriving and staring at Isobel's tears with hungry curiosity. At seven-thirty in the evening merciful dusk was still some time ahead, so I veered away from the entrance and she, wholly without resistance, came with me round the nearest corner.

The Town Hall formed one of the sides of the cobbled square. The Sleeping Dragon took up an adjoining side, with shops (and party headquarters) along the other two. Wide alleyways, that once had been open roads, led away from every corner, and on one of them lay the main Town Hall entrance doors. Along the side of the Town Hall that faced onto the square, there was a sort of cloister – a covered walkway with pillars and benches giving shelter and rest. Isobel Bethune crumpled onto one of the benches and, after a craven moment of wanting to ditch her, I sat beside her and wondered what to say.

I needn't have worried. She compulsively went on sobbing and pouring out her unhappiness and resentment at the unfairness of things. I half listened, watching the wretchedness that twisted her lipsticked mouth, and seeing in her swelling eyes and grey-flecked hair that not long ago she'd been quite pretty, before Usher Rudd had taken a photographic sledgehammer to her complacent world.

Her sons were just as bad, she sobbed. Fifteen, seventeen, they sulked and argued with everything she said and complained non-stop. If Paul got elected it would at least take him away from home more, and, oh dear, she didn't mean to say that, but it was either him or her – and where would she go? She was at her wit's end, she said.

She was on the point of a full breakdown, I thought. I had been only about twelve when my Aunt Susan had screamed and yelled and slammed doors, had driven the family car across the lawn into a hedge and been taken to hospital, and had then got worse when her second son left to join a rap group and grew a beard and got AIDS. My Uncle Harry had gone to my father for help, and somehow or other my parent had restored general order and put some balance back in Susan; and if it was never a rapturously happy household after that, there was no actual abuse.

I asked Isobel Bethune, 'Do your sons want Mr Bethune to be elected?'

'They just grunt. You can't get a word out of them.' She sniffed, wiping her eyes with her fingers. 'Paul thinks he would have beaten Orinda easily, but he says George Juliard is different. Oh! I'd forgotten, you're his son! I shouldn't talk to you like this. Paul will be so cross.'

'Don't tell him.'

'No . . . would you like a drink?' She looked across at the Sleeping Dragon. 'Brandy?'

I shook my head but she said she badly needed a nerve-steadier and she wouldn't drink alone, so I went across the square with her and drank Coke while she dealt with a double Rémy Martin on ice. We sat at a small table in the bar, which was Friday-night busy with couples.

Both of Isobel's hands were shaking.

She left me to go and 'tidy up', returning with combed hair, freshened lipstick and powdered eyelids, still clutching a tissue but much more in control.

She ordered more brandy. I said no to Coke.

'I'm not going back to the Town Hall,' she said. 'I'll walk home from here. It's not all that far.'

When she picked up her refilled glass, the ice still clattered and shook in her grasp.

'Could I get you a taxi?' I asked.

She leaned across the table and put her hand on mine. 'You're a nice boy,' she said, 'whoever your father is.'

There was a familiar bright flash and the whine of a film winding on and there, a few feet away, stood the other Rudd, Bobby Usher himself, grinning triumphantly and radiating ill nature in megawatts.

Isobel Bethune lunged furiously to her feet but Usher Rudd, quick at getaways, was out of the door before she could draw breath to shout. 'I *hate* him,' she said, again near to tears. 'I'll kill him.'

I asked the barman to phone for a taxi.

'Mrs Bethune still owes for the drinks.'

'Oh.'

'I haven't any money,' she said. 'Pay for me, there's a dear.'

I salvaged from my pockets the remains of the

money my father had given me in Brighton and handed her all of it.

'You pay the man for the drinks. I'm not old enough yet to buy alcohol and I'm not getting into that sort of trouble.'

Both the barman and Isobel, open-mouthed, completed the sale.

CHAPTER FIVE

Back at the Town Hall the debate had passed through lukewarm and was heating towards chopping motions with the hands of the two protagonists.

A local chess champion, brought in as referee, had come to the fray with a pinging time clock and, making his own set of rules, he had decreed that each candidate would in turn answer specific questions, the answers to last a maximum of five minutes before being silenced by the time clock's arbitration.

The format seemed to be working quite well, chiefly because both candidates knew how to speak. I was no longer surprised by my father's ability to rouse, amuse and convince, but somehow I'd expected Paul Bethune to be as bombastic and unkind as he'd seemed to his wife. Instead he delivered dryly witty and well-prepared responses to the questions and it was only afterwards that I wondered if he'd learned his best phrases by heart and had used them before.

The Town Hall was full. The seats given by Polly to me and Isobel Bethune now held the Mayor and his missus and, glad to be less exposed, I stood by the door and watched the waves of animation and agreement and fury roll in turn across the faces of the audience, and thought that at least they were *listening*, and obviously cared.

There could be no winner that night. They both won. Everyone applauded and went away talking.

Orinda had several times clapped Bethune. Leonard Kitchens kept his hands for ever in his pockets. Dearest Polly's long face glowed with goodness and pleasure, and freckly Basil Rudd looked even more like his obnoxious cousin when he smiled.

No one produced a gun.

My father and Paul Bethune shook hands.

Like star actors they left the stage last, each surrounded at once by chattering satellites, all with something to say, questions to ask, points to make. My father genuinely enjoyed it, and again his spirits were helium-ballooning as we headed back to our base.

'It's quicker if we walk straight across the square,' my parent objected as I tried to persuade him to take to the cloister. 'Why do you want to walk two sides of a triangle, not one, and you a mathematician?'

'Bullets,' I said.

'My God.' He stopped dead. 'But no one would try again!'

'You'd have said no one would try the first time but they did.'

'We don't know for sure.'

'And the sump-plug?'

He shook his head as if in general disbelief, but he made no further objection to the cloister route, and seemed not to notice that I walked between him and the well-lit open square.

He wanted to talk about the debate. He also wanted to know why I'd missed half of it and where I'd been. I told him all of Isobel's troubles but I could feel he was barely attending: his mind and his tongue were still busy with points made and lost against the lady's unfaithful man.

'He's dedicated, you know. I can't stand his politics.'

I said, 'I hate what you say, but I'll defend to the death your right to say it.'

'Bull's eye. Don't tell me all those school fees weren't wasted.'

'Come down,' I begged. 'You're too high in the sky.'

Again he stopped walking. We had by then left the cloister and were passing dimly lit shop fronts on the way to the bay windows of first the charity gift shop and, next door, the party headquarters.

'You have no idea what it's like to hold an audience in your hand.'

'No.' Winners at long odds got little praise, and I'd never won on a favourite.

We walked on to the doorway.

Dearest Polly waited there, puzzled. 'Where have you been? You left ahead of me.'

'The boy,' my father said, pointing at me though

there were precious few other boys in sight. 'Benedict, my son, has this fixed idea that someone is violently seeking to put paid to my campaign, if not to my life. Dearest Polly, tell him I'll take my chances and I don't want him ever again to risk his own neck to preserve mine.'

'Dearest Polly,' I said – and she smiled vividly with sweetness – 'this is the only father I'm ever likely to have. Persuade him to give me a real job in this election. Persuade him he needs a full-time bodyguard. Persuade him to let me try to keep him safe.'

'I don't need a bodyguard,' he insisted. 'I need you to be a social asset. Isobel Bethune is useless to Paul, but you have this extraordinary gift – which I admit I didn't expect – of getting people to talk to you. Look at Isobel Bethune! Look at Crystal Harley! I haven't got a word out of her and she chatters away to you. Look at Mrs Kitchens, pouring information into your ears.'

Polly nodded, smiling. 'You're so young, you're no threat to anyone. They all need to talk, and you're safe.'

I said pensively, 'How about Orinda? She turned her back on me at the dinner and wouldn't say a word.'

Polly clapped her hands together with laughter. 'I'll give you Orinda. I'll manage it again.'

'But alone,' I said. 'I could talk to her if she was

alone, but the Anonymous Lover never leaves her side.'

'Who?'

'A.L. Wyvern.'

'Anonymous Lover!' Polly exclaimed. 'Enchanting. His name's really Alderney, I think. He plays golf. He used to play golf with Dennis.'

She moved around smoothly, at home in the office, sorting out mugs and making coffee. I couldn't guess her age nearer than ten years: somewhere between forty or fifty, I thought, but knew I could be wrong. She was again wearing the inappropriate crimson lipstick, this time with a green jacket over a long skirt of brownish tweed: heavy for August. Somehow, with the opaque stockings and 'sensible' shoes, one would have expected her to be clumsy, but she was paradoxically graceful, as if she had once been a dancer. She had no rings on her long capable fingers and for jewellery relied on a single strand of maidenly pearls.

One could have felt sorry for Polly at first sight, I thought, but that would have been a great mistake. She had an inner certainty to go with the goodness. She carried the fuddy-duddy clothes without self-consciousness. She was – I fished for the word – serene.

She said, pouring hot water onto instant coffee granules, 'I don't see any harm in Benedict appointing himself officially to look after you. After all, he hasn't done a bad job so far. Mervyn grumbled all over the Town Hall tonight about having to find a lock-up garage because Benedict wanted one. He says he doesn't like Benedict giving him orders.'

'It was a suggestion, not an order,' my father said.

'It felt like an order to Mervyn, therefore to him it *was* an order. Mervyn resents Benedict's influence over you. Mervyn likes to be in charge.'

'Ben's only been here two days,' my father protested.

Polly smiled. 'Ten minutes was probably enough. You're a brilliant politician on a grand scale, George, but it's your son who sees into individual minds.'

My father looked at me thoughtfully.

'He's good at it now,' Polly said, 'and he's not yet eighteen. Just wait ten years or so. You brought him here to give yourself social credibility, proving you had a son, you weren't a bachelor, confirmed or otherwise, and you've found an asset you didn't expect, so use him, George.'

She stirred the mugs of coffee and distributed it black. My father absentmindedly fished a small container out of a pocket and tapped a sweetener into his drink.

'George?' Polly prompted.

He opened his mouth to answer but before he could speak the telephone rang, and as I was nearest I picked up the receiver.

'Juliard?' a voice said.

'Benedict. Do you want my father? He's here.'

106

'No. You'll do. Do you know who you're talking to?'

'Foster Fordham,' I said.

'Right. And have you worked out what was plugging your sump?'

'Something that would melt when the oil got really hot.'

He laughed. 'I refrigerated the oil and filtered it. There were enough wax globules to make a good thick plug. There are also cotton fibres which may have been from the wick of a candle. Now let me talk to your father.'

I handed over the receiver and listened to half of a long discussion that was apparently about whether or not to report the sabotage to the police. There had been no further action that my father knew of over the rifle shot but, he thought, and his opinion persuaded, that his friend Foster should write an account of what he'd done and what he'd found, and that my father should give a copy of it to the boys in blue as a precaution.

Polly and I listened to snatches. 'They don't have the manpower for surveillance . . . they won't do it . . . you can't guard against a determined assassin . . . yes . . .' my father's gaze slid my way, ' . . . but he's too young . . . all right, then . . . we're agreed.' He put down the receiver carefully and with deliberation and a sigh said, 'Foster Fordham will write a report for the police. Ben will nanny me to the best of his ability and Mervyn will have to put up with it. And now, dearest Polly, I'm going to abandon tomorrow's canvassing and go where I'm not expected.'

Hanging from a hook on one wall was a large appointments calendar with an extensive square allocated to each day. Crystal had entered the basics of my father's advance plans in the squares so that one could see at a glance what he would be doing on each day.

The programme had started the previous Tuesday with 'Candidate arrives. Office familiarisation.' Wednesday's schedule of 'Drive round constituency' had been crossed off, and 'Fetch son from Brighton' inserted instead and, underneath that, 'Dinner at Sleeping Dragon'. Nothing about being shot at on the way home.

The Quindle engagements and the infant school evening were listed for Thursday, and door-to-door canvassing and the Town Hall debate for Friday.

More of the same stretched ahead. If I hadn't had the interest of attempting to foil seriously dangerous attacks on said candidate I would have suffered severe strain of the smiling muscles long before polling day.

How could he face it? I wondered. How could he *enjoy* it, as he clearly did?

'Tomorrow,' he said, pleased with his inspiration, 'tomorrow we'll go to Dorset County racecourse. Tomorrow will be for Ben. We'll go to the races.'

My first reaction was joy, which he noted. Fast on

joy's heels came a sort of devastation that I couldn't hope to be riding there, that I would spend the afternoon as an exile, envying my neighbour his ox and his ass and his saddle in the amateurs' steeplechase; but I let only the joy show, I think.

'We'll go in the Range Rover,' my father said decisively, pleased with his plan. 'And Polly will come with us, won't you, Poll?'

Polly said she would love to.

Did Polly ever lie?

We drank the coffee without stress, my father finally as calm as he'd achieved during this whole strange week. Polly went out through the back office to retrieve her car and drive home, which I understood was a house in a wood outside the town, and my father and I, bolting everything securely, climbed the steep little staircase and slept undisturbed until Saturday morning.

Mervyn leaned in heavy annoyance on the bell at breakfast time and of course frowned heavily over the change of destination. How did George ever hope to be successful in a marginal seat if he neglected the door-to-door persuasion routine, which was of *paramount* importance? The Dorset County racecourse, sin of sins, was outside the Hoopwestern catchment area.

Never mind, my father soothed him, the many

Hoopwestern voters who went to the races might approve.

Mervyn, unconvinced, shut his mouth grimly for half an hour, but as the day expanded decided to salvage at least crumbs from what he considered the ruins of canvassing's best weekend opportunity and got busy on the telephone, with the result that we were invited to lunch with the racecourse Stewards and were otherwise showered with useful tickets. Mervyn, from long experience, knew everyone of influence in the county.

He blamed me, of course, for the switch, and perhaps with reason. If he'd had his way he would have been dancing happy attendance on Orinda, walking backwards in her presence. What he would have done with A.L. Wyvern I couldn't guess, but presumably he was used to the enigmatic shadow, as the Anonymous Lover had been deceased Dennis Nagle's best friend also. They played golf.

Mervyn's disappointments, I thought, shrugging off his ill will, were just too bad. In his life's terms, success lay in getting his candidate elected, or, if not elected, a close runner-up. Mervyn was not about to ruin his own reputation as agent out of tetchiness with Juliards, father or son.

The chilly atmosphere in the offices was lightened by an unexpected visit from the woman who ran the charity shop next door. She and Mervyn knew each other well, but she was fascinated to meet the new

110

candidate, she said; she had seen us come and go, she wanted to shake hands with George, she'd heard his son was a doll, she wondered if we would like a home-made apple pie.

She put her offering on my father's desk.

'Kind of you, Amy,' Mervyn said, and in his manner I read that not only had he known his neighbour a long time but he'd undervalued her for probably the whole period.

Amy was one of those people easy to undervalue; an apologetic unassuming middle-aged widow (Polly said) who received gifts of unwanted junk, spruced them up a bit to sell, and would never have dipped into the till before passing on the proceeds to the charity that maintained her. Amy was fluffy, honest and halfway to stupid: also kind and talkative. One day of unadulterated Amy, I thought, would last a lifetime.

It was easy not to listen to every word in the flow, but she did grab our attention at one point.

'Someone broke a pane of glass in our window on Wednesday night and I've had a terrible job getting it mended.' She told us at far too much length how she'd managed it. 'A policeman called, you know, and asked if the window had been broken by a rifle bullet but I said, of course not, I clean the floor first thing when I arrive every morning because, of course, I don't live upstairs like you can here. There's only a bath-room and one small room I use for storage, though

111

sometimes I do let a homeless person sleep there in an emergency. Anyway, of course I didn't find a bullet. I told the policeman, Joe it was, whose mother drives a school bus, and he came in for a look round and made a note or two. I saw it in the paper about the gun going off and maybe someone was shooting at Mr Juliard, you never feel safe these days, do you? And then, just now when I was dusting an old what-not that I can't seem to sell to anybody, I came to this *bump*, and I pulled it out, and I wonder if this was what Joe was looking for, so do you think I should tell him?'

She plunged a hand into a pocket in her drab droopy cardigan and put down on the desk, beside the apple pie, a squashed-looking piece of metal that had certainly flown at high speed from a .22 rifle.

'I do think,' my father said carefully, 'that you should tell your friend Joe, whose mother drives a school bus, that you've found the little lump of metal stuck in a what-not.'

'Do you really?'

'Yes, I do.'

Amy picked up the bullet, squinted at it, and polished it a bit on her cardigan. So much for residual fingerprints, I thought.

'All right, then,' Amy said cheerfully, putting the prize back in her pocket. 'I was sure you would know what I should do.'

She invited him to look around her shop, but he

cravenly sent me instead, and so I found myself staring at an ugly six-foot-high cane and wicker what-not that had stood near the window and had stopped the slug.

'I call it an *étagère* these days,' Amy said sadly. 'But still nobody wants it. I don't suppose *you* . . .?'

'No,' I said. And nor did I want any of the silver spoons or children's toys or second-hand clothes neatly and cleanly arranged to do good.

I retrieved the Range Rover from its safe haven, picked up my father and (following Mervyn's ungracious directions) found Polly's unexpectedly grand house in the woods. She sat on the rear seat for our journey to the races and, with a touch of glee, detailed a few telephone calls she had made; a touch of persuasion here, a dangle of carrot there.

'Mr Anonymous Lover Wyvern,' she said, 'received a lovely last-minute invitation to play golf in the county's top pro-am event of the year, an offer he'd have to have been ice to refuse. So off he was due to go with his precious clubs, and that was *him* out of the way.'

'How did you manage it?' my father asked admiringly.

'Inducements,' she said darkly. 'And, shortly afterwards, Orinda got invited to the Stewards' box at the races . . .'

'That's where we're going to!' exclaimed my father.

'You don't say!' Polly teased him. 'Benedict,' she

admonished me, 'I'm giving you Orinda without the lover, so don't waste the day.'

'But what can he do?' my father protested.

'He knows,' Polly said. 'How he'll do it, I can't tell, but trust your son.' She switched her attention back to me. 'Orinda knows bugger all about racing. She's going today for the snob value of a Duke, who's one of the Stewards. You'll have to contend with that. Think you can do it?'

I said a bit helplessly, 'I don't know.' Polly's forthright language always disconcerted me, although everyday lurid stable-talk passed my ears unnoticed.

'Go for shit,' she said.

Orinda was already into lobster mousse with diced cucumber when we reached the Stewards' luncheon room and although she looked outraged at our arrival she could do little but choke and recover with sips of wine, patted delicately on the back by the Duke at her side.

The Duke rose and gave Polly a conspiratorial kiss on the cheek, and I saw how Orinda had been hooked and reeled in.

Orinda wore a white linen suit with a green silk scarf tied and floating from a black lizard handbag that swung from the back of her chair. Sleek, matt-skinned, her presence easily eclipsed every other woman in the room, especially Polly who had dressed as usual as if not sure of the event or the season.

My father shook hands all round, his innate unmistakable power turning every head his way even in a roomful of powerful men. Orinda hated him.

'My son Benedict,' he said, introducing me: but it was he who claimed their eyes.

The Duke, hesitantly, said to me, 'Haven't I met you before? Haven't you ridden against my son Edward?'

'Yes, sir. At Towcester last Easter. He won.'

The Duke had a remembering smile. 'You finished third! It was Eddie's birthday. We had an impromptu party to celebrate. You were there.'

'Yes, sir.'

'Nothing like racing, is there? Best thing on earth, Eddie says.'

My father looked sharply at my face.

'Best thing,' I said.

'Mind you,' the Duke said to my father, 'for all these young men, it's only a hobby. Amateurs can't make a living at it. The best amateurs used to be able to turn pro but for some reason it's hardly ever done these days. Eddie needs a job. Amateurs can't ride for ever. I expect your Benedict knows all that. A good fellow, your Benedict, Eddie says. Sit down, Mr Juliard. It's an excellent lunch.'

He seated my father on the other side of him from Orinda, whose enjoyment of the day had waned to twilight even though the sun outside shone brightly.

115

She pushed away her unfinished mousse as if she could no longer taste it and had difficulty, with rigid facial muscles, in smiling at her host.

A stocky man of perhaps sixty, the Duke looked less patrician than industrious, a worldly-wise business-man, a managing director more than a figurehead chairman. His son, Eddie, a good fellow himself, had once said he envied the time I could give to racing: his own father insisted he work for his living. Well, I thought ruefully, Vivian Durridge and my own father had more than evened us up. Eddie's father owned horses which the son could ride in races, and mine didn't.

Polly and I were seated several places down the lengthy white-clothed dining table on the other side from the uncomfortable Orinda, and placidly ate our mousse and cucumber which was, as the Duke said, excellent, even though, now I'd been let off near-starvation, I would have preferred a large salami pizza.

There was some sort of curried chicken next. As time ran out towards the first race, the Duke, looking at his watch, told my father that as Chief Steward for the day he (the Duke) would have to leave the party now in order to carry out his duties. As if by accident he saw the near panic on Orinda's face at being left without a buffer zone between herself and her beastly usurper, and found an irresistible and apparently spur-of-the-moment solution.

With a flick of a glance at Polly, who was looking

particularly bland, the Duke said to Orinda kindly, 'Now, Mrs Nagle, I am truly concerned that you should enjoy and understand our splendid sport of steeple-chasing, and as I'll be busily occupied I can think of no one better to entrust you to than young Benedict there. He knows all about racing, in spite of his age, and he will take you round and show you everything, and we will all meet up here again after, say, the second race. So, Benedict,' he spoke to me loudly down the table, 'be a good fellow and take Mrs Nagle down to see the horses walk round the parade ring. Watch the race with her. Answer her questions, right?'

I said, 'Yes, sir,' faintly, and the Duke, nodding benignly, more or less pushed Orinda into my arms. I sensed her begin to stiffen and refuse but the Duke made urging motions towards the door as if there were no possibility of a change of his plans, and over my shoulder, as I followed the white linen suit into the passage outside, I caught glimpses of astonishment on my father's face and a wide grin on Polly's.

Orinda marched along the passage and down the stairs at the end into the open air; and there she stopped dead and said, 'This is ridiculous.'

'Yes,' I said.

'What do you mean, yes?'

'I mean, you're not going to listen to me because you hate my father, which is pretty unreasonable when you look at it, but I'd probably feel the same way, so if you like I'll just leave you here and go and look at the horses which is actually what I want to do anyhow.'

She said irritably, inconsequentially, 'I'm old enough to be your mother.'

'Easily,' I said. Hardly tactful.

In spite of her fury she almost laughed. 'You're supposed to say I couldn't be.'

'Sorry.'

'Mervyn says you're only seventeen.'

'I'll be eighteen in two weeks.'

'What will I do, if you just dump me here?'

'Well,' I said, 'I won't dump you. But if you want me to vanish, well, round that corner you'll find the parade ring where the horses walk round before the race so that everyone can see what they're putting their money on.'

'What if I want to bet?'

'Bookmakers or the Tote?'

'What's going to win?'

I smiled at her with real goodwill. 'If I knew, if anyone knew, I'd be rich.'

'And if you were rich?'

'I'd buy a string of racehorses, and ride them.'

I hadn't expected the question, and the answer I'd given her came straight from the honesty of childhood. I wasn't yet used to being adult. My mind, and also my voice and physical co-ordination, could switch disconcertingly sometimes back to fifteen, even in dreams to thirteen. Some days I could ski downhill with sharp turning certainty: other days I'd crash out on the first bend. Some days I'd move in total harmony with a horse's gallop: other days I'd have gawky arms and legs. Always, so far always, I could shoot and hit the inner or the bull, a two-inch spot at a hundred yards.

Orinda said formally, 'I'd be grateful if you'd accompany me to the parade ring.'

I nodded as if she were conceding nothing, and with minute body signs steered her to where the horses plodded round the ring, the sun shining on their coats, the smell and sound of them piercing my senses, the last four days setting up in me such an acute sense of loss that I wished myself anywhere on earth but on a racecourse.

'What's the matter?' Orinda said.

'Nothing.'

'That's not true.'

'It doesn't matter.'

She had given me a perfect opening for what I wanted to say to her, but I miserably shrank from it. I hadn't expected to feel so grindingly forlorn: an exile looking through a glass barrier at a life denied him.

I found a place for us to stand against the rails of the parade ring, and I gave her my racecard, as she had left her own upstairs. She needed spectacles from her handbag to see small print with, and help in identifying the runners from their number cloths.

'What do all these figures mean?' she asked, scratchily pointing to the card. 'It's double Dutch to me.'

'They tell you the horse's age and how much weight he's carrying in the race. Those very small figures tell you his results in the last races he's run in.' I pointed. 'F means fell, and P means he pulled up and didn't finish.'

'Oh.' She studied the card and read aloud the conditions of entry to the first race, a two-and-a-half-mile hurdle race for novices.

'A race for four-year-olds and upwards, which at the start of the season have not won a hurdle race ... but if they *have* won a hurdle race since the start of the season, they are to carry a 7-lb penalty.' She looked up, disliking me. 'What's a 7-lb penalty?'

'Extra weight. Most often flat thin sheets of lead carried in pockets in the weight cloth which lies over the horse's back under the number cloth and saddle.' I explained that a jockey had to carry the weight allotted to his horse. 'You get weighed before and after a race ...'

'Yes, yes, I'm not totally ignorant.'

'Sorry.'

She studied the racecard. 'There's only one horse in this race carrying a 7-lb penalty,' she announced. 'Will he win?'

'He might if he's very good.'

She turned the pages of the card, looking forward.

'In almost every race a horse carries a penalty if it's won recently.'

'Mm.'

'What's the heaviest penalty you can get?'

I said, 'I don't think there's any set limit, but in practice a 10-lb penalty is the most a horse will be faced with. If he had to carry more than ten pounds extra in a handicap he almost certainly wouldn't win, so the trainer wouldn't run him.'

'But you *could* win with a 10-lb penalty?'

'Yes, just about.'

'A lot to ask?'

'It depends how strong the horse is.'

She put her glasses away and wanted me to go with her to the Tote, where she backed the horse that had won on the first day of the season and earned himself an extra seven pounds of lead. 'He must be the best,' she said.

Almost as tall as I was, Orinda walked always a pace ahead of me as if it were natural to her to have her escort to her rear. She was used to being looked at, and I did see that her clothes drew admiration, even if more geared to Ascot than a country meeting in the boondocks of rural far-from-all-crowds Dorset.

We stood on the steps of the grandstand to watch the race. Orinda's choice finished fourth.

'Now what?' she said.

'Same thing all over again.'

'Don't you get bored with it?'

'No.'

She tore her Tote ticket across and let the pieces flutter to the ground like a seasoned loser.

'I don't see much fun in this.' She looked around at a host of people studying racecards. 'What do you do if it rains?'

The simple answer was 'get wet', but it would hardly have pleased her.

'People come to see the horses as much as to gamble,' I said. 'I mean, horses are marvellous.'

She gave me a pitying stare and said that after the following races she would return to the Stewards' room to thank the Duke for his hospitality, and then she would leave. She couldn't see the fascination that jump racing held for everyone.

I said, 'I can't see what fascination politics has for my father, but for him now it's his whole life.'

We were walking back towards the parade ring where the horses were beginning to appear for the second race. She stopped abruptly from one stride to the next and faced me with frank hostility.

'Your father,' she said acidly, biting off each word as if she could crunch them to splinters of glass, 'has stolen my purpose in life. It is *I* who should represent Hoopwestern in Parliament. It was *I* who was supposed to be fighting this election, and I'd have won it too, which is more than your precious father will do for all his machismo.'

'He didn't know you existed,' I said. 'He was sent by the central party in Westminster to fight the by-election, if he could get selected. He didn't set out to replace you personally.'

She demanded, 'How do you know?'

'He told me. He's been giving me a condensed course in politics since last Wednesday, when he brought me here as window dressing. He respects the way you feel. And actually, if he had you on his side, and if because of that he did get elected, then maybe you could be as good a team with him as you were with Mr Nagle.'

'You're a *child*,' she said.

'Yes... sorry. But everyone here says how outstanding you are at work in the constituency.'

She made no comment, angry or otherwise, but began as before to study her racecard, leaning on the parade ring rails as if at home.

After a bit she said, 'What your father wants is power.'

'Yes.' I paused. 'Do you?'

'Of course.'

Power stalked past us in the muscular rumps of fully grown steeplechasers, animals capable of covering ground at thirty miles an hour or more for distances of from four and a half miles: the length and speed of the Grand National. No animal on earth could better a racehorse for stamina and speed. That power... *that* was power for me. To share it, guide it, jump with it. Oh, dear God, give me that power.

'Usher Rudd,' Orinda said, 'do you know who I mean?'

'Yes.'

'Usher Rudd told my friend Alderney Wyvern – um, do you know who I mean by Alderney Wyvern?'

'Yes again.'

'Usher Rudd says George Juliard is not only lying about you being his legitimate son but maintains you are his catamite.'

'His what?' If I sounded bewildered, it was because I was. 'What's a ... a cat of mice?'

'You don't know what he means?'

'No.'

'A catamite is a boy ... a prostitute boy lover.'

I wasn't so much outraged as astonished. In fact, I laughed.

'Usher Rudd,' Orinda said warningly, 'is a tireless researcher. Don't take him lightly.'

'But I thought Paul Bethune was his sleaze target.'

'Anyone is,' Orinda said. 'He makes up lies. He likes to destroy people. He'll do it for money if he can, but if there's no money in it he'll do it for pleasure. He's a butterfly-wing puller. Are you George Juliard's legitimate son?'

'I look like him, a bit.'

She nodded.

'And he did marry my mother – in front of a lot

124

of witnesses.' (Disapproving witnesses, but never mind.)

The news seemed not to please her.

'I suppose,' I said, 'that you would prefer Usher Rudd to be right? Then you could have got rid of my father?'

'Alderney Wyvern says it will take more than an Usher Rudd fabrication. It's a matter of finding a strong lever.'

She sounded fiercely bitter. Whatever Polly thought of my ability to understand unhappiness and release it, I felt lost in the maze of Orinda's implacable grievances against my father.

'Someone took a shot at him,' I said.

Orinda shook her head. 'Another lie.'

'I was there,' I protested.

'So was Alderney,' she said. 'He saw what happened. George Juliard tripped on the cobbles and someone loosed a single shot out of high spirits and Juliard claimed it had been aimed at him! Utter *rubbish*. He'll do anything for publicity.'

I thought: Orinda herself would never get under a car and unscrew a sump-plug. However careful one might be, oil would run out before one could thrust a candle into the drain. Even if she knew how and where to unscrew the plug, engine oil and Orinda's clothes couldn't be thought of together in a month of canvassing.

Orinda needed glasses to read a racecard: I couldn't envisage her aiming and firing a target rifle.

Orinda might wish my father dead, but couldn't kill him herself, and didn't believe that anyone else had tried.

Orinda, I thought, hadn't asked or paid anyone to get rid of her rival physically. There were limits to her hate.

I took her across the course to watch the second race from near one of the fences, to give her at least some sensation of the speed involved. Her narrow high heels tended to dig into the turf and stick, making walking difficult, which didn't please her. I was not, I acknowledged to myself in depression, making a great success of the afternoon.

She was, though, impressed by the noise and energy of the half-ton horses soaring or crashing through the tops of the big black birch fence, and she could hear the jockeys shouting to each other and to their mounts; could see the straining legs in white breeches and the brilliant colours of the silks in the August sun. And whether she wanted me to know it or not, she did quite suddenly understand why this sort of racing fascinated the Duke and everyone else who had made the effort and the journey to the racecourse.

When the horses had surged past us again and were striving their way to the winning post, while the very air still vibrated with their passage, I said, 'I do

126

understand what you feel about having been passed over by the selectors.'

Orinda said unkindly, 'You can't possibly. You're far too young.'

Almost in desperation I said, 'You've lost what you most wanted, and it's near to unbearable. You were looking forward to a sort of life that would be a joy every day, that would fulfil you and give you inner power to achieve your best dreams, and it's been snatched away. You've been told you can't have it. The pain of it's brutal. Believe me, I do know.'

She stared, the green eyes wide.

'You don't have to be old,' I said. 'You can feel it if you're only six and you passionately want a pony and you've nowhere to keep it and it's not sensible to start with. And I . . .' I swallowed. I wanted to stop again, but this time found the grit for the words. 'I wanted *this*.' I swept an arm to the black fence, to the whole wide racecourse. 'I wanted all of *this*. I've wanted to be a jockey for as long as I can remember. I've grown up in the belief that this would be my life. I've grown up feeling warm and certain of my future, and . . . well . . . this week it's been snatched away from me. This week I've been told I can't live this life, I'm not a good enough rider, I haven't the spark to be the jockey I want to be. The trainer I was riding for told me to leave. My father says he'll pay for me to go to university, but not for me to waste my time riding in races when I'm not going to be brilliant.

It didn't really sink in . . . I didn't know how absolutely *awful* it would be until I came here today . . . but I'd like to scream, actually, and roll on the ground, and if you think you have to be old enough to be my mother to feel as you do, well, you're wrong.'

CHAPTER SIX

At the end of the afternoon I glumly drove the Range Rover back to Polly's house in the woods, feeling that I'd wasted all her planning and not only failed to profit from an unrepeatable opportunity but had positively made things worse.

By the time Orinda and I had recrossed the course (her heels were sticking worse than ever) and regained the Stewards' room, the Duke had disappeared again towards his duties. Orinda watched the third race from the viewing balcony leading out of the luncheon room, her back relentlessly turned towards me, her manner forbidding conversation.

A horse carrying a 7-lb penalty won the race. Orinda hadn't backed it.

When the Duke returned, all smiles at the sight of her, she thanked him charmingly for his hospitality and left. She said nothing to my father or to Polly or to myself, ignoring our existence, and I survived the last three races wishing I were smaller, richer, and at the very least a genius. Settling for the obvious privileges I had seemed dreary compared with the fairy-tale lost.

When Polly invited us into her house my father accepted at once.

'Cheer up,' he commanded to my silent reluctance. 'No one wins all the time. Say something. You haven't said anything for hours.'

'All right ... Orinda said Usher Rudd wants to know if I'm your catamite.'

My father spluttered into the gin that Polly had poured him.

Polly said, 'What's a catamite?', but my father knew.

I said, 'Usher Rudd's trying to prove I'm not your son. If you have a marriage certificate, put it in a bank vault.'

'And your birth certificate, where's that?'

'With my stuff at Mrs Wells.'

He frowned. My things hadn't followed me so far. He borrowed Polly's phone and called my ex-landlady forthwith. 'She's packed everything,' he reported, 'but the carriers I ordered haven't turned up. I'll see to it again on Monday.'

'My bicycle is at the stables.'

He caught some sense of the wreck he'd made of my aspirations, but I also saw quite clearly that he still expected me to face reality thoroughly and grow up.

'Tough it out,' he said.

'Yes.'

Polly looked from one of us to the other and said, 'The boy's doing his best for you, George.'

Leaving her in her house I drove the Range Rover back to Hoopwestern, familiar at last with the four-wheel drive and the weight and size. I disembarked my parent at a church hall (directions from Mervyn) where he was due to meet and thank the small army of volunteers working for him and the party's sake throughout the whole scattered area of the constituency. The volunteers had brought their families and their neighbours, and also tea, beer, wine and cake to sustain them and my father's inexhaustible enthusiasm to energise them for the next three weeks.

'My son . . . this is my son.' He presented me over and over again, and I shook hands and smiled and smiled and chatted up old ladies and talked football with shaky knowledge and racing with piercing regret.

Mervyn moved from group to group with plans and lists. This ward would be canvassed tomorrow, that ward on Monday: leaflets . . . posters . . . visits . . . leave not one of seventy thousand voters unaware of JULIARD.

Three more weeks of it . . . Even with the spice of looking out for stray attacks, the campaign at that point seemed more like purgatory than appealing.

But I'd said I would do it . . . and I would.

I ate chocolate cake. Still no pizza.

At goodbye time I collected the Range Rover from where I'd parked it in a nearby road and was as sure

131

as possible that no one had tampered with it that evening.

Foster Fordham had given me simple instructions on the telephone. 'Always take with you a carton of dishwasher powder in a box with a spout. When you park the vehicle, sprinkle a thin line of powder on the ground from behind each front wheel back to the rear wheel on the same side. If anyone has moved the vehicle or wriggled under it in your absence, the powder will tell you. Understand?'

'Yes. Thank you.'

'Always set the alarms carefully, and disable them and start the vehicle from a distance, however short a time you've been away.'

I'd followed his instructions faithfully, but our sump-plug merchant had tried no other tricks. I ferried my father safely from the church hall back to the bow-fronted head-quarters and left him there with Mervyn, the two of them endlessly discussing tactics, while I housed the Range Rover in its lock-up and finally ran a pizza to earth in the local take-away.

Mervyn and my father absentmindedly ate half of it. Mervyn laid out dozens of stickers and leaflets in piles, ready for distribution. Yes, he said when I asked him, *of course* by-elections were wildly exciting, they were the peaks of an agent's busy life. And there were the final touches to be arranged for the fund-raising fête organised for next week – such a pity Orinda wasn't in charge of it this time . . .

132

I yawned and climbed the narrow stairs, leaving my two elders to lock up: and I woke in the night to a strong smell of smoke.

Smoke.

I sat bolt upright in bed.

Without much more than instinct I disentangled my legs from the sheets and violently shook the unconscious lump on the neighbouring mattress, yelling at him, 'We're on fire!' as I leapt to the half-open door to see if what I said was actually, devastatingly true.

It was.

Down the stairs there were fierce yellow leaping flames, devouring and roaring. Smoke funnelled up in growing billows. Ahead of me the sitting-room blazed yellow with flames from the rear-office underneath.

Gasping at once for breath in the smoke, I swivelled fast on one foot and jumped into the bathroom. If I switched on the taps, I thought, the bath and the washbasin would overflow and help to drown the flames: I pushed the stoppers into the plug-holes and opened all the taps to maximum: and I swept a large bath towel into the toilet bowl and pulled the flush. Whisking the sopping towel into the bedroom, I closed the door against the smoke and laid the wet towel along the bottom of the door with a sort of speed near to frenzy.

'The window,' I yelled. 'The bloody window's stuck.'

The window was stuck shut with layers of paint and had been annoying my father for days. We were both wearing only underpants, and the air was growing hot. 'We can't go down the stairs.' Doesn't he understand? I thought. He smoothly picked up the single bedroom chair and smashed it against the window. Glass broke, but the panes were small and the wooden frames barely cracked. We were above the bow windows facing the square. A second smash with the chair burst through the sticky layers of old paint and swung open both sides of the window – but underneath the fire had already eaten through the bay window's roof and was shooting up the wall.

The bay window of the charity shop next door blazed also with manic energy. If anything the fire next door was hotter and older and had reached the roof, with scarlet and gold sparks shooting into the sky above our heads.

I scrambled over to the door, thinking the stairs the only way out after all, but even if the wet towel was still holding back the worst of the smoke it was useless against flame. The door knob was now too hot to touch. The whole door had fire on the far side.

I shouted with fierceness, 'We're burning. The door's on fire.'

My father stared at me briefly across the room.

'We'll have to take our chances and jump. You first.'

He put the damaged chair against the window wall

and motioned me to climb up and leap out as far as I could.

'You go,' I said.

There were people now in the square and voices yelling, and the raucous siren of the fire engine coming nearer.

'Hurry,' my father said. 'Don't bloody argue. Jump.'

I stood on the chair and held onto the window frame. The paint on it scorched my hands.

'*Jump*!'

I couldn't believe it – he was struggling into shirt and trousers and zipping up his fly.

'Go on. *Jump*!'

I put a bare foot on the frame, pulled myself up and leapt out with every scrap of muscle power . . . with strong legs and desperation: and I sailed through the flames from the bay window and missed the front burning edge of it by terrifying inches and crashed down onto the dark cobbled ground with a head-stunning disorientating impact. I heard people yelling and felt hands grabbing me to pull me away from the fire and I was choking with smoke and winded by hitting the unyielding ground and rolling, and also fighting to free myself from the firmly clutching hands to help to cushion my father's fall when he jumped down after me. I had no strength. Sat on the ground. Couldn't even speak.

Incredibly there were camera flashes. People were *recording* our extreme danger, our closeness to dying.

I felt helplessly angry. Outraged. Near to sobbing. Illogical, I dare say.

Voices were screaming to my father to jump and voices were screaming to my father *not* to jump, to wait for the bellowing fire engine now charging across the square, scattering onlookers and spilling people in yellow helmets.

'Wait, wait,' people screamed as firemen released their swivelling ladder to extend it to my father, but he was standing up silhouetted in the window with a reddish glow behind him. He was standing on the chair – and the door behind him was burning.

Before the ladder reached him there was an outburst of bright sunlike flame in the room at his back and he stood on the window frame and threw himself out as I had done, flung himself through the climbing fire of the bow windows below into the darkness beyond, knowing he might break his neck and smash his skull, knowing the ground was there but unable to judge how far away: but too near. Break-your-bones near.

A camera flashed.

Two men in yellow suits like moonsuits were sprinting, heavy-gloved hands outstretched, dragging as they went a circular trampoline thing for catching jumpers. No time to position it. They simply ran, and my father crashed down into them, all the figures sprawling, arms and legs flying. People crowded to help them and hid the tangle from my sight but my father's legs had been moving with life, and he had *shoes* on, which he hadn't had upstairs.

I was covered in smoky dirt and bleeding from a few cobble-induced scrapes and grazes, and I had tears running down my face, although I didn't know I was crying: and I was dazed still and was coughing and had blisters forming on my fingers and feet, but none of it mattered. Noise and confusion filled my head. I'd aimed to keep my father safe from danger and I hadn't even *contemplated* a smoke alarm.

His voice said, 'Ben?'

I looked up woozily. He was standing above me; he was *smiling*. How could he?

Men in yellow suits unrolled hoses and poured gallons from the tanker onto the killing bow-fronts. There was steam and smoke and unquenched flame: and there were people putting a red blanket round my bare shoulders and telling me not to worry. I wasn't sure where they had come from, or what I didn't have to worry about.

I wasn't actually *sure* of anything.

'Ben,' my father said in my ear, 'you're concussed.'

'Mm?'

'They say your head hit the ground. Can you hear me?'

'No smoke alarm. My fault . . .'

Ben!' He shook me. People told him not to.

'I'll get you elected,' I said.

'Christ.'

137

People's familiar faces loomed into my orbit and went away again. I thought it extraordinary that they were walking around fully dressed in the middle of the night but at one point learned that it was barely twenty minutes past eleven, not five to four. I'd gone early to bed and jumped out of the window wearing only my watch and my underpants and got the time wrong.

Amy was there, wringing her hands and weeping. Amy crying for the charity gifts lost to ashes, the ugly what-not gone for ever, still unsold. What's a what-not, Amy? An *étagère*, you know, an upright set of little shelves for filling an odd corner, bearing plates and photographs and what not.

And bullets?

'Oh dear,' she said. 'I left the bullet in my awful cardigan in the shop, and now I've lost it, but never mind, it was only a lump of old lead.'

Mrs Leonard Kitchens patted my shoulder reassuringly. 'Don't you worry, boy, there was nothing in those old shops but junk and paper. Leaflets. Nothing! My Leonard's here somewhere. Have you seen him? Likes a good fire, does my Leonard, but the fun's all over now. I want to go home.'

Usher Rudd stalked his prey backwards, framing his picture, stepping back and clicking. He grinned over my blanket, took time to focus, aimed his lens.

Flash.

The cameraman from the local TV station arrived with his brighter light that was still out-watted by fire.

Mervyn wrung his hands over the lost heaps of JULIARDS. He'd barely been home half an hour before someone had phoned to warn him the charity shop was on fire.

Crystal Harley knelt beside me, dabbing bloody trickles with tissues and said worriedly, 'Do you think I'd better come into work tomorrow?'

Paul and Isobel Bethune illicitly drove into the pedestrian-only precinct. Emergencies made new rules, the local councillor said, bustling towards my father, presenting a surface of urgent concern, all camaraderie for him and with hail-fellow greetings individually for the firemen.

Isobel asked me weakly if I were all right.

'Of course he's not,' Crystal snapped. 'He jumped through fire and hit the ground. What do you expect?'

'And . . . er . . . his father?'

'His father will win the seat,' Crystal said.

God bless politics, I thought.

'Paul was out at a meeting,' Isobel said. 'He came home to collect me when he heard about the fire, to see if there was anything I could do to help. It always looks better if I'm with him, he says.'

Water plumed out of the huge appliance and sizzled on the flames and ran out of the building again, soaking the cobbles. I and my red blanket dripped and chilled.

Another vast tanker in the car park at the rear raised soaring fountains above the roof so that the two arcs of glittering Niagara met and married and fell together as monstrous rain. Leaflets and junk a fiery furnace; two vulnerable organisms shivering outside.

The yellow-helmets prodigally aimed their hoses at the still dark buildings next to the blazing shops and, in time, inevitably, the ravaging tongues of fire ran out of fuel and began to diminish, to whisper instead of roar, to give up the struggle and leave the battlefield so that what fell from the sky into the square was no longer sparks but hot clinging ash, and what assaulted the senses wasn't heat but the acrid after-smell of burning.

Someone fetched the doctor who had seen to my father's ankle three days earlier; he peered into my eyes with bright lights and into my ears and felt the bump on my head and bound up blisters in huge padded dressings so that they wouldn't burst and get infected, and he agreed with my father that all a healthy boy needed was to see him in the morning.

My father solved the interim by enlisting the sympathy of the manager of the Sleeping Dragon, who gave us a bedroom and whose wife found me some clothes.

'You poor dears ... you poor dears ...' She mothered us, kind, but enjoying it, and both she and her husband happily welcomed the reporters from the

140

London dailies who thronged through the doors the next day.

Usher Rudd's admittedly brilliant photograph of my father in mid-leap with the flaming window behind him made the front pages, not only of the *Hoopwestern Gazette* and the next edition of the *Quindle Diary* (JULIARD JINX) but of every major paper in the land (JULIARD JUMPS) and hot on the heels of the factual news came endless comment and criticism and picking-to-pieces.

People will always tell you what you should have done. People will tell you what *they* would have done if they had woken in the night with fire underneath them. People will say that absolutely the first thing to do was call the fire brigade, and no one could be bothered to say how do I call the brigade when the only telephone is downstairs surrounded by flames? How do you call a fire brigade when the telephone line has melted?

Everyone can think logically afterwards, but in the heat and the smell and the noise and the danger, analytical reasoning is more or less out of the question.

People tend to think that wildly unreasonable behaviour in terrifying circumstances can be called 'panic', and forgiven, but it's not so much panic, a form of ultimate illogical fear, but a lack of time to think things through.

Perhaps my father and I would have done differently if we had been presented with the situation as a

141

theoretical exercise with a correct and an incorrect solution.

Perhaps we should have thrown the mattresses out of the window as a possible way of breaking our fall. Perhaps, if we could have got them through the window. As it was, we both nearly died and, as it was, we both lived, but more by luck than reason.

Don't waste time with clothes, they'll tell you. Better go naked into this world than clothed into the next. But they – 'they', whoever they are – haven't jumped in front of the media's sharpened lenses.

I thought afterwards that I should at least have dashed into the burning sitting-room for my jacket and jockey's helmet, instead of bothering with the taps. Also I should have wrapped towels round my hands and feet before grasping the window frame.

But I don't think my father ever regretted the near-to-lethal seconds he spent in putting on his shirt and trousers. He knew in some way, even in that life-or-death split second, that a photograph of him jumping half naked from the flames would haunt his whole career. He knew, even in that fraught moment, that an orderly presentation was everything. Not even the worst that Usher Rudd could dredge up in the future ever showed George Juliard as anything but a fast-thinking headliner who was at his very best – *who put his shoes on* – in a crisis.

*

The police investigation sauntered upwards from Joe, whose mother drove a school bus, to higher ranks at county level, but the firefighters couldn't swear the two bow-fronts had been torched and no one found a .22 rifle to match the lost-again bullet, and Foster Fordham's report on wax in the Range Rover's sump was judged inconclusive.

George Juliard *might* have been the target of three attempts on his candidature, if not on his life, but again he might not. There were no obvious suspects.

In the August doldrums for news, London editors gave the puzzle two full days of wide coverage. George Juliard shone on television nationwide. Every single voter in the Hoopwestern constituency knew who JULIARD was.

While my father dealt with publicity people and Mervyn Teck drove around like an agitated bluebottle searching for inexpensive substitute headquarters, I spent most of the Sunday sitting in an armchair by the window of our Sleeping Dragon room, letting bruises and grazes heal themselves, and looking across the square at the burnt-out building opposite.

From somewhere up here, I thought, from somewhere here among the many hanging baskets of geraniums (her Leonard, the nurseryman, had designed them, Mrs Kitchens had told me with pride), from among all these big clusters of scarlet pompoms and little blue flowers whose name I didn't know, and from among the fluffy white flowers that filled and

143

rounded the bright living displays decorating the whole long frontage of the Sleeping Dragon, from somewhere up here someone had aimed a .22 rifle at my father.

The marksman probably hadn't been in this room given to us in the night, which was much further along towards the Town Hall than the main door of the hotel from which we'd walked. A shot from where I sat would have had to take into account that the target wasn't walking straight ahead but moving sideways. A stalker's shot; but not a stalker's gun.

A ricochet could, of course, take a bullet anywhere, but I thought it unlikely that a ricochet from where I sat would have turned and hit the charity shop.

At one point, shuffling on the padded blisters, I explored the length of the hotel's first floor, glimpsing the square through an open doorway or two and coming to a little lounge area furnished with armchairs and small tables that I reckoned lay directly above the front hall and main door, accessible to the world. Straight ahead through the window from there was the unmarked path I'd taken with my father across the cobbles.

Anyone ... *anyone* ... if they had the nerve, could have stood among the floor-length curtains, opened the window, rested the barrel of a .22 on the windowsill and shot through the geraniums and the warm night.

My father, interested, asked the manager for the names of the people sleeping in the bedrooms on

144

Wednesday night, but although the register was freely opened, no one familiar appeared.

'Nice try, Ben,' my father sighed; and the police had the same nice try in due course, with similar results.

By Monday morning Mervyn had rented an empty shop in a side street and borrowed a desk for Crystal and some flip-up chairs. The campaign hiccupped for two days while he cajoled his friendly neighbourhood printer into replacement leaflet and poster production at grand-prix speed and near-to-cost prices, but by late Tuesday afternoon the indefatigable witches, Faith, Marge and Lavender, had turned the empty shop into a fully working office complete with teapot and mobile phone.

On Monday and Tuesday George Juliard filled the newspapers, and enlivened some chat shows, and on Wednesday morning a miracle happened.

Mervyn had sticky-taped a new large-scale map onto the wall and was pointing out to me the roads I should drive along (feet OK by now) for Faith and Lavender to ring as yet untroubled door-bells. In the absence of a megaphone (burned) I would please occasionally toot the horn, just enough to announce our presence but *not enough*, he lectured me, to anger anyone trying to get a baby to sleep. The mothers of babies (he wagged a finger at me) swayed Xs in the polls like pendulums. Kiss a baby: win a vote. A hundred thousand politicians couldn't all be historically wrong.

'I'll kiss every baby in sight,' I promised recklessly.

He frowned at me, never one to take a joke. I was reminded of my father's most recent lesson: '*Never ever* make a joke to the police, they have *no* sense of humour. *Never* make a political joke, it will always be considered an insult. Always remember that umbrage can be taken by the lift of an eyebrow. Remember that if offence can possibly be taken, it will be.'

I'd gazed at my father. 'Are people that silly?'

'Silly,' he said with mock severity, 'isn't a word you should ever apply to people. They may be totally stupid, in fact, but if you call them silly you've lost their vote.'

'And you want silly people to vote for you?'

He laughed. 'Don't make jokes.'

He had gone to London on Wednesday morning when the miracle happened. There were just Mervyn, Crystal, Faith, Marge, Lavender and me in the make-shift office, just the bunch of us putting the best face possible on the lack of computer (for the totals spent on tea-bags), copier (schedules for volunteers) and fax (reports from distant galaxies like Quindle).

Orinda walked in.

All business stopped.

She wore pale citrus green: trousers, jacket and headband. Gold chains. She carried, beside the black lizard handbag, a substantial roll of papers.

She looked around the bare room, smiled faintly at Marge and fixed her gaze on me.

'I want to talk to you,' she said calmly. 'Outside.'

I followed where she led. We stood on the pavement in the sun, with shoppers passing by.

'Since Saturday,' she announced, 'I have been considering things. On Sunday morning, at half past eight or so, a newspaperman appeared at my house in an invasive procedure I believe is called "door stepping".'

She paused. I nodded faintly.

'He asked if I was glad or sorry that you hadn't been burned to death. You and your father, that is.'

'Oh.'

'It was the first I'd heard about the fire.'

'I'm surprised no one had phoned you.'

'I unplug the telephone when I sleep. I find it hard to sleep in any case.'

I said, 'Oh,' again, vaguely.

'The journalist wanted to know my opinion of the information he'd been given that close-to-death attacks had been made on George Juliard so that he would have to retire from the candidacy, clearing the way for my return.'

She paused, studying my face, and continued: 'I see that that thought isn't new to you.'

'No, but I don't think you did it.'

'Why not?'

'You're hurt. You're furious. But you wouldn't murder.'

147

'When will you be eighteen?'

'In ten days.'

'Then consider this a coming-of-age present.' She thrust the roll of papers into my hands. 'This is for you. It is because of you...' She stopped abruptly, swallowing. 'Use it in any way you like.'

With curiosity I unrolled the stiff sheets, having to hold them wide to prevent them rolling up again. The top one, in very large capital letters, read:

ORINDA NAGLE SAYS VOTE FOR JULIARD

My mouth, I know, fell open.

'There are ten of them,' she said simply. 'They're all the same. I had them printed this morning. They'll print dozens, if you like.'

'Orinda...' I was all but speechless.

'You showed me... at the races...' she began, and stopped again. 'You're so very *young*, but you showed me it's possible to bear an unbearable disappointment. You made me look into myself. Anyway, I will *not* have people thinking I would set fire to our old headquarters in order to get rid of your father, so I'll *join* him. I'll support him from now on in every way. I should never have listened to all those people who told me he had robbed me. I don't know, to be really truthful, and the truth is awful... I don't know that I wasn't *relieved* not to be forced to go to Westminster, but I do like working in the constituency and that's what hurts most ... that the people I've worked so hard for passed me over for some stranger from outside.'

She stopped talking and looked at me in a sort of desperation to see if I could possibly understand, and I understood so well that I leaned forward impulsively and kissed her on the cheek.

A camera flashed.

'I can't *believe* it,' Orinda screeched. 'He follows me round.'

Usher Rudd, with the advantage of surprise, was already scuttling away down the street to get lost in bunches of shoppers.

'He follows me, too,' I said, putting a hand on Orinda's arm, to deter her trying to catch him. 'You warned me and I told my father ... but unless Usher Rudd breaks the law it seems he can't be stopped, and the law is still on the side of copy-cat Rudds.'

'But my private life is my own affair!' She glanced at me as if it were my fault that it wasn't.

I said, 'Drug dealers would be out of business if people didn't want drugs.'

'What?'

'The so-called war on drugs is fought against the wrong people. Lock up the users. Lock up the demand. Lock up human nature.'

She looked bewildered. 'What have drugs to do with Usher Rudd?'

'If people didn't flock to buy his sleaze, he wouldn't push it.'

'And you mean . . . they always will?'

She needed no answer. She followed me into the shop/office and, after delivering her news, enjoyed a hugging session with Mervyn (no photo) and an ambiguous welcome from the three witches, who had with pink arousal transferred their effective allegiance to the new order.

'Where are you canvassing today, Mervyn?' Orinda asked, and he showed her on the map, with the unexpected result that when I drove the Range Rover round Hoopwestern that morning I had on board Mervyn, Orinda, Faith and Lavender, and all of Orinda's roll of commitment flattened out as placards.

As Mervyn had telephoned the editor of the *Gazette* – gasps of shock at having to U-turn his anti-all-politicians spin – we were greeted in the car park behind the burned shop by a hastily assembled crowd, by the leader-writer of the *Gazette* (the paper was short of news) and by the cameraman who had besottedly followed Orinda with his loving lens round the reception before the dinner a week earlier at the Sleeping Dragon.

Orinda flirted again with his lens (or with him – much the same thing) and told everyone prettily through a non-squeaking microphone that George Juliard, undoubtedly on the brink of becoming a nationally acclaimed politician, was the best possible substitute for her beloved husband Dennis, who had dedicated his life to the good citizens of this glorious part of Dorset.

Applause, applause. She appeared in the sitting-rooms of Hoopwestern on the lunchtime television news against the only slightly orchestrated cheers.

By the time my father returned on the train from London he'd heard of Orinda's media conference with mixed feelings – she might be stealing his limelight or she might just be saving his life – but at another church hall meeting of the faithful that evening he embraced her in a warm hug (reciprocated) that would have been unthinkable a day earlier.

Not everyone was pleased.

Orinda's shadow, Anonymous Lover Wyvern, followed her around like thunder. She, dressed in blackberry-coloured satin and glowing with a sense of generosity and virtue, kept giving him enquiring looks as if unsure of the source of his dudgeon. In her inner release she didn't seem to realise, as I did, albeit only slowly through the evening, that in dumping her anger at not being selected she had in some way lessened his status. He had been Dennis Nagle's best friend, but Orinda was leaving her Dennis behind.

Dearest Polly, to my surprise, positively scowled, even though she had herself delivered Orinda to her change of heart.

'I didn't count on such a radical about-face,' Polly complained. 'She's cast herself in the ongoing role of constituency wife! There's no doubt she was good at it, but she *isn't* George's wife and she can't surely imagine she can go on opening fêtes and things, and I bet that's what she's got in mind. Whatever did you say to her at the races?'

I said, 'I thought you wanted her on my father's side.'

'Well, yes, I do. But I don't want her going around saying all the time that *she* was the one we should have picked.'

'Get him into Parliament, Polly,' I said. 'Put him on the escalator, then he'll deal with Orinda and everything else.'

'*How* old did you say you are?'

'Eighteen at the end of next week. And it was you, dearest Polly, who said I look into people's minds.'

She asked in some alarm, 'Do you see into mine?'

'Sort of.'

She laughed uneasily; but I saw nothing but good.

One could say the opposite about Leonard Kitchens. I had come to notice that the tilt of his prominent moustache acted like a weather-vane, signalling the direction of his feelings. The upward thrust that evening was combative and self-important, a combination looking for a fight. Bulky Mrs Kitchens (in large pink flowers printed on dark blue) followed her Leonard's progress round the meeting with anxiety for a while and then made a straight line to my side.

'Do something,' she hissed into my ear. 'Tell Orinda to leave my Leonard alone.'

It seemed to me that it was the other way round, as Leonard's moustache vibrated by Orinda's neck, but at Mrs Kitchens' urgent and continuous prompting I went over to hear Leonard's agitated and whining drift.

'I would do *anything* for you, Orinda, you know I would, but you're joining the *enemy* and I can't bear to see him slobbering all over you, it's disgusting . . .'

'Wake up, Leonard,' Orinda said lightly, not seeing the seething lava below the faintly ridiculous exterior, 'it's a new world.'

The undercurrents might tug and eddy, but Orinda had definitely unified the party behind JULIARD; yet in our room that night my father would literally not hear a word said about her. In fact, he put a finger decisively against his lips and drew me out into the passage, closing our door behind us.

'What's up?' I asked, mystified.

'Tonight the editor of the *Gazette* asked me if I thought people who voted for me were silly.'

'But that's nonsense. That's – ' I stopped.

'Yes. Think back. When we joked about silly voters we were alone in this bedroom here. Did you repeat what we said?'

'Of course not.'

'Then how did the *Gazette* know?'

I stared at him, and said slowly, 'Usher Rudd.'

He nodded. 'Didn't you tell me that that mechanic – Terry, isn't that what his name is? – got sacked because Usher Rudd had listened to his pillow talk using one of those gadgets that pick up voice waves from the faint vibrations in the windows?'

'Usher Rudd,' I said furiously, 'is trying to prove I'm not your son.'

'Never mind, he's on a loser.'

'He's following Orinda too, not to mention the Bethunes.'

'He thinks if he flings enough mud, some will stick. Don't give him any target.'

As the days went by one could see that Orinda's flip-flop had most impact in Hoopwestern itself, less in Quindle, and not very much in the villages dotting the maps with a church spire, a couple of pubs and a telephone box. Cheers and clapping greeted her near home but news of her arrival to canvass in, say, Middle Lampfield (pop. 637) was more likely to be greeted with a polite 'Oo? Aah' and a swift return to 'Zoomerzet' cider.

More local draught cider flowed down the constituency throats than babies' formula, and my father's head for the frothy fruit of the apple earned him approval. We rolled every day at lunchtime from pub to pub to pub (I drove) and I got used to hearing the verdict. 'A good chap, your father, he understands what we need in the countryside. Reckon I'll vote for him. That Bethune, that they say is a certainty, he's a *town* councillor, and you know what we think of them lot, thumbs down.'

My father made them laugh. He knew the price of hay. They would have followed him to the South Pole.

Orinda thought the villages a waste of time, and so did Mervyn.

'The bulk of the votes is in the towns,' they lectured. Dennis Nagle had been the star of the businessman circle.

'You vote for a man you play darts with,' my father said, missing double top. 'I buy my own drinks, they buy theirs. Neither of us is beholden.'

Orinda didn't like cider, and she didn't like pubs. Lavender, surprisingly, liked both: my father, Lavender and I therefore spent several days soap-boxing the outskirts in the silver and gold Range Rover, seeing to it (as my father said) that not a voter was left unturned.

The following week it was Orinda who nearly died.

CHAPTER SEVEN

On the Tuesday of the last full week of canvassing, my box of possessions, and my bicycle, finally arrived by carrier from Mrs Wells.

Up in our room, my father picked with interest and curiosity through the meagre debris of my life: two trophies for winning amateur 'chases the previous Easter, several photographs of me on horses and skis, and other photos from school with me sitting in one of those frozen team line-ups (this one for target shooting), with the captain hugging a cup. There were books on mathematics, and racing biographies. Also clothes, but not many as, to my dismay, I was still growing.

My father extracted my passport, my birth certificate and the framed photograph of his wedding to my mother. He took the picture out of its frame and after looking at it for several long minutes he ran his finger over her face and sighed deeply, and it was the only time I'd known him show any emotion at all about his loss.

I said incautiously, 'Do you remember her? If she walked into the room now, would you know her?'

He gave me a look of such bleakness that I realised I'd asked a question of unforgivable intrusion, but after a pause all he said was, 'You never forget your first.'

I swallowed.

He said, 'Have you had your first?'

I felt numb, embarrassed almost beyond speech, but in the end I said truthfully, 'No.'

He nodded. It was a moment of almost unbearable intimacy, the first ever between us, but he remained totally calm and matter-of-fact, and let me recover.

He sorted through some papers he had brought in a briefcase from a recent trip to London, put my own identifications in the case, snapped shut the locks and announced that we were going to call on the *Hoopwestern Gazette*.

We called, in fact, on the editor, who was also the publisher and proprietor of the only local daily. He was a man in shirt-sleeves, harassed, middle-aged, and from the tone of his front pages, censorious. He stood up from his desk as we approached.

'Mr Samson Frazer,' my father said, calling him by name, 'when we met the other evening, you asked if I thought people who vote for me are silly.'

Samson Frazer, for all his importance in Hoopwestern, was no match in power against my parent. Interesting, I thought.

'Er . . .' he said.

'We'll return to that in a minute,' my father told him. 'First, I have some things for you to see.'

He unclipped the briefcase and opened it.

'I have brought the following items,' he said, taking out each paper and putting it down in front of the editor. 'My marriage certificate. My son's birth certificate. Both of our passports. This photograph of my wife and myself taken outside the registry office after our wedding. On the back – ' he turned the picture over, 'you will see the professional photographer's name and copyright, and the date. Here also is my wife's death certificate. She died of complications after the birth of our son. This son, Benedict, my only child, who has been at my side during this by-election.'

The editor gave me a swift glance as if he hadn't until that point taken note of my existence.

'You employ a person called Usher Rudd,' my father said. 'I think you should be careful. He seems to be trying to cast doubt on my son's identity and legitimacy. I'm told he has made scurrilous insinuations.'

He asked the editor just how he'd come to hear of 'silly' votes when he, my father, had only used the word – and in a joke – in the privacy of his own room.

Samson Frazer froze like a dazzled rabbit.

'If I have to,' my father said, 'I will send hair samples for DNA testing. My own hair, my son's hair, and some hair from my wife that she gave me in a locket. I hope you will carefully consider what I've said and what I've shown you.' He began methodically replacing the certificates in the briefcase. 'Because, I assure you,' he went on pleasantly, 'if the *Hoopwestern Gazette* should be so unwise as to cast doubt on my son's origins, I will sue the paper and you personally for defamation and libel, and you might quite likely wish you hadn't done it.' He snapped the locks shut so vigorously that they sounded in themselves like a threat.

'You understand?' he asked.

The editor plainly did.

'Good,' my father said. 'If you catch me in sleaze, that will be fair enough. If you try to manufacture it, I'll hang you out by the toes.'

Samson Frazer found nothing to say.

'Good day to you, sir,' my father said.

He was in high good humour all the way back to the hotel and went upstairs humming.

'What would you say,' he suggested, 'to a pact between us?'

'What sort of pact?'

He put the briefcase down on the table and drew out two sheets of plain paper.

'I've been thinking,' he said, 'of making you a promise, and I want you to make the same promise in return. We both know how vulnerable one is to people like Usher Rudd.'

'And it's not impossible,' I interrupted, 'that he's

listening to us at this moment, particularly if he knows where we've just been.'

My father looked briefly startled, but then grinned. 'The red-haired dung-beetle can listen all he likes. The promise I'll make to you is not to give him, or anyone like him, any grounds ever for messy publicity. I'll be dead boring. There will be no kiss-and-tell bimbos and no illicit payment for favours and no cheating on tax and no nasty pastimes like drugs or kinky sex...'

I smiled easily, amused.

'Yes,' he said, 'but I want *you* to make the same promise to *me*. I want you to promise me that if I get elected you'll do nothing throughout my political career that can get me discredited or sacked or disgraced in any way.'

'But I wouldn't,' I protested.

'It's easy for you to say that now while you're young, but you'll find life's full of terrible temptations.'

'I promise,' I said.

He shook his head. 'That's not enough. I want us both to write it down. I want you to be able to see and remember what you promised. Of course, it's in no way a legal document or anything pretentious like that, it's just an affirmation of intent.' He paused, clicking a ball-point pen while he thought, then he wrote very quickly and simply on one sheet of paper, and signed his name, and pushed the paper over for me to read.

It said: 'I will cause no scandal, nor will I perform any shameful or illegal act.'

Wow, I thought. I said, not wanting this to get too serious, 'It's a bit comprehensive, isn't it?'

'It's not worth doing otherwise. But you can write your own version. Write what you're comfortable with.'

I had no sense of binding myself irrevocably to sainthood.

I wrote: 'I'll do nothing that could embarrass my father's political career or drag his name in the dust. I'll do my best to keep him safe from any sort of attack.'

I signed my name lightheartedly and gave him the page. 'Will that do?'

He read it, smiling. 'It'll do.'

He folded both pages together, then picked up the wedding photograph and positioned it face down on the glass in its frame. He then put both of the signed pacts on the photo and replaced the back part of the frame, fastening it with its clips.

'There you are,' he said, turning the frame face up. 'Every time you look at your mother and me, you'll remember the promises behind the photo, inside the frame. Couldn't be simpler.'

He stood the picture on the table and without fuss gave me back my birth certificate and passport.

'Keep them safe.'

'Yes.'

'Right. Then let's get on with this election.'

Stopping only briefly to leave my identity in an envelope in the manager's safe, we went to the new headquarters to collect Mervyn, pamphlets, Faith and Lavender, and start a door-to-door morning round three Hoopwestern housing estates. Light-bulb workers, they said.

Mervyn, proud of himself, had found a replacement megaphone. His friendly printer continued to furnish a torrent of JULIARDS. Mervyn for once seemed content in his world, but his day shone even brighter when Orinda arrived, declaring her readiness for the fray.

With Faith and Lavender cool and Mervyn hot, therefore, six of us squeezed into the Range Rover, leaving behind Crystal (chronically anxious) and Marge (dusting and sweeping).

Only eight days after this one, I thought, and it will be over. And what will I do, I wondered, after that? There would be three or four weeks to fill before the Exeter term started. I mentally shrugged. I would be eighteen. I had a bicycle . . . might get to France . . .

I drove mechanically, stopping wherever Mervyn dictated.

Orinda had come in neat trousers and jacket, light orange-scarlet in colour. As usual, gold chains. Smooth, perfect make-up.

Babies got kissed. My father came across a clutch of child-minding house-husbands, factory shift workers, and learned about tungsten filaments. I chatted up a coffee-morning of old ladies who weren't satisfied until my parent shook their hands. (Pink smiles. A blossoming of votes.) Orinda met old friends. Mervyn alerted the streets to our presence like a musically tinkling fish-and-chip van, and Faith and Lavender left no door-bell un-rung.

When we drove out of the last of the estates we'd seen one or two TITMUSSES, no WHISTLE, not a BETHUNE to speak of, but many a window now proclaimed JULIARD. One could not but hope.

Mervyn and my father decided on one more long street, this time of varied and slightly more prosperous-looking houses. I, by this time, had had enough of door-to-dooring to last me several lifetimes, but as always the others seemed to have an indefatigable appetite. My father's eyes still shone with enthusiasm and people who disagreed with his political theories left him not downcast but stimulated. He never tired, it seemed to me, of trying to convert the heathen.

Without much hope I asked Faith and Lavender if they wouldn't prefer to say they'd done enough; how about lunch? 'No, no,' they insisted with fervour, 'every vote counts.'

Orinda alone seemed uneasy and withdrawn and not her usual positive and extravagant self, and in the end, while she and I waited together on the pavement beside the Range Rover for the others to finish

163

galvanising an old people's home, I asked her what was the matter.

'Nothing,' she said, and I didn't press it, but after a moment or two she said, 'Do you see that white BMW there, along the road?'

'Yes.' I frowned. 'I saw it earlier, in one of the housing estates.'

'He's following us.'

'Who's following us? Is it Usher Rudd?'

'Oh, no.' She found the idea a surprise, which in itself surprised me. 'No, not Usher Rudd. It's Alderney Wyvern.'

It was I, then, who was surprised, and I asked, sounding astonished, 'Why on earth should he follow us?'

Orinda frowned. 'He's still furious with me for supporting your father.'

'Well . . . I'd noticed. But why, exactly?'

'You're too young to understand.'

'I could try.'

'Dennis used to do everything Alderney said. I mean, Alderney actually was how Dennis got advancement. Alderney would tell him what to say. Alderney is very clever, politically.'

'Why doesn't he find a parliamentary seat for himself?'

'He says he doesn't want to.' She paused. 'To be frank, he isn't easy to understand. But I know he expected me to be selected and to retain the seat as

Dennis' widow, and he worked on people like that creepy Leonard Kitchens, with that shudder-making moustache, to make sure I was selected. And then out of the blue the central party in Westminster decided they wanted George Juliard in Parliament, so he came and dazzled the selectors, who always listen to Polly, as a matter of course, and she fell for him like a ton of bricks ... Anyway, Alderney got nowhere with your father. I sometimes think that that's the sort of power Alderney really wants, to be able to pull the levers behind the scenes.'

It seemed to me at that moment a wacky notion. (I still had a lot to learn.)

'So now that I've joined your father,' Orinda said, 'I'm not listening to Alderney as much. I used to do everything he suggested. We always did, Dennis and I, because Alderney would tell us such and such a thing would happen on the political scene and mostly he was right, and now I'm out with you and your father so much of the time ... You'll laugh, but I almost think he's *jealous*!'

I didn't laugh. I'd seen my father's powerful effect on every female in Hoopwestern, from acid-tongued Lavender onwards. It wouldn't have surprised me if he'd left a comet-tail of jealousy through the constituency, except that he needed the men to vote for him as well as the women, and I'd watched him keep a tactical distance from their wives.

Alderney Wyvern, along the road, got out of his

car and stood aggressively on the pavement, hands on hips, staring at Orinda.

'I'd better go and talk to him,' Orinda said.

I said instinctively, 'No, don't.'

She caught the alarm in my voice and smiled. 'I've known him for years.'

I hadn't yet come across the adult grossly matured variety of jealousy, only the impotent rage of adolescence, but I felt intuitively that a great – and disturbing – change had taken place in A.L. Wyvern.

He had been by his own choice self-effacing on every occasion I'd seen him: quiet in manner, self-contained, behaving as if he didn't want to be noticed. All that had now gone. The stocky figure seemed heavier, the shoulders hunched, the face, even from a distance, visibly tense with menace. He had the out-of-control anger of a rioter, or of a militant striker.

I said to Orinda, 'Stay here.'

'Don't be silly.'

She walked confidently towards him in her brave orange-red clothes.

I could hear his voice, low and growling, but not what he said. Her reply was light and teasing. She put out a hand as if to stroke his arm affectionately, and he hit her very hard in the face.

She cried out with shock as much as pain. I ran towards her, and although Wyvern saw me coming he hit her again, back-handed, across her nose and mouth.

She squealed, raising her hands to shield her face,

166

trying at the same time to escape from him, but he clutched the shoulder of her jacket to prevent her running, and drew back his fist for a third blow.

She wrenched herself free. She half-overbalanced. She stumbled off the pavement into the roadway.

The prosperous residential street that had been so peaceful and empty suddenly seemed filled with a heavy lorry that bore down towards Orinda, brakes shrieking, horn blowing in banshee bursts.

Orinda tottered blindly as if disoriented, and I sprinted towards her without calculating speed or distance but simply impelled by the need of the moment.

The lorry driver was swerving about, trying to miss her and actually making things worse because his direction was unpredictable. I might easily have shoved her into his path rather than out of it, but I threw myself at Orinda in a sort of twisting rugby-football tackle so that she fell half under me onto the hard surface and rolled, and the screaming black tyres made skid marks an inch from our feet.

Orinda's nose was bleeding and her eyes were overflowing with pain-induced tears, and beyond that she was dazed and bewildered. I knelt beside her, winded myself and fearful that I'd hurt her unnecessarily when the lorry driver might have avoided her anyway.

The lorry had stopped not far beyond us and the driver, jumping down from his cab and running towards us, was already rehearsing aggrieved innocence.

'She ran out straight in front of me, I didn't have a chance. It isn't my fault . . . I couldn't help it . . . it isn't my fault she's bleeding all down her front.'

Neither Orinda nor I made any reply. It was irrelevant. It hadn't been his fault, and no one would say it had been. The person at fault stood in shocked rage on the pavement directly across the road from us, glaring and rigid and not coming to our aid.

With breath returning I asked Orinda if she was all right. Silly question, really, when her nose was bleeding and there were other marks of Wyvern's dangerous hands on her face. Her jacket was torn. One black shoe was off. The careful make-up was smeared and there was a slack weakness through all her body. The Orinda lying in the road looked far from the assured sophisticated flirter with cameras that I was used to; she looked a shattered, ordinary, middle-aged and rather nice woman trying to gather her wits and understand what had happened.

I leaned forward and slid an arm under her neck to see if she could sit up, and to my relief she let me help her to do that, until she was sitting in the road with her knees bent and her head and her hands on her knees.

She'd broken no bones, I thought gratefully. The fractures were internal and mental and couldn't be mended.

She said tearfully, trying to wipe blood with her fingers, 'Have you got a tissue?'

I hadn't.

'There's one in my bag.'

Her handbag, I knew, was in the Range Rover.

'I'll get it,' I said.

'No . . . Benedict . . . don't leave me!'

'Call an ambulance,' the lorry driver advised bullishly. 'I missed her, I know I did. It's not my fault she's bleeding.'

'No, it's not,' I agreed, standing up. 'But you're a big strong guy and you can help by picking up the lady and carrying her to that goldish Range Rover over there.'

'No fear,' he interrupted. 'I'm not getting her blood on me, it's not my sodding fault, she ran straight out in front of me.'

'Yes. OK,' I said. 'It wasn't your fault. But you did at least stop, so if you'd help and take her along to that vehicle, and if I just jot down your name and the firm you work for, that owns the lorry, then I'm sure you can carry on with whatever you were doing.'

'No police,' he said.

'You don't have to call the police to an accident unless someone's been injured, and you didn't injure this lady, as you said.'

'Straight up? How do you know that? You're only a boy.'

I'd learned it in the course of reading for my driving licence, but I couldn't be bothered to explain. I bent down and tried to get Orinda to her feet, and she stood up shakily, clutching me to stop herself from falling.

I put my arms round her awkwardly. She was trembling all over. My father would simply have scooped her up and carried her to the Range Rover, but apart from my doubt of having adequate strength, I was embarrassed by the difference in our ages. Ridiculous, really. I felt protective, but unsure.

A couple of cars went by, the passengers craning their necks with curiosity.

'Oh, come on, missus,' the driver said suddenly, picking up her scattered shoe and putting it on for her, 'hold onto my arm.'

He offered her a rock-like support, and between the two of us Orinda walked unsteadily, setting her feet down gingerly as if not sure where the ground lay. In that fashion we reached the Range Rover and installed Orinda in the front passenger seat, where she relaxed weakly and thanked the driver.

'Hey!' he said suddenly, surveying the highly noticeable vehicle. 'Doesn't this motor belong to that politician? Some funny name?'

'Juliard.'

'Yeah.'

'I'm his son,' I said. 'This lady, that you cleverly missed hitting, and that you've helped just now, is a Mrs Orinda Nagle, whose husband was the MP here before he died.'

'Cor!' Surprise at least stopped the whine of self-

170

justification. I reckoned he was already rehearsing a revised tale to his masters. 'I live in Quindle,' he said. 'They say your father's got no chance, the way things are, but maybe I'll vote for him now anyway. Can't say fairer than that!'

I wrote down his name, which he gave willingly, and the name of the furniture firm he worked for, and the telephone number, and he positively beamed at Orinda and told her not to worry, and drove off in his lorry giving us a smile – a *smile* – and a wave.

Alderney Wyvern, all this time, had remained as if the soles of his shoes were glued to the ground.

A few people had come out of the houses because of the noise of horn and brakes, but as there'd been no actual crash, and as Orinda had stood up and walked away, their curiosity had died quickly.

For once, with a real story to record, Usher Rudd and his lens had been missing.

My father, Mervyn, Faith and Lavender came out from a triumphant conversion of the old people's home and exclaimed in horror at Orinda's blood and distress. The tissue from her handbag had proved inadequate. Her tears by now were of uncomplicated misery, rolling half-mopped down her cheeks.

'What happened?' my father demanded of me fiercely. 'What have you done?'

'Nothing!' I said. 'I mean . . . nothing.'

Orinda came to my defence. 'George, Benedict

171

helped me ... I can't believe it ...' Her voice wailed. 'Alderney ... *Alderney* ... h-h-hit me.'

'He *what*?'

We all looked along the road to where Wyvern still pugnaciously stood his ground, and if I had needed an explanation of the emotions involved, my father didn't. He strode off with purposeful anger towards the visibly unrepentant ex-best friend and challenged him loudly, though we couldn't hear the actual words. Wyvern answered with equal vigour, arms waving.

'Benedict ...' Orinda begged me, increasingly upset, 'go and stop them.'

It was easy enough for her to say it, but they were both grown men whereas I ... Well, I went along there fast and caught my father's arm as he drew back his fist for an infuriated swipe at Wyvern who was, incredibly, sneering.

My father swung round and shouted at me, raging, 'Get out of my bloody way.'

'The pact,' I yelled at him. 'Remember the pact.'

'*What*?'

'The *pact*,' I insisted. 'Don't hit him. Father ... Dad ... don't hit him.'

The scorching fury went out of his eyes as suddenly as if he were waking up.

'He *wants* you to hit him,' I said. I didn't know how I knew or why I was so certain. It had something to do with the fact that Wyvern had remained on the spot instead of driving off, but it was mostly intuition

172

derived from his body language. He was looking for trouble. He meant all sorts of harm to my father, not least adverse publicity before polling day.

My father gave me a blank look, then walked past me to go back to the Range Rover. I half turned to follow him but was grabbed and spun round by Wyvern, whose always unsmiling face was now set fast with brutal malice. If he couldn't get what he wanted from the father, he would take it out on the son.

I hadn't learned boxing or karate, but I did have naturally fast reflexes and, thanks to riding and skiing, an instinctive command of balance. Wyvern might have had weight in his fists, but I ducked and dodged two sizzling punches to the face that would have laid me out flat if they'd connected, and concentrated solely on staying on my feet.

He drove me back against the shoulder-height rough stone wall that divided a garden from the pavement, but I squirmed out of his grasp and simply ran, intent on escape and containment, not on winning any battles.

I could hear Wyvern coming after me, and saw my father with renewed fury turning back to my aid.

I yelled at him in frenzy, 'Get in the Range Rover. *Get in the vehicle*,' and he wavered and turned again and marvellously did as I said.

Three steps from the Range Rover I stopped running and swung round fast to face Wyvern, in whom calculation had never been wholly overwhelmed by emotion: he sized up the gallery he was playing to – Orinda, my father, Mervyn, Faith and Lavender – and under the glare of all those sets of eyes he abruptly conceded that further attack would have legal consequences he wouldn't relish and stopped a bare six paces from where I stood.

The venom in his expression shrivelled the saliva in my mouth.

'One day,' he said, 'I'll get you one day.'

But not today, I thought; and today was all that mattered.

He took a few steps backwards, his face smoothing out to its customary flatness, then he turned and walked towards his car as if nothing had happened. Easing into the driver's seat he started the engine and drove collectedly away with no burning of tyres or other histrionics.

He left a lot of speechlessness in and around the Range Rover.

In the end Mervyn, clearing his throat, said, 'Orinda needs a doctor.'

Orinda disagreed. 'I need a tissue.'

Faith and Lavender between them produced some crumpled white squares. Orinda wiped her face, looked in a small mirror and moaned at the wreck it revealed. 'I'm not going anywhere like this.'

'The police . . .?' suggested Faith.

'*No*,' Orinda said, and no one argued.

With everyone subdued I drove the Range Rover

back to the headquarters where my father transferred himself and Orinda into her nearby parked car and set off to her home, with me following to bring him back.

He was silent for the whole of the return journey, but as I braked to a halt at the end of it he said, finally, 'Orinda thinks you saved her from being run over by the lorry.'

'Oh.'

'Did you?'

'The lorry driver missed us.'

He insisted I tell him what had happened.

'Her eyes were watering,' I explained. 'She couldn't see where she was going.'

I made as if to get out of the vehicle, but he stopped me.

'Wait.' He seemed to be searching for words and not finding them.

I waited.

He said in the end, 'I'm afraid I've let you in for more than I expected.'

I half laughed. 'It hasn't been boring.'

He went to Quindle with Mervyn early on the following Saturday to undertake an all-embracing round of the town's suburbs and, because of a dinner that evening and yet more commitments on the Sunday morning, he stayed in Quindle overnight.

175

That Sunday was my eighteenth birthday. My father had told me he would leave me a birthday card with Crystal, and I was to go along at nine in the morning to collect it. He would return that afternoon, he said, and we would dine together that evening to celebrate. No more political meetings, he said. Just the two of us, with champagne.

When I arrived at the party office at nine the door was locked and fifteen minutes passed before Crystal arrived and made her way inside. Yes, she agreed, my father had left me a card: and many happy returns and all that.

She took an envelope out of the desk and gave it to me, and inside I found a card with a joke on it about growing old, and nothing else. 'Yours, Dad,' he'd written.

'George said,' Crystal told me, 'that you are to go out into the street and find a black car with a chauffeur in it. And don't ask me what it's about, George wouldn't tell me, but he was smiling fit to crack his cheeks. So off you go, then, and find the car.'

'Thanks, Crystal.'

She nodded and waved me off, and I went outside and found the black car and the chauffeur a hundred yards away, patiently parked.

The chauffeur without speaking handed me a white envelope, unaddressed.

The card inside read '*Get in the car.*'

And underneath, '*Please.*'

With a gleam and a breath of good spirits I obeyed the instructions.

It wasn't much of a surprise when the chauffeur (not the same man as before, nor the same car) refused to tell me where we were going. It was, however, clear shortly that the direction was westwards and that many signposts distantly promised Exeter.

The chauffeur aimed at the heart of that city and pulled up outside the main doors of its grandest hotel. As before, the car's rear door was ceremoniously opened for me to step out and again, smiling broadly (not in the script), he pointed silently towards the interior and left me to the uniformed porters enquiring sniffily about my luggage.

My luggage this time again consisted of what I wore: a white long-sleeved sweatshirt, new blue jeans, and well-tried running shoes. With undoubtedly more self-confidence than at Brighton I walked into the grand lobby and asked at the reception desk for George Juliard.

The receptionist pressed buttons on a computer.

'Sorry, no one called Juliard staying at the hotel.'

'Please check again.'

She checked. Gave me a professional smile. Still no one called Juliard, past, present or future.

I was definitely not this time in sawn-off shorts and message-laden T-shirt land. Even on the last summer Sunday of August, business suits here prevailed. Ladies were fifty. In a cathedral city, people had been to church. The chauffeur, I gloomily concluded, had taken me to the wrong place.

The hotel's entrance lobby bulged at one side into a glass-roofed conservatory section with armchairs and green plants, and I sat there for a while considering what I should do next. Had my father intended me to get to know Exeter before I went to its university? Or what?

After about half an hour a man dressed much as I was myself, though a good ten years older, appeared in the lobby. He looked around and drifted unhurriedly in my direction.

'Juliard?' he said. 'Benedict?'

'Yes.' I stood up, taller than he by an inch or two, which seemed to surprise him. He had yellow-blond hair, white eyelashes and outdoor skin. A man of strong muscles, self-confident, at home in his world.

'I'm Jim,' he said. 'I've come to collect you.'

'Who are you?' I asked. 'Where are we going?'

He smiled and said merely, 'Come on.'

He led the way out of the hotel and round a few corners, fetching up beside a dusty dented red car that contained torn magazines, screwed-up sandwich papers, coffee-stained polystyrene cups and a mixed-parentage dog introduced as Bert.

'Disregard the mess,' Jim said cheerfully, sweeping crumpled newspapers off the front passenger seat onto the floor. 'Happy birthday, by the way.'

'Uh ... thanks.'

He drove the way I'd been taught not to; jerking acceleration and sudden brakes. Start and stop. Impulse and caution. I would have gone a long way with Jim.

It turned out to be only eight miles westward, as far as I could judge. Out of the city, past a signpost to Exeter University's Streatham Campus (home among much else of the department of mathematics), deep into rural Devon, with heavy thatched roofs frowning over tiny-windowed cottages.

Jim jerked to a halt in front of a larger example of the basic pattern and pointed to a heavy wooden front door.

'Go in there,' he instructed. 'Down the passage, last room on the left.' He grinned. 'And good luck.'

I was quite glad to be getting out of his car, even if only to stop the polymorphous Bert from licking my neck.

'Who lives here?' I asked.

'You'll find out.'

He left me with a simple choice: to do as I'd been told or find a way of returning to Exeter. Alice down the bleeding rabbit hole, I thought.

I opened the heavy door and went along the passage to the last room on the left.

CHAPTER EIGHT

In the last room on the left a man sat behind a large desk, and at first I thought with an unwelcome skipped heart-beat that he was Vivian Durridge, intent on sacking me all over again.

He looked up from his paperwork as I went in and I saw that though he wasn't Vivian Durridge himself he was of the same generation and of the same severe cast of mind.

He gave me no warm greeting, but looked me slowly up and down.

'Your father has gone to a great deal of trouble for you,' he said. 'I hope you're worth it.'

No reply seemed suitable, so I didn't make one.

'Do you know who I am?' he demanded.

'I'm afraid not . . . sir.'

'Stallworthy.'

He waited for the name to trickle through my brain, which it did pretty fast. It was the implication of his name that slowed my reply. Too much hope was bad for the pulse.

'Er . . . do you mean Spencer Stallworthy, the race-horse trainer?'

'I do.' He paused. 'Your father telephoned me. He wants to buy a horse and put it in training here with me, so that you can bicycle over from the university to ride it out at exercise. He asked me to enter it in amateur events so that you can ride it in races.'

He studied my face. I must have looked pretty ecstatic because a slow wintry smile lightened his heavy expression.

'I just hope,' he said, 'that you can ride well enough not to disgrace my stable.'

I just hoped he hadn't been talking to Vivian Durridge.

'Your father asked me to find a suitable horse. We discussed price, of course, I told him I train forty or so horses and one or two of them are always for sale. I have two here at present which might fit the bill. Your father and I agreed that you should come here today and have a ride on both. You are to choose which of them you prefer. He wanted it to be a surprise for your birthday – and I see it is.'

I breathlessly nodded.

'Right. Then go out of the back door. My assistant, Jim – he was the one who brought you here – he'll drive you along to the stables where the horses are ready for you. So off you go, then.'

'Er . . .' I said. 'Thank you . . . very much.'

He nodded and bent his head to his paperwork;

and Jim, grinning widely, drove half a mile to the stable yard that was old, needed paint and had sent out winners by the dozen over the years to small races on West Country courses. Stallworthy didn't aim for Cheltenham, Sandown or Aintree. He trained for local farmers and businessmen and ran their horses near home.

Jim stood in the yard and laconically pointed. 'Tack-room there.' He half turned. 'Horse in number twenty-seven. OK?'

'OK.'

I took a look at the occupant of box 27 and found a heavily muscled chestnut gelding standing there, anxious, it seemed, to be out on the gallops. He had nice short legs, with hocks not too angular, and a broad chest capable of pushing his way over or through any obstacle which came his way. More the type of a tough hardy steeplechaser than an ex-flat racer graduating to jumps.

I guessed at stamina and an unexcitability that might take a tiring amateur steadfastly towards the finish line, and if there were anything against him at first sight it was, perhaps, that he was a bit short in the neck.

Jim whistled up a lad to saddle and bridle the chestnut, though I had the impression that he had at first intended that I should do it myself.

Jim had considered me a sort of a joke. Perhaps my actual presence in the yard had converted me from joke to customer. In any case, neither Jim nor the lad saw anything but ordinary sense when I asked if I could see the chestnut being led round the yard at a walk. Somewhere along the way in my scrappy racing education I'd been told and shown by an avuncular old pro jockey that a horse that walked well galloped well. A long slow stride boded well for long-distance 'chases. A tittupping scratchy little walker meant a nervous scratchy little galloper.

The stride of the chestnut's walk was long enough and slow enough to suggest a temperament that would plod for ever. When he and his lad had completed two circuits of the yard I stopped him and felt his legs (no bumps from past tendon trouble) and looked in his mouth (which perhaps one shouldn't do to a gift horse) and estimated him to be about seven years old, a good solid age for a steeplechaser.

'Where do I ride him?' I asked Jim, and he pointed to a way out of the yard which led to a gate into a vast field that proved to be the chief training ground for the whole stable. There were no wide open down-land gallops, it seemed, in that cosy part of Devon.

'You can trot or canter down to the far end,' Jim said, 'and come back at a half-speed gallop. He ... the chestnut ... knows the way.'

I swung onto the chestnut's back and put the toes of my unsuitable running shoes into the stirrups, lengthening the leathers while getting to know the 'feel' of the big creature who would give me half speed and at least an illusion of being where I belonged.

I might never be a great jockey, and I might at times be clumsy and uncoordinated owing to growing in spurts and changing shape myself, but I'd ridden a great many different horses in my school holidays by working for people who wanted a few horses cared for while they went away on trips. I'd begged racehorse experience from trainers, and for the past two years had ridden in any race offered: I had had twenty-six outings to date, with three wins, two thirds and three falls.

The Stallworthy chestnut was in a good mood and let me know it by standing still patiently through the stirrup-leather lengthening and the pause while Jim sorted out a helmet in the tack-room, insisting that I wear it even though it was a size too small.

The chestnut's back was broad with muscles and I hadn't sat on a horse for three and a half weeks; and if he'd been mean-spirited that morning he could have run away with me and made a fool of my deficient strength, but in fact he went out onto the exercise ground as quietly as an old hack.

I didn't enjoy his trot, which was lumpy and threw me about, but his canter was like an armchair. We went in harmony down to the far end of the exercise field where the land dropped away a bit, so that the first part of the gallop home was uphill, good for strengthening legs.

At a half-speed gallop, riding the chestnut was a bit like sitting astride a launched rocket: powerful, purposeful, difficult to deflect. I reined to a slightly breathless walk and went over to where Jim waited beside the gate. 'Right,' he said noncommittally, 'now try the other one.'

The other horse – a bay gelding with a black mane – was of a leaner type and struck me as being more of a speed merchant than the one I'd just ridden. He carried his head higher and was more frisky and eager to set off and get into his stride. Whether that stride would last out over a distance of ground was, perhaps, doubtful.

I stood with my toes in the irons all the way down the field, letting the trot and canter flow beneath me. This was not a horse schooled to give his rider a peaceful look at the countryside; this was a fellow bred to race, for whom nothing else was of interest. At the far end of the field, instead of turning quietly, he did one of those swerving pirouettes with a dropped shoulder, a manoeuvre guaranteed to fling an unwary jockey off sideways. I'd seen many horses do that. I'd been flung off myself. But I was ready for Stallworthy's bay to try it; on his part more from eagerness to gallop than from spite.

His half-speed gallop home was a battle against my arms all the way: he wanted to go much faster. Thoughtfully I slid off his back and led him to Jim at the gate.

'Right,' Jim said. 'Which do you want?'

'Er . . .' I patted the bay's neck. He shook his handsome head vigorously, not in disapproval, I gathered, but in satisfaction.

'How about,' I suggested, 'a look at the form books and the breeding over a sandwich in a pub?'

I was quite good at pub life after three and a half weeks with my father.

Jim briefly laughed. 'I was told I was to fetch a school kid. You're some school kid.'

'I left school last month.'

'Yeah. Makes a difference!'

With good-natured irony he collected the necessary records from inside Stallworthy's house and drove us to a local pub where he was greeted as a friendly regular. We sat on a high-backed wooden settle and he put the form books on the table beside the beer (him) and the diet Coke (me).

In steeplechase breeding it's the dams that matter. A dam who breeds one winner will most likely breed others. The chestnut's dam had never herself won, though two of her progeny had. The chestnut so far hadn't finished nearer than second.

The bay's dam had never even raced, but all of her progeny, except the first foal, had won. The bay had won twice.

Both horses were eight.

'Tell me about them,' I said to Jim. 'What ought I to know?'

There was no way he was going to tell me the absolute truth if he had any commission coming from the sale. Horse traders were as notorious as car salesmen for filling the gear box with chaff.

'Why are they for sale?' I asked.

'Their owners are short of money.'

'My father would need a vet's certificate.'

'I'll see to it. Which horse do you want?'

'I'll talk to my father and let you know.'

Jim gave me a twisted smile. He had white eyebrows as well as white lashes. I needed to make a friend of him if I were to come often to ride exercise, so regrettably, with all my father's wily political sense, I deliberately set about canvassing Jim's pro-Ben vote, and thought that maybe I'd learned a few reprehensible techniques, while being willing to listen to people's troubles and desires.

Jim told me, laughing, that he'd hitched himself to Stallworthy because he hadn't been able to find a comparable trainer with a marriageable daughter. A good job I wasn't Usher Rudd, I thought.

Spencer Stallworthy apparently slept on Sunday afternoons, so I didn't see him again that day. Jim (and Bert) drove me back to Exeter by three o'clock and with a grin and a warm slap on the back he handed me over to the black car with the silent chauffeur.

'See you, then,' Jim said.

'I can hardly wait.'

The future had spectacularly clarified. My father,

instead of giving me a monthly allowance, had through my teens sent me one lump sum at Christmas to last me for the year: consequently I had enough saved away both to find myself a temporary lodging within cycling distance of Spencer Stallworthy and to immerse my brain in the racing press.

The chauffeur took me not to the headquarters from where he'd collected me, but to a playing field on the edge of Hoopwestern where, it appeared, an afternoon amalgam of fête and political rally was drawing to a close. Balloons, bouncy castle, bright plastic chutes and roundabouts had drawn children (and therefore voting parents) and car-boot-type stalls seemed to have sold out of all but hideous vases.

Painted banners promised 'GRAND OPENING BY MRS ORINDA NAGLE AT 3.00' and 'GEORGE JULIARD, 3.15.' Both of them were still present at 5.30, shaking hands all round.

Dearest Polly saw the black car stop at the gate and hurried across dry dusty grass to greet me.

'Happy birthday, Benedict. Did you choose a horse?'

'So he told you?' I looked across the field to where he stood on the soapbox surrounded by autograph books.

'He's been high as a kite all day.' Polly's own smile stretched inches. 'He told me he'd brought you here to Hoopwestern originally as window-dressing for the campaign, and he'd got to know you for the first time ever, and he'd wanted to give you something you would like, to thank you for all you've done here . . .'

'Polly!'

'He told me he hadn't realised how much he'd asked you to give up, with going to university instead of racing, and that you hadn't rebelled or walked out or cursed him. He wanted to give you the best he could.'

I swallowed.

He saw me from across the field and waved, and Polly and I walked over and stopped just outside the hedge of autograph seekers.

'Well?' he said over their heads. 'Did you like one?'

I couldn't think of adequate words. He looked, however, at my face, and smiled at what he saw there, and seemed content with my speechlessness. He stepped off the soapbox and made his way through the offered books, signing left and right, until he was within touching distance, and there he stopped.

We looked at each other in great accord.

'Well, go on,' Polly said to me impatiently, 'hug him.'

But my father shook his head and I didn't touch him, and I realised we had no tradition between us of how to express greeting or emotion, and that until that moment there had never been much intense mutual emotion to express. Far from hugging, we had never shaken hands.

'Thanks,' I said to him.

It sounded inadequate, but he nodded: it was enough.

'I want to tell you about it,' I said.

'Did you choose one?'

'More or less, but I want to talk to you first.'

'At dinner, then.'

'Perfect.'

Orinda was smiling warmly at me, fully recovered, make-up hiding any residual marks, all traces of the shaking, frightened woman in blood-spattered clothes overlaid by Constituency Wife, Mark I, the opener of fêtes and natural hogger of cameras.

'Benedict, daaahling!' She at least had no inhibitions about hugging, and embraced me soundly for public consumption. She smelled sweetly of scent. She wore a copper-coloured dress with green embroidery to match her eyes, and Polly beside me stiffened with the prehistoric reaction of Martha to butterfly.

Dearest Polly. *Dearest* Polly. I was far too young externally to show I understood her, let alone insult her by offering comforts. Dearest Polly wore remnants of the awful lipstick, a chunky necklace of amber beads and heavily strapped sandals below a muddy-green dress. I liked both women, but on the evidence of their clothes, they would never equally like each other.

Instinctively I looked over Orinda's shoulder, expecting the everlasting Anonymous Lover to be back at his post, but Wyvern had once and for all abandoned Hoopwestern as his path to influence. In his place behind Orinda loomed Leonard Kitchens with a soppy grin below his out-of-control moustache. Close on his heels came Mrs Kitchens, looking grim.

Usher Rudd was wandering about with his intrusive malice trying to catch people photographically at a disadvantage but, interestingly, when he caught my eye he pretended he hadn't, and veered away. I had no illusions that he wished me well.

Mervyn Teck and a retinue of dedicated volunteers, stoutly declaring the afternoon a success, drove my father and me back to the Sleeping Dragon. Four days to polling day, I thought; eternity.

Over a good dinner in the hotel dining-room I told my father about the two Stallworthy horses. A phlegmatic chestnut stayer and a sprinting excitable bay with a black mane.

'Well . . .' he said, frowning, 'you love speed. You'll take the bay. What makes you hesitate?'

'The horse I want has a name that might disturb you. I can't change his name: one isn't allowed to, after a thorough-bred has raced. I won't have that horse unless it's OK with you.'

He stared. 'What name could possibly disturb me so much?'

After a pause I said flatly, 'Sarah's Future.'

'Ben!'

'His dam was Sarah Jones; his sire, Bright Future. It's good breeding for a jumper.'

'The bay – ?'

'No,' I said. 'The chestnut. He's the one I want. He's never won yet, though he's been second. A novice has a wider – a better – choice of a race. Apart from that, he felt right. He'd look after me.'

My father absentmindedly crumbled a bread roll to pieces.

'*You,*' he said eventually, '*you* are literally Sarah's future. Let's say she would be pleased. I'll phone Stallworthy in the morning.'

Far from slackening off during the run-up to polling day, the Juliard camp spent the last three days in a non-stop whirl.

I drove the Range Rover from breakfast to bedtime. I drove to Quindle three times, and all around the villages. I screwed together and unclipped the soapbox until I could do it in my sleep. I loaded and unloaded boxes of leaflets. I made cooing noises at babies and played ball games with kids and shook uncountable hands and smiled and smiled and smiled.

I thought of Sarah's Future, and was content.

On the last evening, Wednesday, my father invited all his helpers and volunteers to the Sleeping Dragon for a thank-you supper. Along in a room off the Town Hall, Paul Bethune was doing the same.

The Bethune cavalcade had several times crossed our path, their megaphone louder, their travelling circus larger, their campaign vehicle not a painted

Range Rover but a roofless double-decker bus borrowed from his party headquarters. Bethune's message followed him everywhere: 'Dennis Nagle was out of touch, old-fashioned. Elect Bethune, a local man, who knows the score.'

A recent opinion poll in the constituency had put Bethune a few points ahead. Titmuss and Whistle were nowhere.

The *Gazette* had trumpeted merely 'An End to Sleaze' and waffled on about 'the new morality' without defining it. Though by instinct a Bethune man, the editor had let Usher Rudd loose and thereby both increased his sales and scored an own-goal. The editor, I thought in amusement, had dug his own dilemma.

My father thanked his faithful workers.

'Whatever happens tomorrow,' he said, 'I want you to know how much I appreciate all you've done ... all the time you've given ... your tireless energy ... your friendly good nature. I thank our agent, Mervyn, for his excellent planning. We've all done our best to get the party's message across. Now it's up to the voters to decide.'

He thanked Orinda for rallying to his side. ' ... All the difference in the world to have her support ... immensely generous ... reassuring to the faithful ...'

Orinda, splendid in gold chains and emerald green, looked modest and loved it.

Polly, beside me, made a noise near to a retch.

I stifled a quivering giggle.

'Don't think I've forgotten,' she said to me severely, 'that it was you who changed Orinda from foe to angel. I bear it only because the central party wants to use your father's talents. Get him *in*, they said. Just like you, they more or less told me to put his feet on the escalator, and he would rise all the way.'

But someone, I thought, had tried to prevent that first step onto the escalator. Had *perhaps* tried. A bullet, a wax plug, an unexplained fire. If someone had tried to halt him by those means and hadn't left it to the ballot-box... then *who*? No one had seriously tried to find out.

The speeches done, my father came over to Polly and me, his eyes gleaming with excitement, his whole body alive with purpose. His strong facial bones shouted intelligence. His dark hair curled with healthy animal vigour.

'I'm going to win this by-election,' he said, broadly smiling. 'I'm going to win. I can feel it.'

His euphoria fired everyone in the place to believe him, and lasted in himself through breakfast the next morning. The glooms crowded in with his second cup of coffee and he wasted an hour in doubt and tension, worrying that he hadn't worked hard enough, that there was more he could have done.

'You'll win,' I said.

'But the opinion polls...'

'The people who compile the opinion polls don't go round the village pubs at lunchtime.'

'The tide is flowing the wrong way...'

'Then go back to the City and make another fortune.'

He stared and then laughed, and we set out on a tour of the polling stations, where the volunteers taking exit polls told him they were pretty even, but not to lose hope.

Here and there we came across Paul Bethune on a similar mission with similar doubts. He and my father were unfailingly polite to each other.

The anxiety went on all day and all evening. After weeks of fine weather it rained hard that afternoon. Both sides thought it might be a disaster. Both sides thought it might be to their advantage. The rain stopped when the light-bulb workers poured out of the day shift and detoured to the polling booths on their way home.

The polls closed at ten o'clock and the counting began.

My father stood at our bedroom window staring out across the cobbled square to the burned-out shell of the bow-fronted shops.

'Stop worrying,' I said. As if he could.

'I was head-hunted, you know,' he said. 'The party leaders came to me and said they wanted to harness my economic skills for the good of the country. What if I've let them down?'

'You won't have,' I assured him.

He smiled twistedly. 'They offered me a marginal

seat to see what I was made of. I was *flattered*. Serves me right.'

'Father . . .'

'Dad.'

'OK, Dad. Good men do lose.'

'Thanks a lot.'

We went in time along the square to the Town Hall where, far from offering peace, the atmosphere was electric with hope and despair. Paul Bethune, surrounded by hugely rosetted supporters, was trying hard to smile. Isobel Bethune, in dark brown, tried to merge into the woodwork.

Mervyn talked to Paul Bethune's agent absentmindedly and I would have bet neither of them heard what the other was saying.

Usher Rudd took merciless photographs.

There was a smattering of applause at my father's entrance and both Polly (in pinkish grey) and Orinda (in dramatic glittering white) sailed across the floor to greet him personally.

'George, daaahling,' Orinda crowed, offering her smooth cheek for a kiss. 'Dennis is with us, you know.'

George daaahling looked embarrassed.

'It's going quite well, George,' Polly said, giving succour. 'First reports say the town votes are fairly even.'

The counting was going on under all sorts of rigorous supervision. Even those counting the Xs weren't sure who had won.

My father and Paul Bethune looked as calm as neither was feeling.

The hall gradually filled with supporters of both sides. After midnight, getting on for one o'clock, the four candidates and their close supporters appeared on the platform, shuffling about with false smiles. Paul Bethune looked around irritably for his wife, but she'd hidden herself successfully in the crowd. Orinda stood on the platform close beside my father as of right and no one questioned it, though Polly, beside me on the floor, fumed that it should be me up there, not that ... that ...

Words failed her.

My father told me afterwards that the result had been whispered to the candidates before they faced the world, presumably so no one would burst into tears, but one couldn't have guessed it from their faces.

Finally the returning officer (whose function was to announce the result) fussed his way onto the centre stage, tapped the microphone to make sure it was working (it was), grinned at the television cameras, and rather unnecessarily asked for silence.

He strung out his moment of importance by looking around as if to make sure everyone was there on the platform who should be and, finally, slowly, in a silence broken only by a throng of heartbeats, read the result.

Alphabetically.

Bethune ... thousands.

Juliard ... thousands.

Titmuss . . . hundreds.

Whistle . . . 69.

It took a moment to sink in. Staring down a preliminary cheer from the floor, the returning officer completed his task.

George Juliard is therefore elected . . .

The rest was drowned in cheers.

Polly worked it out. 'He won by just under two thousand. Bloody well done.'

Polly kissed me.

Up on the stage Orinda was loudly kissing the new MP.

It was too much for Dearest Polly, who left my side to go to his.

I found poor sad Isobel Bethune at my elbow instead.

'Look at that *harridan* with your father, pretending it was *she* who won the votes.'

'She did help, to be fair.'

'She would never have won on her own. It was your *father* who won the election. And my Paul lost. He positively *lost*. Your father never mentioned that bimbo of his, not once, though he could have done, but the public never forget those things. Sleaze sticks, you know.'

'Mrs Bethune . . .'

'This is the third time Paul's contested the seat,' she told me hopelessly. 'We knew he would lose to Dennis Nagle the last two times, but this time the party said he was bound to win, with the way the recent by-elections have been swinging in our favour, and with the other party ignoring Orinda and bringing in a stranger, and they'll never let Paul stand again. He's lost worse than ever this time with everything on his side, and it's that *horrid* Usher Rudd's fault and I could *kill* him . . .' She smothered her face in a handkerchief as if to shut out the world and, stroking my arm, mumbled, 'I'll never forget your kindness.'

Up on the stage her stupid husband still looked self-satisfied.

A month ago, I thought, I hadn't known the Bethunes existed.

Dearest Polly had bloomed unseen.

I hadn't heard of Orinda, or of Alderney Wyvern.

I hadn't met Mrs Kitchens nor her fanatical unlovable Leonard, and I hadn't known plump efficient Mervyn or worried Crystal. I never did know the last names of Faith or Marge or Lavender, but I was certain even then that I would never forget the mean-spirited red-haired terror whose delight in life was to find out people's hidden pleasures in order to destroy them. Bobby Usher bleeding Rudd.

CHAPTER NINE

So my father went to Westminster and I to Exeter, and the intense month we had spent in getting to know each other receded from a vivid present experience into a calmer, picture-filled memory.

I might not see him for weeks at a time but we talked now often on the telephone. Parliament was still in its summer recess. He would go back as a new boy, as I would, when my first term began.

Meantime, I rode Sarah's Future every morning under Stallworthy's critical eye and can't have done as badly as for Vivian Durridge because when I asked if he would enter the chestnut in a race for me – any race would do – he chose a novice 'chase at Wincanton on an inconspicuous Thursday and told me he hoped I'd be worth it as it was costing my father extras in the way of horse transport and shoeing with racing plates, not to mention the entry fee.

Laden thus half with glee and half with guilt I went with Jim in his car to Wincanton, where Jim declared and saddled the horse and then watched him win with as much disbelief as I felt when I sailed past the post first.

'He *flew*!' I said, thrilled and astonished, as I unbuckled the saddle in the winner's enclosure. 'He was brilliant.'

'So I saw.'

Jim's lack of much enthusiasm, I discovered, was rooted in his not having had the faith for a bet. Neither was Stallworthy overjoyed. All he said the next morning was, 'You wasted the horse's best win. You haven't any sense. If I'd thought for a moment you would go to the front when the favourite fell, I'd have told you to keep the chestnut on a tight rein so we could have put the stable money on him next time out. What your father will say, I can't imagine.'

What my father said was, 'Very well done.'

'But nobody backed it ...'

'Don't you listen to Stallworthy. You listen to *me*. That horse is for you to do your best on. To win whenever you can. And don't think I didn't back it. I have an arrangement with a bookmaker that wherever – *whenever* – you ride in a race, I am betting on you at starting price. I won on you at twenties yesterday ... I'm even learning racing jargon! *Always* try to win. Understand?'

I said, 'Yes,' weakly.

'And I don't care if you lose because some other horse is faster. Just keep to the rules and don't break your neck.'

'OK.'

'Is there anything else you want?'

'Er . . .'

'You'll get nowhere if you're afraid to tell me.'

'I'm not exactly afraid,' I said.

'Well, then?'

'Well . . . will you telephone Stallworthy? Will you ask him to run your horse in the novice 'chase at Newton Abbot a week tomorrow? He's entered him but now he won't want to run him. He'll say it's too soon. He'll say the horse will have to carry a 5-lb penalty because I won on him yesterday.'

'And will he?'

'Yes, but there aren't many more races – suitable races, that is – that I can ride him in before term starts. Stallworthy wants to win but I just want to *race*.'

'Yes, I know.' He paused. 'I'll fix it for Newton Abbot. Anything else?'

'Only . . . thanks.'

His laugh came down the wire. 'Give my regards to Sarah's Future.'

Feeling a bit foolish I passed on the message to the chestnut, though in fact I had fallen into a habit of talking to him, sometimes aloud if we were alone, and sometimes in my mind. Although I had ridden a good many horses, he was the first I had known consistently from day to day. He fitted my body-size and my level of skill. He undoubtedly recognised me and seemed almost to breathe a sigh of relief when I appeared every morning for exercise. We had won the race at Wincanton because we knew and trusted each other, and when I'd asked him for maximum speed at the end he'd understood from past experience what was needed, and had seemed positively to exult in having at last finished first.

Jim forgave the success and grew interested. Jim was by nature in tune with horses and, as I gradually realised, did most of the actual training. Stallworthy, although he watched the gallops most mornings, won his races with pen and entry forms, totting up times and weights and statistical probabilities.

Up the centre of the long exercise field there were two rows of schooling fences, one of three flights of hurdles, and one of birch fences. Jim patiently spent some mornings teaching both me and the chestnut to go up over the birch with increasing precision, measuring our stride for take-off from further and further back before the actual jump.

The riding I'd learned to that date had been from watching other people. Jim taught me, as it were, from inside, so that in that first month with Sarah's Future I began to develop from an uncoordinated windmill with a head full of unrealistic dreams into a reasonably competent amateur rider.

Grumbling at great length about owners who knew nothing at all about racing and should leave all decisions to their trainer, Stallworthy complainingly sent the chestnut to carry his 5-lb penalty at Newton Abbot.

I'd never before ridden on the course and at first sight of it felt foolish not to have listened to Stallworthy's judgment. The steeplechase track was an almost one-and-a-half-mile flat circuit with sharpish turns, and the short grass gave little purchase on rock-hard ground, baked by the sun of August.

Stallworthy, with several other runners from his yard, had brought his critical eye to the course. Jim, saddling Sarah's Future, told me the chestnut knew the course better than I did (I'd walked round it a couple of hours earlier to see the jumps, and the approaches to them, at close quarters) and to remember what I'd learned from him at home, and not to expect too much because of the weight disadvantage and because the other jockeys were all professionals, and this was not an amateur race.

As usual, it was the speed that seduced me and fulfilled, and the fact that we finished third was enough to make my day worthwhile, though Stallworthy, who had incidentally also trained the winner, announced to me several times, 'I told you so. I told your father it was too much to expect. Perhaps you'll listen to me next time.'

'Never mind,' Jim consoled. 'If you'd won today you'd have to have carried a 10-lb penalty at Exeter races next Saturday, always supposing you can persuade the old man to let him run there after this. He'll say it's too soon, which it probably *is*.'

The old man (Stallworthy) conducted a running battle over the telephone with my father.

My father won.

So, blisteringly, by six lengths, did Sarah's Future, because the much longer galloping track, up on Haldon Moor above Exeter, suited him better. He carried a 5-lb penalty, not 10, and made light of it. The starting price, my father assured me later, would pay the training fees until Christmas.

Two days after that, in cooler blood, I went to learn mathematics.

My father learned back-bench tactics, but that wasn't what the party had sent him to Hoopwestern for. He tried to explain to me that the path upward led through the Whips' office, which sounded nastily about flagellation to me, though he laughed.

'The Whips' office is what gives you the thumbs up for advancement towards the ministerial level.'

'And their thumbs are up for you?'

'Well ... so far ... yes.'

'Minister of what?' I asked, disbelievingly. 'Surely you're too young?'

'The really forward boys are on their way by twenty-two. At thirty-eight, I'm old.'

'I don't like politics.'

'I can't ride races,' he said.

To have the Whip withdrawn, he explained, meant the virtual end to a political career. If getting elected was the first giant step, then winning the Whips' approval was the second. When the newly elected member for Hoopwestern was shortly appointed as Under-Secretary of State in the Department of Trade and Industry, it was apparently a signal to the whole fabric of government that a bright fast-moving comet had risen over the horizon.

I went to listen to his maiden speech, sitting inconspicuously in the gallery. He spoke about light bulbs and had the whole House laughing; and Hoopwestern's share of the illumination market soared.

I met him for dinner after his speech, when he was again in the high exaltation of post-performance spirits.

'I suppose you haven't been back to Hoopwestern?' he said.

'Well, no.'

'I have, of course. Leonard Kitchens is in trouble.'

'Who?'

'Leonard ...'

'Oh, yes. Yes, the unbalanced moustache. What sort of trouble?'

'The police now have a rifle which may be the one fired at us that evening.'

'By the police,' I asked as he paused, 'do you mean Joe the policeman whose mother drives a school bus?'

'Joe whose mother drives a school bus is actually Detective Sergeant Joe Duke, and, yes, he's now received from the Sleeping Dragon a very badly rusted .22 rifle. It seems that after the trees shed their leaves the guttering round the roof of the hotel got choked with them, as happens most years, and rainwater overflowed instead of draining down the pipes as it should, so they sent a man up a ladder to clear out the leaves, and they found it wasn't just leaves clogging the guttering, it was the .22 rifle.'

'But what's that got to do with Leonard Kitchens?'

My father ate peppered steak, rare, with spinach.

'Leonard Kitchens is the nurseryman who festoons the Sleeping Dragon with all those baskets of geraniums.'

'But – ' I objected.

'Apparently in a broom cupboard on that bedroom level he keeps a sort of trolley with things for looking after the baskets. Clippers, a long-spouted watering can, fertiliser. They think he could have hidden the gun in the trolley. If you stand on a chair by the window you can reach up far enough outside to put a rifle up in the gutter. And someone *did* put a gun up there.'

I frowned over my food.

'You know what people are like,' my father said. 'Someone says, "I *suppose* Leonard Kitchens could have put the rifle in the gutter, he's always in and out of the hotel," and the next person drops the "I suppose" and repeats the rest as a fact.'

207

'What does Leonard Kitchens himself say?'

'Of course, he says it wasn't his gun and he didn't put it in the gutter, and he says no one can prove he did.'

'That's what guilty people always say,' I observed.

'Yes, but it's true, no one can prove he ever had the gun. No one has come forward to connect him to rifles in any way.'

'What does Mrs Kitchens say?'

'Leonard's wife is doing him no good at all. She goes around saying her husband was so besotted with Orinda Nagle that he would do anything, including shooting me in the back, to get me out of Orinda's way. Joe Duke asked her if she had ever seen a rifle in her husband's possession, and instead of saying no, as any sensible woman would, she said he had a garden shed full of junk, and it was possible he had *anything* lying around in there.'

'Did Joe by any chance search the shed? I mean, did he have a look round to see if Leonard had any bullets?'

'Joe couldn't get a warrant to search, as there were no real grounds for suspicion. Also, as I suppose you know, it's quite easy to buy high-velocity bullets, and even easier to throw them away. There's no chance of telling that it was indeed that rifle that was used because, even if you could remove all the rust, there is no bullet to match it to, as the one from the what-not finally got lost altogether in the fire. No one ever found any cartridge cases in the hotel either.'

My father continued with his steak. Putting down his knife and fork he said, 'I took the Range Rover to Basil Rudd's garage and had him dismantle the engine for a thorough check of the oil system. There was nothing in the sump except oil. It was actually extremely unprofessional for that mechanic – Terry, I think he is – to push the substitute plug up into the sump, but Basil Rudd won't hear a word against him, and I suppose there was no harm done.'

'There might have been,' I said. I thought for a moment and asked, 'I suppose Leonard Kitchens isn't accused of being in possession of candles?'

'You may laugh,' my father said, 'but in the shop at his garden centre, where they sell plastic gnomes and things, they do have table centre-pieces with candles and ribboned bows and stuff.'

'You can buy candles anywhere,' I said. 'And what about the fire? Was that Leonard Kitchens, too?'

'He was there,' my father reminded me, and I remembered Mrs Kitchens saying her Leonard liked a good fire.

'Did the firemen ever find out how that fire started?'

My father shook his head. 'They didn't at the time. Some of them are now saying unofficially that it could have been started with candles. Leonard Kitchens fiercely denies he had anything to do with it.'

'What do you think, yourself?'

My father drank some wine. He was trying to indoctrinate me into liking burgundy but, to his disgust, I still liked diet Coke better.

He said, 'I think Leonard Kitchens is fanatical enough to do almost anything. It's easy enough to think of him as a bit of a silly ass, with that out-of-proportion moustache, but it's people with obsessions who do the real harm in the world, and if he still has a grudge against me, I want him where I can see him.'

I did my best with the wine, but I didn't really like it.

'There's no point in his arranging accidents for you any more, now that you're elected.'

My father sighed. 'With people like Kitchens you can't be sure that good sense will be in control.'

I stayed with him that night in his Canary Wharf apartment by the Thames. His big windows looked down the wide river where once a flourish of cranes had been busy with shipping, though he himself couldn't remember 'the Docks' except as a long-ago political lever. His old office (he ran his investment-consultant business from home) gave him a two-mile walk along the Embankment to his new office in Whitehall, a leg-stretching that was clearly keeping him muscularly fit. He blazed with vigour and excitement. Even though he was my father I felt both energised and overwhelmed by his vitality.

In a way, I deeply loved him.

In a way I felt wholly incapable of ever equalling

his mental force or his determination. It took me years to realise that I didn't have to.

On the morning after his maiden speech I caught the early train from Paddington to Exeter, clicketing along the rails from reflected fame to anonymity.

In Exeter, one of eight thousand residential students, I coasted through university life without attracting much attention, and absorbed reams of calculus, linear algebra, actuarial science and distribution theory towards a Bachelor of Science degree in Mathematics with Accounting: and as a short language course came with the package I also learned French, increasing my vocabulary from *piste* and *écurie* (track and stable) to law and order.

As often as possible I cycled to Stallworthy's stable to ride Sarah's Future, and on several Saturdays set off from starting gates. After the first flourish as a novice, finding winning races for a steady but unspectacular jumper proved difficult, but also-ran was fine by me: fourth, fifth, sixth, one easy fall and no tailed-offs.

On one very cold December Saturday towards the end of my first term I was standing on the stands at Taunton watching one of Stallworthy's string scud first towards the last flight of hurdles when it crashed and fell in a cascading cartwheel of legs, and snapped its neck.

211

They put screens round the disaster and winched the body away, and within ten minutes I came across Stallworthy trying to comfort the female owner. Crying ladies were not Stallworthy's speciality. He first asked me to find Jim and then cancelled that instruction and simply passed the weeping woman into my arms, and told me to take her for a drink.

Many trainers went white and shook with emotion when their horses died. Stallworthy shrugged and drew a line across a page.

Mrs Courtney Young, the bereaved owner, wiped away her tears and tried to apologise, while a large bracer of gin took its effect.

'It's all right,' I assured her. 'If my horse died, I'd be devastated.'

'But you're so young. You'd get over it.'

'I'm sure you will too, in time.'

'You don't understand.' Fresh tears rolled. 'I let the horse's insurance lapse because I couldn't afford the premium, and I owe Mr Stallworthy a lot of training fees, and I was sure my horse would win today so I could pay off my debts, and I backed it with a bookie I have an account with, and I haven't any money to pay him. I was going to have to sell my horse anyway if he didn't win, but now I can't do even that . . .'

Poor Mrs Courtney Young.

'She's mad,' Jim told me later, saddling Sarah's Future. 'She bets too much.'

'What will she do?'

'Do?' he exclaimed. 'She'll sell a few more heir-looms. She'll buy another horse. One day she'll lose the lot.'

I grieved very briefly for Mrs Courtney Young, but that evening I telephoned my father and suggested he insure Sarah's Future.

'How did you get on today?' he asked. 'I heard the results and you weren't in the first three.'

'Fourth. What about insurance?'

'Who arranges horse insurance?'

'Weatherbys.'

'Do you want to?'

'For your sake,' I said.

'Then send me the paperwork.'

Weatherbys, the firm that arranged insurance for horses, were the administrators for the whole of racing. It was Weatherbys who kept the records, who registered horses' names and ownership details including colours; Weatherbys to whom trainers sent entries for races; Weatherbys who confirmed a horse was running and sent details of racing programmes to the press; Weatherbys who printed racecards in colour by night and despatched them to racecourses by morning.

Weatherbys published the fixture list, kept the thorough-bred Stud Book and acted as a bank for the transfer of fees to jockeys, prize money to owners, anything to anyone. Weatherbys ran a safe computer database.

There wasn't much in racing, in fact, that Weatherbys didn't do.

It was because of mad, tearful, silly Mrs Courtney Young that I began to think that one distant day I might apply to Weatherbys for a job.

In the spring of my third year of study my father came to Exeter to see me (he had been a couple of times before) and to my surprise brought with him Dearest Polly.

I had spent a week of each Christmas holidays skiing (practising my French!) and I'd been riding and racing in every spare minute, but I also played fair and passed all my exams and assessments with reasonable grades if not with distinction, so when I saw him arrive a quick canter round the guilt reflexes raised no wincing spectres, and I shook his hand (we had at least advanced that far) with uncomplicated pleasure.

'I don't know if you realise,' my father said, 'that we are fast approaching a General Election.'

My immediate reaction was 'Oh, God. No.' I managed not to say it aloud, but it must have been plain on my face.

Dearest Polly laughed and my father said, 'This time I'm not asking you to canvass door to door.'

'But you need a bodyguard . . .'

'I've engaged a professional.'

I felt instantly jealous: ridiculous. It took me a good

ten seconds to say sincerely, 'I hope he'll mind your back.'

'He's a she. All sorts of belts in martial arts.'

'Oh.' I glanced at Polly, who looked merely benign.

'Polly and I,' my father said, 'propose to marry. We came to hear if you had any objections.'

'Polly!'

'Dear Benedict. Your father is so abrupt. I would have asked you more gently.'

'I've no objections,' I said. 'Very much the opposite.' I kissed her cheek.

'Goodness!' she exclaimed. 'You've grown.'

'Have you?' my father enquired with interest. 'I hadn't noticed.'

'I've stopped at last,' I sighed. 'I'm over an inch taller and fifteen pounds heavier than I was at Hoop-western.' Too big, I might have added, for much scope as a professional jockey, but an excellent size for an amateur.

Polly herself hadn't changed, except that I saw with interest that the hard crimson lipstick had been jetti-soned for an equally inappropriate scarlet. Her clothes still looked unfashionable even by charity shop stan-dards, and no one had taken recent scissors to her hair. With her long face and thin stringy body, she looked a total physical mismatch for my increasingly powerful father, but positive goodness shone out of her as always, and her sincerity, it seemed to me, was now tinged with amusement. There had never been anything gauche or self-conscious in her manner, but only the strength to be her own intelligent, uncompromising self.

More than a marriage of true minds, I thought. A marriage of true morality.

I said sincerely to my father, 'Congratulations,' and he looked pleased.

'What are you doing next Saturday?' he asked.

'Racing at Chepstow.'

He was shaking his head. 'I want you to stand beside me.'

'Do you mean...' I hesitated, 'that you are marrying... next Saturday?'

'That's right,' he agreed. 'Now that we've decided, and since you seem quite pleased, there's no point in delaying. I'm going to live with Polly in her house in the woods, and I'll also find a larger flat in London.'

Polly, I learned by instalments through that afternoon, had inherited the house in the woods from her parents, along with a fortune that set her financially free to work unpaid wherever she saw the need.

She was two years older than my father. She had never been married: a mischievous glint in her eye both forbade and answered the more intimate question.

She didn't intend, she said, to make a wasteland of Orinda Nagle's life. Orinda and Mervyn Teck had been running the constituency day to day and making a success of it. Polly didn't hunger to open fêtes or flirt with cameras. She would organise, as always, from behind the scenes. And she would be listened to, I thought, where influence mattered.

Six days later she and my father married in the ultimate of quiet weddings. I stood by my father and Polly was supported by the Duke who'd lured Orinda to the races, and all of us signed the certificates.

The bride wore brown with a gold and amber necklet given by my father, and looked distinguished. A photographer, at my request, recorded the event. A discreet paragraph appeared in *The Times*. The *Hoopwestern Gazette* caught up with the story later. Mr and Mrs George Juliard, after a week in Paris, returned to Hoopwestern to keep the light-bulb workers faithful.

I still disliked politics and I was extremely grateful that the approach of my final exams made it impossible for me to repeat my by-election stint.

There were many politically active students at Exeter, but I kept my head down with them too and led a double life only on Stallworthy's gallops and various racetracks. I won no races that spring, but the sensation of speed was all that mattered: and, in an oddity of brain activity, the oftener I raced the more clearly I understood second-order differential equations.

The General Election swelled and broke under me like a Pacific surf, and my father, along with his party, were returned to power. A small majority, but enough.

No one shot at him, no one plugged his sump-drain

with wax, no one set fire to Polly's house, and no one let the martial arts expert earn her fee.

Suspicion of shooting and arson still lay heavily on Leonard Kitchens, but no one could accuse him of anything this time as his formidable and unforgiving wife insisted on his taking her on a double Mediterranean cruise. They were in Athens on polling day.

Poor Isobel Bethune had been right: Paul Bethune's party dumped him as a candidate in favour of a worthy woman magistrate. Though it was no longer hotly scandalous news, Paul Bethune's roving eye had settled again outside his home, and Isobel, at last fed up with it, had shed her marriage and her sullen sons and gone to live with her sister in Wales.

Polly kept me informed, her humour dry. My father couldn't have married anyone better.

I told him to beware of bikini-clad bimbos falling artistically into his lap with Usher Rudd in attendance for accusations of sleaze. Hadn't I heard, he asked, that Usher Rudd had been sacked by the *Gazette* for manufacturing sleaze where it didn't exist? Usher Rudd, my father cheerfully said, was now telephoto-lens-stalking a promiscuous front-bencher of the Opposition.

When the party in power reassembled after the whole country had voted, there was a major reshuffle of jobs. To no one's surprise at Westminster, my father's career skipped upwards like helium and he became a Minister of State in the Ministry of Transport, one step down from a seat in the Cabinet.

I had the best photograph of his wedding to Polly framed and stood it beside the one of him and my mother. I took the pacts we'd signed out of my mother's frame and read them thoughtfully, and put them back. They seemed to belong to a different life. I had indeed grown up at Exeter, and I'd had 'the first' that I would never forget: but the basic promises of those pacts had so far been kept, and although now it might seem a melodramatic statement, I knew that if it ever became necessary, I would indeed defend my father against any form of attack.

I took my final exams and, seeing that I'd probably done enough to gain a Bachelor of Science degree of a reasonable standard, I wrote to Weatherbys and asked for a job.

They replied, what job?

Any, I wrote. I could add, subtract and work computers, and I had ridden in races.

Ah, *that* Juliard. Come for an interview, they said.

Weatherbys, a family business started in 1770 and currently servicing racing in increasingly inventive and efficient ways, stood quietly in red brick surrounded by fields, trees and peaceful countryside near the small ancient town of Wellingborough, some sixty miles north-west of London in Northamptonshire.

Inside, the atmosphere of the furiously busy secretariat was notably calm and quiet also. Knowing the vast scope and daily pressure of the work being done there, I suppose I'd expected something like the clattering frenzy of an old-fashioned newspaper office, but what I walked into was near to silence, with rows of heads bent over computer monitors and people walking among them with thoughtfulness, not scurrying, carrying papers and boxes of disks.

I was handed from department to department and shown around, and in an undemanding interview at the end was asked for my age and references. I went away in disappointment: they had been polite and kind but had asked none of the piercing questions I would have expected if they'd had a job to offer.

Back at Exeter, living in rooms halfway between the university and Stallworthy's yard, I began dispiritedly to send job applications to a list of industries. Weatherbys had seemed my natural home: too bad they didn't see me as their child.

They did, however, follow up on the references I'd given them: my tutor at the university and Stallworthy himself.

The gruff old trainer told me he'd said my character and behaviour were satisfactory. Thanks a lot, I thought. Jim laughed. 'He doesn't want you to leave and take Sarah's Future with you. It's a wonder he didn't call you a loud-mouthed trouble-maker!'

There was a letter from my tutor:

Dear Benedict,

I enclose a photocopy of a reference I have sent to an institution called Weatherbys, that has something to do with horse racing, I believe.

His testimonial in full read:

'Benedict Juliard is likely to have gained a creditable degree in Mathematics with Accounting, though not a brilliant one. He took very little part in student activities during his three years at University, as it seems he was exclusively interested in horses. There are no adverse reports of his character and behaviour.'

Shit, I thought. Oh, well.

Much to my astonishment, I also received a letter from Sir Vivian Durridge:

My dear Benedict,

I am delighted to have seen over the past three years that you have had the opportunity to ride successfully as an amateur on your father's horse, Sarah's Future. I am sure that he has told you he enlisted my help in making you face the fact that you were not cut out for rising to the top three in the steeplechase jockeys' list. Looking back, I see that I was unnecessarily brutal in accusing you of drug-taking, as I knew perfectly well at the time

that with your sort of character you did not, but
on that particular morning it seemed to me – and
I regret it – that it was the only thing that would
disturb you so badly that you would do as your
father wanted, which was to go to university.

I have now heard from a friend of mine at Weatherbys that you have applied to them for a job. I
enclose a photocopy of a letter I have written to
them, and I hope that some way this may straighten
things between us.

Yours sincerely,
Vivian Durridge

His enclosure read:

To whom it may concern:
Benedict Juliard rode my horses as a sixteen- and
seventeen-year-old amateur jockey. I found him
completely trustworthy in every respect and would
give him my unqualified endorsement in any position he applied for.

I sat down, the pages shaking in my hands. Vivian
Durridge was about the last person I would ever have
applied to for a thumbs up.

I had vaguely been looking for a safe place to keep
my birth certificate, so as not to lose it while I moved
from lodgings to lodgings. I knew I wouldn't lose the
marriage photographs so I decided to put my birth

certificate behind my father and Polly, and as I'd been doing that when Vivian Durridge's remarkable letter arrived, I folded his pages into the frame too.

Three days later the mail brought an envelope bearing the Weatherbys logo, a miniature representation of a stallion standing under an oak tree, from a painting by George Stubbs.

I was cravenly afraid of opening it. It would begin 'We regret . . .'

Well, it had to be faced.

I opened the envelope, and the letter began 'We are pleased . . .'

Pleased.

That evening my father telephoned. 'Is it true you've got yourself a job at Weatherbys?'

'Yes. How do you know?'

'Why didn't you ask for my help?'

'I didn't think of it.'

'I despair of you, Ben.' He didn't, though, sound particularly annoyed.

He had been talking to one of the Weatherby cousins at a dinner in the City, he said. The web of insider chat in the City far outdid the Internet.

I asked if I could move Sarah's Future from Devon.

'Find a trainer.'

'Thanks.'

Spencer Stallworthy grumbled. Jim shrugged: life always moved on. I parted from them with gratitude and boxed my chestnut pal to a new home.

Weatherbys took me into their Racing Operations department which handled entries, runners, weights, riders, the draw: all the details of every race run in Britain, amounting to about a thousand transactions most days and up to three thousand at busy times.

All this computer speed took place in airy light expanses of desks and floor space, and in the calm quietness so impressive on my first visit. I'd thought that at a couple of days over twenty-one I might be at a disadvantage from youth, but I found at once that the whole staff were young, and enjoyed what they were doing. Within a month I couldn't imagine working anywhere else.

Every so often my own name cropped up, both whenever I was actually racing, but also in the next door department of Racing Administration that dealt with records of owners. It became a sort of running joke – 'Hey, Juliard, if you race that nag again at Fontwell, he'll suffer a 7-lb penalty,' or 'Hey, Juliard, you carried overweight at Ludlow. Cut down on the plum duff!'

Sarah's Future, as far as I could tell, enjoyed the exchange of the soft air of Devon for the brisker winds of further north. He still acknowledged my morning arrivals with much head-nodding and blow-breathing down his wide black nostrils, and he seemed to think it normal that I should embrace his neck and tell him he was a great fella, and mean it.

Anyone who says there can be true fusing of animal/

human consciousness is probably deluding themselves, but after several intimate years of speed together, that chestnut and I were probably as near to brothers as interspecies relationships could get.

One Saturday, about a year after I'd started at Weatherbys, the horse and I lined up at Towcester for an uneventful three mile 'chase, my father's inconspicuous colours of gold and grey made even less discernible by a persistent drizzle.

No one on the stands seemed afterwards to be sharply clear what happened. From my point of view we were rising cleanly in a well-judged take-off to a big black open ditch fence coming up the hill towards the straight. Another horse tripped and crashed into us, knocking Sarah's Future completely off balance. He had jumped that fence expertly several times over the past years: neither he nor I was expecting disaster. His feet were knocked sideways. He landed in a heap, throwing me off forwards. I connected with the ground in one of those crunching collisions that tells you at once that you've broken a bone without being sure *which* bone. I heard it snap. I rolled, tucking my head in to save it from the hooves of the runners behind me. The remainder of the field of half-ton horses clattered over my head as I lay winded and anxious on the slippery grass with blades of it in my mouth and up my nose, and dislodging my goggles after an uncontrollable slide.

The clamour of the contest faded away towards the

next fence. Two horses and two jockeys weren't going to be worrying about that. The horse that had crashed into Sarah's Future scrambled to its unsteady feet and trotted off as if dazed, and his unseated rider bent over me with 'Are you all right, mate?' as his best effort at an apology.

I gripped his hand to haul myself to my feet and found that the bone I'd broken was somewhere in my left shoulder.

Sarah's Future, also on his feet, was trying to walk but succeeding only in hobbling around in a circle. He couldn't put any weight on one of his forelegs. A groundsman caught him by the bridle and held him.

In hopeless love for the horse I walked over to him and tried to will it not to be true, not to be possible that after so long this closest of companionships should have so suddenly come to the edge of a precipice.

I knew, as every rider of any experience knew, that there was nothing to be done. Sarah's Future, like Sarah herself, was going to eternity in my hands.

I wept. I couldn't help it. It looked like the rain. The horse had broken his near foreleg. His jockey, his left collar-bone.

The horse died.

The jockey lived.

CHAPTER TEN

My father discontinued the insurance of Sarah's Future when I went to work for Weatherbys; partly, he'd said, because the horse was getting old and lessening in value and partly, punctiliously, so that if the horse were killed, Weatherbys would not have to pay up.

He would hear no apologies when I telephoned him. He briefly said, 'Bad luck.'

When I went back to work two days after Towcester, the man who had originally interviewed me drew up a chair at my desk and said, 'We used to insure that horse of yours, of course.'

I explained why my father had let the insurance lapse.

'I didn't come to talk to you about your loss,' the Weatherbys man said, 'though you do have all my sympathy. And is your arm all right? I came to ask you whether you would be interested in transferring yourself from here into our Insurance Services department, to work there from now on.'

The insurance department, mainly one long room

walled by books, more books and files and more files, was inhabited also by two men in their twenties. One was leaving the firm. Would I like his place?

Yes, I would.

Promotion struck the Juliards twice in one week. Another internal upheaval shuffled the cards in the government, and when the hurt feelings settled my father had moved upwards to the Cabinet as Minister of Agriculture, Fisheries and Food.

I congratulated him.

'I would have preferred Secretary of State for Defence.'

'Better luck next time,' I said flippantly.

My father's resigned sigh came down the wire. 'I suppose you've never heard of Hudson Hurst?'

'No.'

'If you think I'm going up fast, he's going up faster. He beat me to Defence. He's currently the can-do-nothing-wrong flavour-of-the-year with the Prime Minister.'

'How's Polly?' I asked.

'You're incorrigible.'

'I'm sure the jellied eels and the brontosaurus-burgers will be safe in your hands.'

There were for once no agricultural crises looming, and both he and I spent the autumn of that year rooting ourselves comfortably in new realms.

Not a great deal to my surprise, I took to insurance with energy: it not only satisfied my inclination to numbers and probabilities, but I got sent out fairly often on verification trips, to see, for instance, if the polo ponies I was asked to set a premium for actually existed.

As Evan, my co-worker and boss in the insurance department, preferred office work and computers, I did more and more of the leg work, and it seemed to be a useful arrangement all round, as I knew what good stables looked like and fast developed a nose and an instinct for the preparatory arrangements for a rip-off. Preventing insurance fraud at the planning stage became a game like chess: you could see the moves ahead and could put the knights where they would zig-zag sideways for the chop.

A great advantage, it transpired, was my youth. I might not look seventeen any more, but often at twenty-two I wasn't taken seriously enough. A mistake.

In the normal everyday honestly intentioned work of the department, Evan (twenty-nine) and I handled bona fide policies on every sort of horse and need, from the chance of infertility in a stallion to barrenness in a mare.

We also arranged cover for stable yards, all buildings, personal accident, public liability, fire, theft and measles. Anything for everyone. As agents, we kept underwriters busy.

I did abominably miss my early mornings on Sarah's Future, but as dawn grew later and colder towards winter, I would have found, as I had the previous year, that only weekends gave me much scope.

As for riding in races, I was lucky in that: the Northamptonshire trainer who'd taken the chestnut phoned me one day to say an owner of his, a farmer, wanted a free jockey – in other words, an amateur – for a runner he thought had no chance.

Why run it? I thought. I happily took the ride and plugged away, and the horse finished third. Delighted, the farmer put me up again, and although I never actually won for him, I got handed around to his friends like a box of chocolates, and cantered down to a start somewhere most Saturdays.

It wasn't the same without Sarah's Future, but I wasn't ready to try to replace him, even if I could have afforded it. One day, I thought. Perhaps. When I'd paid off the instalments on a car.

I had rationalised my liking for speed. Taking intoxicating risks was normal in growing up. Warrior genes were in-bred: it was necessary to fight the birch fences and the ski slopes, perhaps, in lieu of war.

Nearing Christmas my father said we'd been invited to a reception at No. 10 Downing Street – himself, Polly and I – for the customary jolly given by the current Prime Minister to the members of his Cabinet and their families.

Polly wore a reasonable dress and my father hired a chauffeur, and the Juliards in good formation walked through the famous front door. Staff greeted my father as one who belonged there. Polly had been through the portals before, but I couldn't help but feel awed as I trod through the crimson-walled entrance hall over the black-and-white squared floor and through into the inner hall and up the historic staircase in a river of other guests. The brilliant yellow staircase wall, going up round a central wall, was hung with portraits of all the past Prime Ministers; and I knew from the friendly way he looked at them that my father would try his best to join them, one of these days.

Never mind that there were about twenty other Cabinet ministers with the same dream, let alone all the 'shadow' ministers in the Opposition: one never got to hang on that wall without ambition.

The reception was chattering away in the large formal area upstairs known as the pillared drawing-room. (It had pillars. Two.)

We were greeted sweetly by Mrs Prime Minister – her husband was *bound* to arrive shortly – and were wafted onwards to trays of filled glasses and tiny Christmassy mince pies surrounded with holly.

I no longer asked annoyingly for diet Coke. I drank the Prime Ministerial champagne and liked it.

I knew almost no one, of course, even by sight. Polly kept me in tow for a while, though her husband had drifted away as if on wheels, greeting and laughing and making no enemies. Polly could identify all the Cabinet after eighteen months with my father, but

231

knew none of them – as Orinda would have done – as 'daaahling'.

The Prime Minister did arrive (he was *bound* to, after all) and my father saw to it that the great man shook Polly's hand with warm recognition and mine with at least a show of interest.

'You win races, don't you?' he asked, brow furrowed.

'Er . . . sometimes,' I said weakly.

He nodded. 'Your father's proud of you.'

I did, I suppose, look astounded. The Prime Minister, a gently rounded man with a steel handshake, gave me an ironic smile as he passed to the next group, and my father didn't know whether or not to call him a liar.

Dearest Polly squeezed my arm. 'George doesn't *say* he's proud of you. He just certainly sounds it.'

'That makes us equal.'

'You really are a dear boy, Benedict.'

'And I love you too,' I said.

My father's attention had purposefully wandered. 'You see that man over there?'

There were about twenty men 'over there'.

Polly said, 'Do you mean that one with flat white hair and circular eyes? The Home Secretary?'

'Yes, dearest. But I meant the one he's talking to. The one who's looking presidential and suitable for high office. He's Hudson Hurst.'

Polly shook her head. 'Surely not. Hudson Hurst has

an oiled black pony-tail and one of those silly little black moustache and beard combinations that frame a man's mouth and distract you from what he's saying.'

'Not any more.' My father smiled, but not with joy. 'Someone must have persuaded Hudson Hurst that the topiary work was a political no-no. He's cut off the hair and shaved off the beard. What you see now are the unadorned petulant lips of the Defence Secretary, God help us all.'

Five minutes later my father was putting a seemingly affectionate hand on the Defence Secretary's shoulder and saying, 'My dear Hud, have you met my wife and my son?'

Love thine enemies . . .

I hated politics.

Hud had a damp cold handclasp that I supposed he couldn't help, and if he had lately had an oiled black pony-tail and a black moustache-beard mouth-circling combination, they had very likely been dyed. His present hair colour was the dark-lightly-flecked-with-grey that a passing girl-friend had told me couldn't be faked, and he'd had a cut in a swept-back and duck-tailed style straight from the films of James Bond. Distinguished. Impressive, one had to admit. It inspired trust.

My father's own mat of natural dark close curls was cut to display to advantage the handsome outline of his skull. Expert stuff. Ah, well.

Hudson Hurst was overpoweringly pleasant to Polly.

Smile and smile, I thought, remembering Hoop-western: smile and smile and shake the hands and win the votes. He flicked me a glance, but I wasn't important.

Sweet Mrs Prime Minister appeared at my elbow and asked if I was having a good time.

'Oh, yes. Splendid, thank you.'

'You look a bit lost. Come with me.' She led me across to the far side of the big room and stopped beside a sharply dressed woman who reminded me strongly of Orinda. 'Jill, dear, this is George Juliard's son. Do look after him.'

Jill gave me a comprehensive head-to-toe and stared at Mrs Prime Minister's retreating back without enthusiasm.

'I'm really sorry,' I said, 'I don't know your name.'

'Vinicheck. Education.'

'Minister of?'

Her grim lips twitched. 'Certainly.'

She was joined by another woman in the simplest and best of current fashion: another Orinda-clone. Secretary of State for Social Security.

She said bluntly, 'Where does your mother get her clothes?'

I followed her gaze across the room and saw Polly talking unself-consciously to the man with flat white hair and circular eyes: the Home Secretary. Polly's clothes, as always, had nothing to do with popular opinion but very clearly revealed her individual character.

Jill Vinicheck (Education) kindly said, 'Your father may have a bright career in front of him, but your mother will have to change the way she dresses or she'll be clawed to bits by those bitches who write about fashion in the newspapers.'

The Secretary of State for Social Security agreed. 'Every woman in politics gets the hate treatment. Haven't you noticed?'

'Oh, not really, no.'

'Your mother's skirt is the wrong length. You don't mind me telling you? I'm only being helpful. Frankly, it would be the wrong length whatever length it was, according to the fashion bitches. But you can pass on some tips to her from us, if you like.'

'Er . . .'

'Tell her,' Jill Vinicheck said, enjoying herself, 'never to buy clothes in shops.'

Social Security nodded. 'She must have them made.'

Jill Vinicheck: 'Always wool or silk or cotton. Never polyester, or tight.'

'There's a marvellous man who could make your mother really elegant, with her long thin figure. He totally changed the way the papers write about us now. They discuss our policies, not our clothes. And he doesn't do it only for women. Look at the change in Hudson Hurst! Hud frankly looked a bit of a gangster, but now he's a statesman.'

'No time like the present,' Jill Vinicheck said with the briskness that had no doubt propelled her up the ladder. 'Our wand-waving friend is here somewhere. Why don't we introduce him to your mother straight away?'

'Er ...' I said. 'I don't think she – '

'Oh, *there* he is,' said Social Security, stepping sideways and pouncing. 'Let me introduce you ...'

She had her hand on his arm and he turned towards her, and I came face to face with A.L. Wyvern.

Alderney Anonymous Lover Wyvern.

No wonder Education and Social Security had reminded me of Orinda. All those years ago his ideas had dressed her, too.

I knew him instantly, but it took him several seconds to add four years to my earlier appearance. Then his face hardened to ill-will and he looked disconcerted, even though with my father in the Cabinet he might have considered that he and I might both be asked to the families' Christmas reception. Maybe he hadn't given it a thought. In any case, my presence there was to him an unwelcome surprise.

So was his to me.

Education and Social Security were looking puzzled.

'Do you two know each other?' one of them asked.

'We've met,' Wyvern said shortly.

His own appearance, too, had changed. At Hoopwestern he had made a point of looking inconspicuous, of being easily forgettable. Four years later he wasn't finding it so simple to fade into the wallpaper.

I had thought him then to be less than forty, but I now saw that to have been probably an underestimate. His skin had begun to show a few wrinkles and his hair to recede, and he was now wearing glasses with narrow dark frames. There was still about him, though, the strong secretive aura of introverted clout.

At the Downing Street Christmas party there was no overt sign of the sleeping anger that had blazed across Orinda's face and nearly killed her. He was not this time saying to me aloud in fury, 'One day I'll get you,' but I could see the intent rise again in his narrowed eyes as if no interval for second thoughts had existed.

The extraordinary response I felt was not fear but excitement. The adrenalin rush in my blood was for fight, not flight. And whether or not he saw my reaction to him as vividly as I felt it, he pulled down the shutters on the malice visible behind the dark-framed lenses and excused himself with the briefest of courtesies to Education and Social Security: when he moved slowly away it was as if every step were consciously controlled.

'Well!' exclaimed Jill Vinicheck. 'I know he's never talkative, but I'm afraid he was ... impolite.'

Not impolite, I thought.

Murderous.

*

237

After the reception Polly, my father and I all ate in one of the few good restaurants in London that had taken the din out of dinner. One could mostly hear oneself speak.

My father had enjoyed a buddy-buddy session with the Prime Minister and Polly said she thought the circular eyes of the Home Secretary were not after all an indication of mania.

Didn't the Home Secretary, I asked, keep prisoners *in* and chuck illegal immigrants *out*?

More or less, my father agreed.

I said, 'Did you know there was a list on a sort of easel there detailing all the jobs in government?'

My father, ministerially busy with broccoli that he didn't actually like, nodded, but Polly said she hadn't seen it.

'There are weird jobs,' I said, 'like Minister for Former Countries and Under Secretary for Buses.' Polly looked mystified but my father nodded. 'Every Prime Minister invents titles to describe what he wants done.'

'So,' I said, 'theoretically you could have a minister in charge of banning yellow plastic ducks.'

'You do talk nonsense, Benedict dear,' Polly said.

'What he means,' my father said, 'is that the quickest way to make people want something is to ban it. People always fight to get what they are told they cannot have.'

'All the same,' I said mildly, 'I think the Prime

Minister should introduce a law banning Alderney Wyvern from drinking champagne at No. 10 Downing Street.'

Polly and my father sat with their mouths open.

'He was there,' I said. 'Didn't you see him?'

They shook their heads.

'He kept over the far side of the room, out of your way. He looks a bit different. He's older, balder. He wears spectacles. But he is revered by the Minister of Education, the Secretary of State for Social Security and the Secretary of State for Defence, to name those I am sure of. Orinda and Dennis Nagle were kindergarten stuff. Alderney Wyvern now has his hands on levers he can pull to affect whole sections of the nation.'

'I don't believe it,' my father said.

'The dear ladies of Education and Social Security told me they had a friend who would do wonders for my . . . er, mother's wardrobe. He had already, they said, turned Hudson Hurst from a quasi mobster into a polished gent. What do you think they give Alderney in return?'

'No,' my father said. 'Not classified information. They couldn't!'

He was scandalised. I shook my head.

'What then?' Polly asked. 'What do they give him?'

'I'd guess,' I said, 'that they give him attention. I'd guess they listen to him and act on his advice. Orinda said years ago that he had a terrific understanding of what would happen in politics. He would predict things and tell Dennis Nagle what to do about them and Orinda said he was nearly always right. Dennis Nagle had his feet on the upward path, and if he hadn't died I'd think he'd be in the Cabinet by now with Wyvern at his shoulder.'

My father pushed his broccoli aside. A good thing his broccoli farmers weren't watching. They were agitating for a broccoli awareness week to make the British eat their greens. A law to ban excess broccoli would have had healthier results.

'If he's so clever,' Polly asked, 'why isn't he in the Cabinet himself?'

'Orinda told me the sort of power Alderney really wants is to be able to pull the levers behind the scenes. I thought it a crazy idea. I've grown up since then.'

'Power without responsibility,' my father murmured.

'Allied,' I said ruefully, 'to a frighteningly violent temper which explodes when he's crossed.'

My father hadn't actually seen Wyvern hit Orinda. He hadn't seen the speed and the force and the heartlessness; but he had seen the blood and tears and they alone had driven him to try to retaliate. Wyvern had wanted to damage my father's reputation by provoking my father to hit him. I dimly understood, but still hadn't properly worked it out, that attacking Wyvern would, in the end, destroy the attacker.

My boss Evan agreeing, I'd tied in the No. 10 Thursday evening reception with a Friday morning trip to meet a claims inspector to see if a haybarn had burned by accident or design (accident) and was due to stay again on Friday night in London with Polly and my father, before going to ride at Stratford-upon-Avon on Saturday, but en route I got a message to return to meet my father in Downing Street by two that Friday afternoon.

'I thought you might like to see more of the house,' he said cheerfully. 'You can't see a thing at those receptions.'

He had arranged for one of the household staff – called a messenger – to accompany us and show us round officially, so we went up the yellow staircase again, spending longer over the pictures, and wandered round the three large drawing-rooms leading off the ante-room at the top of the stairs: the white drawing-room, the green drawing-room and the pillared drawing-room where they'd held the reception.

The messenger was proud of the house which he said looked better and was better looked after than at any time in its rickety history. It had once been two houses back to back (rather like the burnt shops of Hoopwestern): the small Downing Street house facing one way, and a mansion to the rear of it facing the other. The interior layout over two and a half centuries had been constantly redesigned, and a modern refurbishment had bestowed overall an eighteenth-century ambience that hadn't been there before.

'The green drawing-room used to be the blue

drawing-room,' the messenger said happily. 'All the beautiful plaster work on nearly all the ceilings is relatively new. So are the classical mantels over the doorways. It all looks now like it always should have done, and never did.'

We admired it all copiously, to his satisfaction.

'Through here,' he said, marching off into one corner of the pillared drawing-room, 'is the small dining-room.' (It seated twelve in comfort.) 'Beyond that is the State Dining-Room.' (Dark panelled walls, seats for twenty-four.)

He told us about all the paintings in every room. I thought of all the past prime ministers for whom this graceful splendour had not existed, who had used this building as an office. It seemed a shame and a waste, somehow.

Back in the ante-room to the drawing-rooms our guide told us, pointing, 'Up those stairs is the Prime Minister's private apartment, and behind that locked door is his own personal room where no one goes unless he invites them. And downstairs . . .' he led the way expertly, via a lift to the ground floor ' . . . along this passage, as of course you know well, sir, is the ante-room to the Cabinet Room itself, sir, and I'll leave you to show those yourself to your son, sir, and I'll see you again just on your way out.'

My father thanked him sincerely for his trouble, and I reflected, slightly overwhelmed, that I'd never before given much of a thought to the living legacy of history my father hoped to inhabit.

The ante-room was any ante-room: just a gathering place, but with brilliant red walls.

The Cabinet Room, at the rear of the old mansion section, was long, with tall windows down one side and across one end, facing out into a peaceful-looking walled garden.

Irish terrorists had lobbed a bomb into that garden while all the Cabinet ministers were in the building. The bomb had done little damage. The grass now looked undisturbed. Peace was relative. Guy Fawkes could rise again.

Extraordinarily, Sir Thomas Knyvet, the magistrate who arrested Guy Fawkes red-handed with his barrels of gun-powder, lived in a house on the exact spot where the developer George Downing later built No. 10.

'This is where I usually sit,' my father said, walking down the room and coming to rest behind one of the two dozen chairs. 'That chair with arms, halfway along the table, that is the Prime Minister's chair. It's the only one with arms.'

The long table down the centre of the room wasn't rectangular but a much elongated oval, in order, my father explained, for the Prime Minister to be able to see the various members more easily.

'Go on, then,' I teased him. 'Take the arms.'

He was half embarrassed, half shy, but he couldn't

243

resist it. There was only his son to see. He crabbed sideways round the table and sat in the chair with arms; he nestled into it, resting his wrists, living the dream.

Above and behind him on the wall hung the only picture in that room, a portrait of Sir Robert Walpole, the first to be given the title Prime Minister.

'It all suits you,' I said.

He stood up self-consciously and said, as if to take the emotion out of the moment, 'The chair opposite the Prime Minister is normally where the Chancellor of the Exchequer sits.'

'And how many of you put your feet up on the table?'

He gave me a disgusted look. 'You're not fit to be taken anywhere.'

We returned to the front hall, my father looking at his watch. The messenger appeared as if on cue to see us off the premises, and I wondered vaguely if there were interior monitoring video cameras – which would be merely normally prudent – to trace the comings and goings of visitors.

While we said lengthy farewells the front door opened and in walked the Prime Minister, followed by two alert young men: bodyguards.

The Prime Minister said, 'Hello, George,' without surprise and glanced at his own watch revealingly. 'Come this way. And you ... er ...'

My father said, 'Ben.'

'Ben, yes. The racerider. You come too.'

He led the way through the front hall and past the staircase into a crowded and busy office crammed with desks, office paraphernalia and people, who all stood up at his approach.

'Now, Ben, you stay here with these good people while I talk to your father.'

He went through the office, opened a door and gestured to my father to follow. The office staff gave me a chair and a friendly welcome and told me that I was in the room where all the real work got done; the running of the Prime Minister's life as opposed to his politics.

They told me that quiet though the house might seem on a Friday afternoon, almost two hundred people worked there in the buildings in connected offices and that someone had once counted how many times the front door of No. 10 had been opened and closed in twenty-four hours, and it was more than nine hundred.

At length, in response to one of the constant telephone calls, I was invited through the office and into the next room in the wake of my father, and found myself in a large quiet tidy place that was part office, part sitting-room.

My father and the Prime Minister sat in the two fattest armchairs, looking relaxed, and I was waved to join them.

'Your father and I,' the Prime Minister said, 'have

been discussing Alderney Wyvern. I've met him once or twice, but I've seen no harm in him. I know that Jill Vinicheck and other women in the Cabinet say they owe him a great deal, and Hudson Hurst, above all, has benefited from a change of presentation. I've seen nothing sinister or unacceptable in any of this. The man is quiet, tactful, and as far as I can see, he hasn't put a foot wrong politically. Jill Vinicheck, in particular, has once or twice found his considered advice helpful, and certainly the Press have stopped making frivolous comments on her clothes, and take her as the serious politician that she is.'

'Er . . .' I said. 'Yes, sir.'

'Your father says that he and you have seen a different side of Alderney Wyvern. A violent side. He says you believe this capacity for violence still exists. I have to tell you that I find this hard to believe, and until I see something of it myself I have to give Wyvern the benefit of the doubt. I am sure you have both acted with the best of intentions in drawing my attention to the influence Wyvern may have with my ministers but, George, if you'll excuse my saying so, your son is a very young man without much experience of the world, and he may be exaggerating trouble where little exists.'

My father looked non-committal. I wondered what the Prime Minister would have thought if he himself had seen Wyvern hit Orinda. Nothing less, it seemed, was going to convince him that the outer shell of the man he'd met hid a totally different creature inside,

246

rather like a beautiful spiky and shiny conch-shell hiding the slippery slug-like mollusc inside, a gastropod inching along on its stomach.

The Prime Minister said, 'I will take note and remember what you have both said, but at the moment I don't see any real grounds for action.'

He stood up, indicating that the meeting was over, and shook hands with my father with unabated good nature; and I remembered my father's teaching on the very first day when I'd driven with him from Brighton to Hoopwestern, that people only believe what they want to believe. It applied, it seemed, even to prime ministers.

After we'd left No. 10 I said glumly to my father, 'I did you no good.'

'He had to be told. He had to be warned. Even if it does my career no good, it was the right thing to do.'

My father's strict sense of right and wrong might destroy him yet, I thought.

CHAPTER ELEVEN

After Christmas that year several things happened that changed a lot of lives.

First of all, on New Year's Eve, a wide tongue of freezing air licked down from the Arctic Circle and froze solid all of Canada, all of northern Europe, and all of the British Isles. Weathermen stopped agitating about global warming and with equally long faces discussed permafrost. No one seemed to mention that when Stonehenge was built in around 3000 B.C. the prevailing climate was warm, and no one remembered that, in the nineteenth century, Britain was so cold in the winters that on the Thames in London, they skated, held fairs and roasted oxen.

In the houses of that time people huddled in wing chairs with their feet on footstools to avoid draughts, and women wore a dozen layers of petticoats.

In the winter when I was twenty-two it rained ice on top of snow. People skated on their lawns and built igloos for their children. Diesel oil congealed to jelly. All racing came to a halt, except on a few specially built all-weather tracks, but even they had to be swept clear of snow. Owners cursed as their training bills kept rolling in, professional jockeys bit their fingernails and amateurs were grounded.

Claims for frost damage avalanched into Weatherbys, and in the middle of all this Evan, my boss, announced that he was leaving the firm to join a growing insurance company as managing director. I expected Weatherbys to replace him, over my head, but instead they told him to spend his three months' notice teaching me his job. I thought I was too young, even by Weatherbys' standards, but they seemed oblivious to my date of birth and merely told me that in following Evan I had a great deal to live up to.

Evan, tall, thin and with a bird-like head on a long neck, had taken over a department that had formerly acted mainly as a convenience for racing's owners and trainers, and in five years had fertilised it with imagination and invention into an agency major by any standard.

In his last three months, in addition to our ordinary busy work, he took me to meet personally all the underwriters he fixed deals with on the telephone, so that in the end I could wander round the 'boxes' at Lloyds knowing and being known in the syndicates and speaking their language.

He taught me scams. 'Beware the friendship scam,' he said.

'What's that?'

'Two friends conspire,' he told me, amused. 'One friend has a horse with something fatally wrong, a kidney ailment, say. OK? Instead of calling in a vet, Friend A sends his sick fellow to the sales. Friend B buys the sick animal at auction, insuring his purchase onwards from the fall of the hammer. Fall-of-the-hammer insurance was introduced to cover accidents like a million-pound colt stumbling on its way out of the sale ring and breaking a leg. Fall-of-the-hammer insurance comes into effect *before* a vet's inspection, see? So Friend B buys and insures a dud horse from the fall-of-the-hammer. Friend A acts all innocent . . . "would never have sold such a horse if I'd known . . ." Friend B humanely kills his dud and collects the insurance. Friends A and B split the proceeds.' He laughed. 'You've a nose for crooks, Ben. You'll do all right.'

During that same three months my father became the front man in an ongoing fish war, discussing at international high level who could take how many fish of such and such a species of such and such a size out of any particular area of the world's oceans. With wit and understanding, and by going to sea himself in freezing salt-crusted net-festooned seasickness factories, he learned the gripes and the legitimate arguments of men who lived close to Davy Jones and his ever-ready locker.

The Press took notice. Headlines appeared: 'JULIARD HOOKS AGREEMENT' and 'JULIARD IN JAPAN'.

250

People in insurance began to say, 'This Juliard person – no relation of yours, I suppose?'

'My father.'

'Seems to be doing a good job for my fish and chips.'

Fish and chips – the potatoes in agriculture – put my father on the map.

A television station sent a cameraman to sea with him: the cameraman, though sick the whole time, shot fearsomely memorable footage of my father hanging half-overboard in oilskins above the breaking waves and *grinning*.

Schoolchildren recognised pictures of 'the Fish Minister' instantly: his Cabinet colleagues didn't like it.

One of the top tabloids dug up the five-year-old stunning photograph of my father in mid-jump from the burning constituency office and printed it big in a centre-page spread extolling virility and presence of mind and the 'hands-on' policy out on the deep blue sea.

Even the Prime Minister didn't much like *that*. George Juliard as a relative newcomer with a normally quiet department in his charge was fine. George Juliard on the fast track upwards in public acclaim was a threat.

'One mustn't make a Minister a *cult*,' the Prime Minister said in a television interview: but others talked of 'leadership qualities' and 'getting things done', and Polly advised Dearest George to damp it down a bit and not let his success antagonise his colleagues.

My father therefore paid lavish tribute to the army of civil servants behind his fish-war solutions. 'Without their help...' and so on and so on. He did a lot of modest grovelling in Cabinet.

Towards the end of the long winter freeze the racing papers – frantic for something to fill their pages after weeks of near stagnation – gave a lot of space to the news that Sir Vivian Durridge, at seventy-four, had decided to retire from training.

The article, full of sonorous clichés like 'long and distinguished career', detailed his winners of the Derby (four) and other great races ('too numerous to mention') and listed both the chief owners he'd trained for ('royalty downwards') and the chief jockeys he'd employed ('champions all').

Tucked away near the end came the riveting information that, according to the form book, 'Benedict Juliard had, for two years, ridden the Durridge horses as an amateur.'

'*Benedict Juliard, as everyone in racing knows, is the son of George Juliard, charismatic Minister of Agriculture, Fisheries and Food. Ben Juliard won three races on horses trained by Sir Vivian, and then left.*'

End of Vivian Durridge. *A happy retirement, Sir Vivian.*

It seemed the freezing temperatures had put a brake even on adultery. Usher Rudd, still active with

252

his telephoto-lens and his mean spirit, had hit a dry patch in his relentless pursuit of the unfortunate Opposition front-bencher, whose progress from bimbo to spanked bimbo (with the odd choir-boy for variety) had either temporarily ceased or he had gone into hiding.

Usher Rudd, sacked by the *Hoopwestern Gazette* as a sleaze generator and definitely now *non grata* under many flags, had all the same as a freelance found a market in weekly sex magazines on the edge of perversion.

The motto he everlastingly lived by: SLEAZE SELLS.

And where it doesn't exist, invent it.

The Opposition front-bencher killed himself.

Shock reverberated through Parliament, and shivered in many a conscience.

He had been the Shadow Chancellor, the one who would have written the country's budget if his party had been in power. Rudd, for all his digging, had found no cent out of place.

Leader writers, hands raised in semi-mock horror, pointed out that though adultery (like suicide) might be a sin, it was not, under British law, a crime. Hounding a man to despair – was that a sin? Was that a crime?

Usher Rudd, smirking and unrepentant, repeated his credo again and again: if people in the public eye chose to behave disgustingly in private, the public had a right to know.

Did they? What was disgusting? Who should judge? Chat shows discussed it endlessly.

Usher Rudd was either 'the watchdog of the people', or a dangerous voyeur.

My father, walking with me in the woods round Polly's house, believed Usher Rudd would now be looking for another target.

'Until he's safely locked on to some other poor bastard,' he said. 'Just you remember how he listened to us in the Sleeping Dragon, so be very careful. He had a go at us then, and we got him sacked.'

'Yes, but,' I said, 'I'm certain you've stuck to what you wrote that day in those pacts: "That you would do nothing shameful or unlawful and would cause no scandal." Usher Rudd can't therefore touch you.'

He smiled. 'Those pacts! Yes, I've kept my bargain. But a small thing like innocence wouldn't stop that red-haired shit. Have you found your side of the promise difficult to keep?'

I shook my head. 'I've kept it.'

It was undoubtedly true, though, that the pact I'd written myself had shaped and inhibited what one might call my sex life. More accurately, my lack of sex life. I'd had two brief but pretty satisfactory interludes, one at university, one in racing, but both times I'd drawn back from any deep involvement. As for promiscuity – Usher Rudd had proved a bigger threat than AIDS.

When the sun at last shone warmingly on the house

in outer Wellingborough where I lived in a 'granny flat' built for a dear-departed granny, the ceilings first drizzled rain from burst pipes in the attic and then fell down completely. As major replastering was obviously required, I packed my stuff again in nomadic boxes and drove them to the office, storing them in the leg-room under my desk.

Evan was stripping the office of the clutter of his five-year tenure. Pin-ups, long lusted over, disap-peared. He arranged a thousand files in easy order and gave me an index. He bequeathed me three straggly green plants suffering from sunlight deficiency.

'I can't manage without you,' I said.

'You can always phone me.' His bird-like head inspected his non-personalised end of the room. 'You won't, though. You'll make your own decisions. If anyone thought you couldn't, you wouldn't be taking my place.'

He left in a flurry of farewell beers, and I spent the whole summer at first tiptoeing and then striding into new responsibilities, and in six swift months shed the last remnants of boy and grew in confidence and perhaps in ability until I had settled into the person I would be for the rest of my life.

When I mentioned how I felt to Polly, she said the change was obvious and that I was lucky: some people weren't sure who they were till the far side of thirty.

My father, who'd known who he was at nineteen, had during the early summer consolidated himself in the Cabinet, and by conscientious work had converted his colleagues' jealousy into acceptance, if not admiration. George Juliard had arrived as a political fact.

I asked him about Alderney Wyvern.

My father frowned. 'I haven't seen Wyvern anywhere since Christmas, but he's somewhere about – though the Prime Minister still won't hear a word against him. I'd say both Hudson Hurst and Jill Vinicheck are voting to his tune. They're both apt to say on one day that they haven't made up their minds on a point of discussion, but a couple of days later their minds and opinions are firm, and they always agree with each other... and I think those opinions are Wyvern's, though I've no way of proving it.'

'And are they good opinions?'

'Sometimes *very* good, but that's not the point.'

Parliament went into summer recess. Polly and the member for Hoopwestern spent the first part of the break in the constituency, living in Polly's house and working with Mervyn and Orinda. The four of them had settled into an energetic and harmonious team to the great benefit of all the voters, floating or not.

My father then took Polly round the world with stopovers in capital cities to learn about famine and fertilisers and freaks of climate, and came back with a fair understanding of how a billion people fed themselves on the blue planet.

I, in my little world at Wellingborough, computed numbers and risks and moved back into my granny flat when the new ceilings were dry.

Usher Rudd began stalking a bishop. Everyone except His Reverence sighed with relief.

I rode a winner in August and another in September.

Beneath this surface, although none of us knew it, little upheavals were growing and coalescing like cumulonimbus. My father had once said that they always killed Caesar, and when Parliament reconvened the knives were ready to drive into the toga.

My father, worried, told Polly and me that Hudson Hurst intended to challenge the Prime Minister for the leadership of the party. Hudson Hurst was cosying up to each Cabinet member in turn to ask for support. With his now polished manner he was smoothly saying that the party needed a tougher, younger leader who would galvanise the nation to prepare for the big build-up towards the next General Election, three years ahead.

'Alderney Wyvern,' I said, 'is writing the script.'

Polly said, horrified, 'He couldn't.'

My father said, 'It's been Wyvern's aim all along to rule by stealth.'

'Then stop him!' Polly exclaimed.

But Hudson Hurst resigned from the Cabinet and announced to the world that a majority of the party in power was dissatisfied with the decisions being made in its name and that he could do better.

'Stop him,' Polly said again. 'Oppose him.'

The three of us, sitting round the kitchen table in Polly's house, were silenced by the suddenness and size of the task. Sure, my father had aimed if possible one day to be Prime Minister, but had thought of acceding peacefully after a resignation, not of being a contender for the Ides of March.

My father, considering loyalty to be a paramount virtue, went to Downing Street and declared himself the Prime Minister's man. The Prime Minister, however, seeing that the party wanted a change, decided it was time to go just as soon as a new leader was elected. The way was now clear for my father to declare himself as a candidate for the ultimate job. The battle was now joined.

On a harmless-looking Tuesday morning in October I went into Weatherbys as usual and found that no one would look at me. Puzzled but unalarmed I made my way into my office and found that someone had kindly – or unkindly – left on my desk a copy of *SHOUT!* open at the centre pages.

SHOUT! was the weekly magazine that regularly printed Usher Rudd's most virulent outbursts.

There was a photograph, not of my father, but of myself, dressed as a jockey.

The headline in huge letters read, 'DOPE!'

Underneath it said: '*Jockey son of George Juliard, self-aggrandising Minister of Agriculture, Fisheries and Food, was fired for snorting cocaine, says trainer.*'

In disbelief I read the trailing paragraphs.

'*I had to get rid of him,*' says Sir Vivian Durridge. '*I could not have a glue-sniffing, drug-taking bad apple, infecting my good stable's reputation. The boy is no good. I am sorry for his father.*'

His father, the magazine pointed out, had entered the ring in the power struggle currently rending apart the Party. How could George Juliard proclaim himself a paragon of all the virtues (including family values) when he had failed as a parent himself, as his only child was a drug addict?

I felt as I had in Vivian Durridge's study on that morning five years earlier; numb from the ankles down. It hadn't been true that I had ever sniffed glue or cocaine or anything else, and it still wasn't true, but I wasn't fool enough now to think that everyone would believe me.

I picked up the magazine and, with eyes speculatively following every step I took, went to see the chairman, the working boss of Weatherbys, in his office. He sat at his desk. I stood before him.

I needn't have taken the magazine with me. He had a copy of it already on his desk.

'It's not true,' I said flatly.

'If it's not true,' the chairman asked, 'why on earth

would Vivian Durridge say it is? Vivian Durridge is one of the most highly respected men in racing.'

'If you'll give me the day off, I'll go and ask him.'

He stared up at me, considering.

'I think,' I said, 'that this is an attack on my father more than on myself. This article was written by a journalist called Usher Rudd who tried to discredit my father once before, in fact five years ago, when he first stood for Parliament in a by-election. My father complained to the editor of the newspaper and Usher Rudd was sacked. This looks like revenge. You'll see that this article says my father is involved in a power struggle in the party and, well, he is. Whoever wins the struggle will be the next Prime Minister. Usher Rudd is determined it won't be George Juliard.'

The chairman still said nothing.

'When I applied here for a job,' I said, 'Sir Vivian sent you a reference about me, and, oh' – I remembered in a blinding flash of joy – 'he sent me a letter, which I'll show you . . .' I turned towards the door. 'It is actually here in this building, in the insurance office.'

I didn't wait for him to comment but hurried back to the long insurance office and retrieved the cardboard box full of my stuff from under my desk. I simply hadn't bothered to take it back to my reconstructed room and clutter the place up again with bits and pieces. Somewhere in that box were my father's wedding photos with wives one and two.

In the frame behind the picture of himself and Polly

260

the letter from Vivian Durridge was as clean and fresh as the day I received it.

As a precaution, I made several copies of the letter and put them in one file among hundreds, and took the original to the chairman.

He had already, fair man that he was, retrieved from his records the short 'To whom it may concern' reference that Sir Vivian had spontaneously sent. It was lying on his desk on top of the magazine.

I handed him the letter, which he read twice.

'Sit down,' he said, pointing to the chair opposite his desk. 'Tell me what happened the day Sir Vivian Durridge accused you of taking drugs.'

'Five years ago' – it seemed a lifetime – 'like it says in the letter, my father wanted to make me face the reality that I would never be a top jockey.'

I told the chairman about the car and the chauffeur, and the hotel in Brighton facing the sea. I told him that my father had asked me to give him family background to help with his by-election campaign.

The chairman listened and at the end asked, 'Who, besides you and your father, knew that Vivian Durridge had accused you of drug taking?'

'That's just it,' I said slowly. 'I certainly told no one, and I don't think my father did either. Will you let me go and find out?'

He looked at the letter again, and at the reference and at the magazine article with its malice and lies, and made up his mind.

'I'll give you a week,' he said. 'Ten days. Whatever it takes. Before you came, Evan was second in command to an insurance specialist who is now on our board of directors. He will do your job until you come back.'

I was grateful and speechless in the face of his generosity. He merely waved me away with a gesture towards the door and, looking back as I left, I saw him slide the magazine, the letter and the reference into a drawer in his desk and lock it.

Back in my own office the telephone was ringing. My father's voice said, 'What the hell's going on? What does Vivian Durridge think he's doing? I can't get any answer from his telephone.'

The reason he couldn't get any answer from Vivian Durridge's telephone, I discovered three hours later, was because he was not in his own home.

The gravel in the drive was tidily raked. The porticoed front of the near-mansion spoke as usual of effortless wealth, but no one answered the doorbell.

Along in his stable yard there were no horses, but the head lad, who lived in an adjoining cottage, was pottering aimlessly about.

He recognised me without hesitation, though it was over five years since I'd left.

'Well, Ben,' he said, scratching his head, 'I never knew you took drugs.'

He was old and small and bandy-legged and had loved and been loved by the great beasts in his care.

The life he'd lived in their service had pathetically gone, leaving him without anchor, without purpose, with only a fading mental scrap-book of victories past.

'I never did take drugs,' I said.

'No, I wouldn't have thought so, but if Sir Vivian says . . .'

'Where is he?' I asked. 'Do you know?'

'He's ill, of course.'

'Ill?'

'He's gone in the wits, poor old man. He was walking round the yard with me one day at evening stables, same as usual, when all of a sudden he clapped a hand to his head and fell down, and I got the vet to him –'

'The *vet*?'

'There's a telephone in the tack-room and I knew the vet's number.' The head lad shook his own old head. 'So, anyway, the vet came and he brought with him the doctor and they thought Sir Vivian had had a stroke or some such. So an ambulance came for him, and his family, they didn't want us to say he was ga-ga, but he couldn't go on training, poor old man, so they just told everybody he'd retired.'

I wandered round the yard with the once supreme head lad, stopping at each empty box for him to tell me what splendid winners had once stood in each.

All the owners, he said, had been asked to take their horses away and send them somewhere else temporarily, but the weeks had passed and the old man wasn't coming back; one could see that now, and nothing was ever going to be the same again.

'But where,' I asked gently, 'is Sir Vivian at this moment?'

'In the nursing home,' he simply said.

I found the nursing home. A board outside announced 'Haven House'. Sir Vivian sat in a wheelchair, smooth of skin, empty of eye, warmed by a rug over his knees.

'He's confused. He doesn't know anyone,' the nurses warned me; but even if he didn't recognise me, he garrulously talked.

'Oh dear, yes,' he said in a high voice, not like his own gruff tones. 'Of course, I remember Benedict Juliard. He wanted to be a jockey, but I couldn't have him, you know! I couldn't have anyone who sniffed glue.'

Sir Vivian's eyes were wide and guileless. I saw that he now did believe in the fiction he had invented for my father's sake. I understood that from now on he would repeat that version of my leaving him because he truly believed it.

I asked him, 'Did you yourself ever actually see Benedict Juliard sniffing glue, or cocaine, or anything else?'

'Had it on good authority,' he said.

Five years too late I asked him, 'Whose authority?'

'Eh? What? Whose authority? Mine, of course.'

I tried again. 'Did anyone tell you that Benedict

Juliard was addicted to drugs? If anyone told you, who was it?'

The intelligence that had once inhabited the Durridge brain, the worldly experience that had illuminated for so long the racing scene, the grandeur of thought and judgment, all had been wiped out by a devastating haemorrhage in some tiny recess of that splendid personality. Sir Vivian Durridge no longer existed. I spoke to the shell, the chaos. There was no hope that he would ever again remember anything in detail, but he would be for ever open to suggestion.

I sat with him for a while, as it seemed he liked company and, even if he didn't know who I was, he didn't want me to go.

The nurses said, 'It settles him to have people near him. He was a great man once, you know. And you're the second person, outside his family, who has been to see him recently. He is so pleased to have visitors.'

'Who else came?' I asked.

'Such a nice young man. Red hair. Freckles. So friendly, just like you. A journalist, he said. He was asking Sir Vivian about someone called Benedict Juliard, who had ridden his horses for him once. Oh, my goodness – ' the nurses said, clapping hands to surprised mouths. 'Benedict Juliard ... isn't that who you said you were?'

'That's right. What would Sir Vivian like that he hasn't got?'

The nurses giggled and said, 'Chocolate biscuits and gin, but he isn't supposed to have either.'

'Give him both.'

I handed them money. Vivian Durridge sat in his wheelchair and understood nothing.

I telephoned my father.

'People believe what they want to believe,' I said. 'Hudson Hurst will want to believe your son is a drug addict and he'll go around asserting to your colleagues that that makes you unfit to be Prime Minister. Well, you remember what I wrote that day when we made the pacts ... that I would do my best to keep you safe from attack?'

'Of course I remember.'

'It's time to do it.'

'But Ben ... how?'

'I'm going to sue him for libel.'

'Who? Hurst? Usher Rudd? Vivian Durridge?'

'No. The Editor of *SHOUT!*'

After a pause my father said, 'You need a lawyer.'

'Lawyers are expensive. I'll see what I can do myself.'

'Ben, I don't like it.'

'Nor do I. But if I can make a charge of libel stick to *SHOUT!*, Hudson Hurst will have to shut up. And there's no time to lose, is there, as didn't you say the first round of voting for the new leader is next week?'

'It is, yes. Monday.'

'Then you go back to your fish and chips, and I'll take a sword to Usher bleeding Rudd.'

From Durridge's place in Kent I drove across much of southern England to Exeter and round to the training stables that to me seemed like home, the domain of Spencer Stallworthy.

I arrived at about six-thirty, when he was just finishing his round of evening stables.

'Hello,' he said, surprised. 'I didn't know you were coming.'

'No . . .' I watched him feed carrots to the last couple of horses and wandered over to look into the box that had held Sarah's Future for three splendid years. It was inhabited now by a long-necked grey, and I grieved for the simple happiness of days gone.

Jim was still there, closing the boxes for the night, checking that the lads had filled the hay nets and positioned the water buckets: all so familiar, so much missed.

The evening routine finished, I asked if I could talk to them both for a while, which meant a short drive to Stallworthy's house and an issue of well-remembered sherry.

They knew my father was in the Cabinet and I explained about the power struggle. I showed them the centre pages of *SHOUT!*, which shocked them back to the bottle.

Jim blinked his white eyelashes rapidly, always a sign of disturbance, and Stallworthy said, 'But it's not true, is it? You never took drugs. I'd have known it.'

'That's right,' I said gratefully, 'and that's what I'd like you to write for me. A statement that I rode from your stables for three years and won races and showed no sign of ever being interested in drugs. I want as many affidavits as I can get to say that I am not a drug addict and never was as far as you can possibly tell. I'm going to sue this magazine for libel.'

Both Stallworthy and Jim were outraged on my behalf and wrote more fiercely in my defence than I could have asked for.

Stallworthy gave me a bed for the night and a horse to ride in the early morning, and I left after breakfast and drove along the familiar country roads back to the university.

The two years since I'd graduated seemed to vanish. I parked the car in the road outside the Streatham Campus and walked up the steep path to the Laver Building, home of the mathematics department. There, after a good deal of casting about, I found my tutor – the one who had written for me the reference sought by Weatherbys – and explained to him, as to Stallworthy and Jim, what I was asking of him.

'*Drugs*? Of course, a lot of the students experiment and, as you know, we try to get rid of the hard core, but you were about the last student I would have suspected of getting hooked. For a start, drugs and mathematics don't mix, and your work was particularly clear-headed. This magazine article is all rubbish.'

I beseeched him to put those views in writing, which he did with emphasis.

'Good luck,' he said when I left. 'These journalists get away with murder.'

I hiked back to my car and drove across country to my old school at Malvern.

There on its hillside campus, steep like Exeter University, though not so big, I sought out the man who had taught me mathematics. He passed the buck to my one-time house-master, who listened and sent me to the Head.

The Headmaster walked with me down the broad familiar stone-floored passage in the Main Building and up the stone stairs to his study, where I showed him a copy of *SHOUT!* and also a copy of Vivian Durridge's letter.

'Of course I'll support you,' he said without hesitation and wrote, and handed me the handwritten page to read.

It said:

Benedict Juliard attended Malvern College for five years. During the last two, while he was successfully working towards his A levels and university entrance, he spent all breaks either riding racehorses

– he won three steeplechases – or skiing, in which sport he won a European under-18 downhill race.

In addition to those skills he was a considerable marksman with a rifle: he shot in the school team that won the prestigious Ashburton Shield.

In all these activities he showed clear-headedness, natural courage and a high degree of concentration. It is ludicrous to suggest that he was ever under the influence of hallucinatory drugs.

I looked up, not knowing quite what to say.

'I admire your father,' the Headmaster said. 'I'm not saying I agree with him all the time politically, but the country could certainly do worse.'

I said, 'Thank you,' rather feebly, and he shook hands with me on a smile.

Onwards I went to Wellingborough where I briefly called in to see the chairman to tell him what I'd been doing and what I proposed to do. Then, taking a couple of the photocopies of Vivian Durridge's letter and his reference from their folder, and making copies of all the letters I'd collected, I drove to Wellingborough station and, tired of the roads, I caught the train to London.

SHOUT! emanated, it transpired, from a small and grubby-looking building south of the Thames. The editor wouldn't in the least want to see me but, late in the afternoon, I marched straight into his office shedding secretaries like bow-waves. He was sitting in a sweatshirt behind a cluttered desk typing on the keyboard of a computer.

He didn't recognise me, of course. When I told him who I was he invited me to leave.

'I am going to sue you for libel,' I said, opening the copy of *SHOUT!* at the centre pages. 'I see from the small print at the beginning of this magazine that the name of the editor is Rufus Crossmead. If that's who you are, I'll be suing Rufus Crossmead personally.'

He was a small pugnacious man, sticking his chest out and tucking his chin in like a pugilist. I supposed briefly that dealing with wronged and furious victims of his destructive ethos was a regular part of his life.

I remembered how, five years earlier, my father had pulverised the editor of the *Hoopwestern Gazette*, but I couldn't reproduce exactly that quiet degree of menace. I didn't have the commanding strength of his vibrant physical presence. I left Rufus Crossmead, however, in no doubt as to my intentions.

I laid down in front of him copies of the strong letters from Spencer Stallworthy, Jim, my Exeter tutor and the Headmaster of Malvern College, and I gave him finally a copy of the letter Vivian Durridge had sent.

'The only good defence in a libel suit,' I said, 'is to prove that the allegations are true. You can't use that defence, because you've printed lies. It will be easy for me to establish that Sir Vivian Durridge is now hopelessly confused after a stroke and doesn't know what he's saying. Usher Rudd must have been aware of it. He was trying to revenge himself for my father having got him sacked from the *Hoopwestern Gazette*. No reputable paper has employed him since. He suits your style, but he's dropped even you in the shit.'

Rufus Crossmead gloomily read the various papers.

'We'll settle out of court,' he said.

It sounded to me as if he'd said it often before, and it wasn't at all what I'd expected. I wasn't sure it was even what I wanted.

I said slowly, 'I'll tell you what I'll settle for . . .'

'It's up to the proprietors,' Crossmead interrupted. 'They'll make you an offer.'

'They always do?' I asked.

He didn't exactly nod, but it was in the air.

'Then you tell the proprietors,' I said, 'that I'll settle for a retraction and a statement of sincere regret from you that your magazine's accusations were based on incorrect information. Tell your proprietors that I'll settle for a statement appearing very visibly in next Tuesday's issue of *SHOUT*! In addition, you will send immediately – by registered post – a personally signed copy of that retraction and statement of regret to each of the 650 or so Members of Parliament.'

CHAPTER TWELVE

It wasn't enough, I thought, to defend.

I should have written in that pact, 'I will attack my father's attackers.' I should have written that I'd go to war for him if I saw the need.

At almost eighteen, I'd written from easy sentiment. At twenty-three, I saw that, if the pact meant anything at all, it pledged an allegiance that could lead to death. And if that were so, I thought, it would be feeble just to sit around waiting for the axe.

It had been Tuesday when *SHOUT!* had hit the newsagents, and late afternoon on Wednesday when I'd crashed into Rufus Crossmead's editorial office. On Friday I drove from Wellingborough to Hoopwestern, and spent the journey looking back to the end of that confrontation and the answers I'd been given.

I'd asked *SHOUT!*'s editor why he had sent Usher Rudd to see Vivian Durridge, and he'd said he hadn't, it had been Usher Rudd's own idea.

'Usher – well, his name is Bobby – said he'd been asked to dig into everything you'd ever done, and come up with some dirt. He was getting ultra frustrated because he couldn't find any sludge. He went blasting on a bit that no one could be as careful to stay out of trouble as you had been, and then there was this announcement of Sir Vivian Durridge's retirement, which said you had ridden for his stable, so Bobby went off on the off-chance, and he came back laughing. Crowing. He said he'd got you at last. So he wrote the story and I printed it.'

'And you didn't check.'

'If I had to check every word I print,' the editor had said with world-weariness, 'our sales would plummet.'

On Wednesday, early evening, I'd phoned Samson Frazer, the editor of the *Hoopwestern Gazette*.

'If you're thinking of reprinting a story about me from *SHOUT!*,' I'd said, 'don't do it. Usher Rudd wrote it. It's not true and it'll get you into court for libel.'

Gloomy silence.

Then, 'I'll re-set the front page,' he'd said.

On Thursday, with prudent speed, *SHOUT!*'s proprietors had acted to avoid the heavy expenses of a libel action and had written and posted the retractions I'd asked for to the Members of Parliament.

My father, attending the House of Commons on Friday morning, found that several registered letters had already reached their targets. In addition, he gave everyone – from the Prime Minister downwards – a copy of Vivian Durridge's letter to me, along with a brief confirmation from himself that he'd asked Durridge to think of a way of persuading me to leave. Apparently the general reaction had been relief and relaxation, though Hudson Hurst had insisted there had to be some truth in the dope story somewhere.

'Why do you think so?' my father related that he'd asked, and the only reply had been stutter and dismay.

My father said, 'I asked Hudson Hurst if he himself had sent Usher Rudd to Vivian Durridge. He denied it. He looked bewildered. I don't think he did it.'

'No, I agree.'

I now negotiated a roundabout. Fourteen more miles to Hoopwestern.

I thought about Hudson Hurst, the ugly duckling converted to swan by scissors and razor. On television he was smooth, convincing and read his speeches from an auto-cue. No inner fire. A puppet.

Alderney Wyvern pulled his strings.

How to prove it? How to stop him?

Attacking Alderney Wyvern could destroy the attacker. I sensed it strongly. History was littered with the laments of failed invasions.

I arrived at Hoopwestern at noon and parked in the car park behind the old party headquarters. Polly had told me that the charity that had owned the whole of the burned double bow-fronted building had chosen to rebuild it much as before, with new bow windows fronting onto the cobbled square and new shops matching the row at the rear. When I walked in from

275

the car park all that seemed different were heavy fire doors and a rash of big scarlet extinguishers.

Mervyn Teck was there, and greeted me with ambivalent open arms and wary eyes.

'Benedict!' He was plumper than ever. Rotund, nowadays.

'Hi, Mervyn.'

He shook hands awkwardly, and glanced past me to where, on his desk, lay two newspapers, both *SHOUT!* and the *Hoopwestern Gazette*.

'I didn't expect you,' Mervyn said.

'No, well, I'm sorry. I expect my father telephoned to say he couldn't get down this weekend for the surgery?' Most Saturday mornings the public came to headquarters with their complaints. 'I expect you'll do fine without him.'

My father, in fact, was busy in London with secretive little lunches and private dinners, with hurried hidden meetings and promises and bargains, all the undercover manoeuvring of shifts of power. I hoped and trusted that A.L. Wyvern was fully occupied in doing the same.

A young woman sitting behind a computer stood up with unaffected welcome.

'Benedict!'

I said, 'Crystal?' tentatively.

'I'm so glad to see you,' she said edging round her desk to give me a kiss. 'It's such ages since you were here.'

A great change here too had taken place. She was no longer thin and anxious, but rounded and secure; and she wore a wedding ring, I saw.

They gave me coffee and local news, and I read with interest what the *Gazette* had made of *SHOUT!*. 'An unfair attack on our MP through his son. No truth in this allegation ... shocking ... libellous ... retractions and regrets are in the pipeline.'

'The by-line in *SHOUT!* says Usher Rudd.' Mervyn pointed. 'Vicious little nerd.'

'Actually,' I said as their indignation boiled on, 'I came hoping to see Orinda, but she doesn't answer her phone.'

'Oh dear,' Crystal said, 'she isn't here. She went away for the weekend. She won't be back till Monday.'

They didn't know where she'd gone.

I'd made a short list of people I aimed to see. Mervyn, helpful with addresses, knew where to find Isobel Bethune at her sister's house in Wales, and as she – telephoned – was not only at home but would be glad to see me, I drove to Cardiff that afternoon and discovered Paul Bethune's rejuvenated wife in a pretty terraced house in the suburbs.

I'd never before seen her happy. She too was a different woman: the grey lines of worry had smoothed into peaches and cream.

It was she, however, who exclaimed, 'How you've changed. You've grown older.'

'It happens.'

Her sister had gone shopping. I sat with Isobel and listened to her remembering for my benefit how Usher Rudd had uncovered her husband's bimbo affair.

'Usher Rudd just dug away and wrote it up sensationally, but it was all Paul's fault. Men are such bloody fools. He confessed to me in snivelling tears in the end that he'd boasted – *boasted*, I ask you – to some stranger that he was playing golf with that he was having an affair his wife didn't know about. Snigger, snigger. Can you believe it? And that stranger turned out to be that weird nobody that was always hanging about round the Nagles. He used to play golf with Dennis.'

'His name's Wyvern.'

'Yes, I know that now. When Dennis died, that Wyvern person wanted to make sure Orinda got elected, so he arranged to play golf with Paul, to see where Paul was weakest ... I hated Usher Rudd, but it wasn't until after your father got elected that Paul broke down and told me what had happened.' She sighed. 'I was shattered then, but I don't care now, isn't that odd?'

'How are your sons?'

She laughed. 'They've joined the army. Best place for them. They sometimes send postcards. You're the only one that was kind to me in those days.'

I left her with a kiss on the peaches-and-cream cheek and drove tiredly back to Hoopwestern for the night, staying in Polly's house in the woods and eating potted shrimps from her freezer.

On Saturday morning I went to the police station and asked to see Detective Sergeant Joe Duke, whose mother drove a school bus.

Joe Duke appeared questioningly.

'George Juliard's son? You look older.'

Joe Duke was still a detective sergeant, but his mother no longer drove a bus. 'She's into rabbits,' he said. He took me into a bare little interview room, explaining he was the senior officer on duty and couldn't leave the station.

He thoughtfully repeated my question. 'Do I know if that fire you could have died in was arson? It's all of five years ago.'

'A bit more. But you must have files,' I said.

'I don't need files. Mostly fires in the night are from cigarettes or electrical shorts, but none of you smoked and the place had been re-wired. Is this off the record?'

'On the moon.'

A dedicated policeman in his thirties, Joe had a broad face, a Dorset accent and a realistic attitude to human failings. 'Amy used to let tramps sleep above the charity shop sometimes, but not that night, she says, though that's the official and easy theory of the cause of fire. They say a vagrant was lighting candles downstairs and knocked them over, and then ran away. Nonsense, really. But the fire did start, the fire-fighters reckoned, in the charity shop, and the back door there wasn't bolted, and both shops of the old place were lined and partitioned with dry old wood, though they've rebuilt it with brick and concrete now, and it's awash with smoke alarms. Anyway, I suppose you heard the theory that crazy Leonard Kitchens set light to the place to frighten your father off so that Orinda Nagle could be our MP?'

'I've heard. What do you think?'

'It doesn't much matter now, does it?'

'But still . . .'

'I think he did it. I questioned him, see? But we hadn't a flicker of evidence.'

'And what about the gun in the Sleeping Dragon's gutter?'

'No one knows who put it there.'

'Leonard Kitchens?'

'He swears he didn't. And he's heavy and slow. It needed someone pretty agile to put that gun up high.'

'Did you ever find out where the rifle came from?'

'No, we didn't,' he said. 'They're so common. They've been used in the Olympics for donkey's years. They're licensed and locked away and accounted for these days, but in the past . . . and theft . . .' He shrugged. 'It isn't as if it had killed anyone.'

I said, 'What's the penalty for attempted murder?'

'Do you mean a deliberate attempt that didn't come off?'

'Mm.'

'Same as murder.'

'A 10-lb penalty?'

'Ten years,' he said.

From the police station I drove out to the ring road and stopped in the forecourt of Basil Rudd's car-repair outfit. I walked up the stairs into his glass-walled office that gave him a comprehensive view over his wide workshop below, only half busy on Saturday morning.

'Sorry,' he said, without looking up. 'We close at noon on Saturdays. Can't do anything for you till Monday.'

He was still disconcertingly like his cousin; red hair and freckles and a combative manner.

'I don't want my car fixed,' I said. 'I want to find Usher Rudd.'

It was as though I had jabbed him with a needle. He looked up, and said, 'Who are you? Why do you want him?'

I told him who and why. I asked him if he remembered the Range Rover's questionable sump-plug, but his recollection was hazy. He was quite sharply aware, though, of the political damage that could be done to a father by a son's disgrace. He had a copy of *SHOUT!* on his desk, inevitably open at the centre pages.

'That's me,' I said, pointing at the photograph of the jockey. 'Your cousin is lying. The *Gazette* sacked him for lying once before, and I'm doing my best to get him finally discredited – struck off, or whatever it's called in newspaper-speak – for what is called dishonourable conduct. So where is he?'

Basil Rudd looked helpless. 'How should I know?'

'Find out,' I said forcefully. 'You're a Rudd. Someone in the Rudd clan must know where to find its most notorious son.'

'He's brought us nothing but trouble . . .

'Find him,' I said, 'and your troubles may end.'

He stretched out a hand to the telephone, saying, 'It may take ages. And it'll cost you.'

'I'll pay your phone bills,' I said. 'When you find him, leave a message on the answer-phone at my father's headquarters. Here's the number.' I gave him a card. 'Don't waste time. It's urgent.'

I went next to the Sleeping Dragon to see the manager. He had been newly installed there at the time of the by-election, but perhaps because of that he had a satisfactorily clear recollection of the night someone had fired a gun into the cobbled square. He was much honoured, he said, to be on first-name terms with my father.

'There were so many people coming and going on that night, and I was only beginning to know who was who. Someone left a set of golf clubs in my office and said they were Dennis Nagle's but, of course, the poor man was dead and I didn't know what to do with them, but I offered them to Mrs Nagle and she said she thought they belonged to her husband's friend, Mr

Wyvern, so I gave them to him.' He frowned. 'It was so long ago. I'm afraid I'm not being much help.'

I left him and walked upstairs and from the little lounge over the main lobby looked down again onto the cobbled square where, on that first night, my father and I had by good luck not been shot.

Golf clubs . . .

Mervyn Teck, at the end of a busy morning surgery, told me where to find Leonard and Mrs Kitchens, and on Saturday afternoon, without enthusiasm, I found their substantial semi-detached house on the outskirts of the town.

The house, its lack of imagination, and the disciplined front garden were all somehow typical of a heavy worthiness: no manic sign of an arsonist.

Mrs Kitchens opened the front door at my ring and, after a moment's hesitation for recognition, said, 'My Leonard isn't in, I'm afraid.'

She took me into a front sitting-room where the air smelled as if it had been undisturbed for weeks, and talked with bitterness and freedom about 'her Leonard's' infatuation for Orinda.

'My Leonard would have done *anything* for that woman. He still would.'

'Er . . .' I said, 'looking back to that fire at the party headquarters – '

'Leonard said,' Mrs Kitchens interrupted, 'that he didn't do it.'

'But *you* think – ?'

'The silly old fool did it,' she said. 'I know he did. But I'm not going to say it to anyone except you. It was that Wyvern who put him up to it, you know. And it was all pointless, as your father is much better for the country than Orinda would have been. Everyone knows that now.'

'People say,' I said gently, 'that Leonard shot a rifle at my father and then put the gun up into the gutter of the Sleeping Dragon.'

Clumsy, large, unhappy Mrs Kitchens wouldn't hear of it. 'My Leonard doesn't know one end of a gun from the other!'

'And does your Leonard change the oil in his own car?'

She looked utterly bewildered. 'He can make plants grow, but he's hopeless at anything else.'

I left poor Mrs Kitchens to her unsatisfactory marriage, and slept again in Polly's house.

For most of Sunday I sat alone in the party's headquarters, wishing and waiting for Basil Rudd to dislike his cousin enough to help me, but it wasn't until nearly six in the evening that the telephone rang.

I picked up the receiver. A voice that was not Basil Rudd's said, 'Is it you that wants to know where to find Bobby Usher Rudd?'

'Yes, it is,' I said. 'Who are you?'

'It doesn't matter a damn who I am. Because of his snooping, my wife left me and I lost my kids. If you want to fix that bastard Usher Rudd, at this very moment he is in the offices of the *Hoopwestern Gazette*.'

The informant at the other end disconnected abruptly.

Usher Rudd was on my doorstep.

I'd expected a longer chase, but the *Hoopwestern Gazette's* offices and printing presses were simply down the road. I locked the party headquarters, jumped in my car, and sped through the Sunday traffic with the devil on my tail, anxious not to lose Usher Rudd now that I'd found him.

He was still at the *Gazette*, though, in mid-furious row with Samson Frazer. When I walked into the editor's office it silenced them both with their hot words half spoken.

They both knew who I was.

Bobby Usher Rudd looked literally struck dumb. Samson Frazer's expression mingled pleasure, apprehension and relief.

He said, 'Bobby swears the dope story's true.'

'Bobby would swear his mother's a chimpanzee.'

Usher Rudd's quivering finger pointed at a copy of Thursday's *Gazette* that lay on Samson's desk, and he found his voice, hoarse with rage.

'You know what you've done?' He was asking me, not Samson Frazer. 'You've got me sacked from *SHOUT!*. You frightened Rufus Crossmead and the proprietors so badly that they won't risk my stuff any more, and I've increased their bloody sales for them over the years . . . it's bloody *unfair*. So now they say they're the laughing stock of the whole industry, printing a false story about someone whose father might be the next Prime Minister. They say the story has backfired. They said it will *help* George Juliard, not finish him. And how was I to know? It's effing unfair.'

I said bitterly. 'You could have seen Vivian Durridge didn't know what he was saying.'

'People who don't know what they're saying are the ones you listen to.'

That confident statement, spoken in rage, popped a light bulb in my understanding of Usher Rudd's success.

I said, 'That day in Quindle, when I first met you, you were already trying to dig up scandal about my father.'

'Natch.'

'He tries to dig up dirt about anyone,' Samson put in.

I shook my head. 'Who,' I asked Usher Rudd, 'told you to attack my father?'

'I don't need to be told.'

Though I wasn't exactly shouting, my voice was loud and my accusation plain. 'As you've known all about cars for the whole of your life, did you stuff up my father's Range Rover's sump-plug drain with a candle?'

'*What?*'

'Did you? Who suggested you do it?'

'I'm not answering your bloody questions.'

The telephone rang on Samson Frazer's desk.

He picked up the receiver, listened briefly, said, 'OK,' and disconnected.

Usher Rudd, not a newspaperman for nothing, said suspiciously, 'Did you give them the OK to roll the presses?'

'Yes.'

Usher Rudd's rage increased to the point where his whole body shook. He shouted, 'You're printing without the change. I insist . . . I'll kill you . . . *stop the presses* . . . if you don't print what I told you to, I'll kill you.'

Samson Frazer didn't believe him, and nor, for all Rudd's passion, did I. Kill was a word used easily, but seldom meant.

'What change?' I demanded.

Samson's voice was high beyond normal. 'He wants me to print that you faked Sir Vivian's letter and forged his signature and that the story about sniffing glue is a hundred per cent sterling, a hundred per cent kosher, and you'll do *anything* . . . *anything* to deny it.'

He picked a typewritten page off his desk and waved it.

'It's Sunday, anyway,' he said. 'There's no one here but me and the print technicians. Tomorrow's paper is locked onto the presses, ready to roll.'

'You can do the changes yourself.' Usher Rudd fairly danced with fury.

'I'm not going to,' Samson said.

'Then don't print the paper.'

'Don't be ridiculous.'

Samson put the typewritten page into my hands.

I glanced down to read it and, as if all he'd been waiting for had been a flicker of inattention on my part, Bobby Rudd did one of his quickest getaways and was out through a door in a flash – not the door to the outside world, but the swinging door into the passage leading deeper into the building; the passage, it transpired, down to the presses.

'Stop him!' yelled Samson, aghast.

'It's only paper,' I said, though making for the door.

'No . . . sabotage . . . he can destroy . . . catch him.'

His agitation convinced me. I sprinted after Usher Rudd and ran down a passage with small empty individual offices to both sides and out through another door at the end and across an expanse inhabited only by huge white rolls of paper – newsprint, the raw material of newspapers – and through a small print-room beyond that with two or three men tending clattering machines turning out coloured pages, and finally through a last swinging door into the long high room containing the heart and muscle of the *Hoop-western Gazette*, the monster printing presses that every day turned out twenty thousand twenty-four-page community enlightenments to most of Dorset.

The presses were humming quietly when I reached them. There were eight in a row with a tower in the centre. From each end of four, the presses put first a banner in colour – red, green, blue – on the sheets that would be the front and back pages, and then came the closely edited black and white pages set onto rollers in an age-old, but still perfectly functional, offset litho process.

I learned afterwards how the machines technically worked. On that fraught Sunday I saw only wide white paper looping from press to press and in and out of inked rollers as it collected the news page by page on its journey to the central tower, from where it went up in single sheets and came down folded into a publishable newspaper, cut and counted into bundles of fifty.

There were two men tending the presses, adjusting the ink flow and slowly increasing the speed of the paper over the rollers and through the mechanism. Warning bells were ringing. Noise was building.

When I ran into the long thundering area, Usher Rudd was shouting at one of the men to turn everything off. The technician blinked at him and paid no attention.

His colleague activated another alarm bell and switched the presses to a full floor-trembling roar. Monday's edition of the *Hoopwestern Gazette*, twenty thousand copies of it, flowed from press to press and up the tower and down at a speed that reduced each separate page to a blur.

Samson Frazer, catching up with me as I watched with awe, shouted in my ear, 'Don't go near the presses while they're running. If you get your little finger caught in any of the rollers it would pull your whole arm in – it would wrench your arm right out of your body. We can't stop the presses fast enough to save an arm. Do you understand?'

'Yes,' I yelled.

Usher Rudd was screaming at the technician.

Samson Frazer's warning was essential.

There was a space of three or four feet between each machine where one was wholly exposed to the revolving accelerating rollers. When the presses were at rest, the printers – the technicians – walked with safety into these spaces to fit the master sheets onto the cylinders and to check the state of the inking rollers. When the presses, switched on, ran even at minimum inch-by-inch speed, the danger began. An arm could be torn out, not in one jerking terror but worse, in inch by excruciating inevitable inch.

I asked later why no guarding gates kept people away. The machines were old, built before safety standards sky-rocketed, Samson Frazer said, but they did indeed now have gates. It was illegal in Britain to operate without them. These gates pulled across like trellises and locked into place, but they were fiddly, and an extra job. People who worked round these presses knew and respected the danger, and sometimes didn't bother with the gates. He didn't approve, but he'd had no tragedies. There were computerised programs and printers to be had, but the old technology worked perfectly, as it had for a hundred years, and he couldn't afford to scrap the old and to install the new, which often went wrong anyway, and one couldn't guard against maniacs like Usher Rudd. No one had to insure against lunatics.

I could have sold him a policy about that: but on that particular Sunday evening, what we needed for Usher Rudd was a straitjacket, not a premium.

He was still swearing at the technician who looked over the Rudd shoulder and saw Samson Frazer's arrival as deliverance.

Stopping the presses, I learned later, meant hitting one particular button on one of the control panels to be found on the end of each press that regulated the overall speed of the printing. The buttons weren't things the size of door-bells, but scarlet three-inch-diameter flat knobs on springs. Neither the technician nor Samson Frazer pushed the overall stop control, and neither Rudd himself nor I knew which of several scarlet buttons ruled the roost. The presses went on roaring and Bobby Usher Rudd completely lost control.

He knew the terrible danger of the presses. He'd worked for the *Hoopwestern Gazette*. He'd been in and out of newspapers all his adult life.

He grabbed the technician by his overalls and swung him towards unimaginable agony.

The technician, half in and half out of one of the lethal spaces, screamed.

Samson Frazer screamed at Usher Rudd.

The second technician sprinted for refuge in the smaller print-room next door.

I, from instinct, leapt at Usher Rudd and yanked him backwards. He too started screaming. Still clutched by the overalls, the technician stumbled out of the fearsome gap, ingrained awareness keeping his hands close to his body: better to fall on the floor than try to keep his balance by touching the death-dealing machinery.

Usher Rudd let go of the overalls and re-routed his uncontrolled frenzy onto me. He was no longer primarily trying to stop the print-run, but to avenge himself for the cataclysms he had brought on himself.

The glare in his eyes was madness. I saw the intention there of pushing me instead of the technician onto the rollers and had we been alone he might have managed it. But Samson Frazer jumped to grab him while the technician, saved from mutilation, gave a horror-struck final shout as he made his terrified stumbling run for the door, and by unplanned chance barged into Usher Rudd on the way, unbalancing him.

Rudd threw Samson off him like an irrelevance, but it gave me time to put space between me and the nearest press, and although Rudd grasped and lurched in an effort to get me back again into the danger zone, I was fighting more or less for my life and it was amazing how much strength ultimate fear generated.

Samson Frazer, to his supreme credit – and maybe calculating that any death on his premises would ruin him – helped me struggle with the demented kicking and punching and clutching red-haired tornado: and it was Samson who delivered a blow to Rudd's head with a bunched fist that half-dazed his target and knocked him to the ground face downwards. I sat on his squirming back while Samson found some of the wide brown sticky tape used for parcels and with my active help, circled one of Usher Rudd's wrists, and then the other, and fastened his arms behind his back in makeshift handcuffs. Samson tethered the wildly kicking legs in the same way and we rolled Rudd onto his back and stood over him panting.

Then with each of us looping an arm under Rudd's armpits we dragged him into the comparative quiet of the secondary print-room next door and propped him in a chair.

All of the technicians were in that room, wide-eyed and upset. Samson told them unemotionally to go back to work, there was a paper to be got out; and slowly, hesitantly, they obeyed him.

In his chair, Rudd began shouting, 'It's all his fault. Wyvern did it. Wyvern's the one you want, not me.'

'I don't believe it,' I contradicted, though I did.

Usher Rudd tried to convince me. 'Wyvern wanted your father out of the way. He wanted Orinda in Parliament. He wanted to get her promoted, like Dennis. He would have done anything to stop your father being elected.'

'Like sabotaging his car?'

'I didn't want to do it. I would write what he wanted. I trailed Paul Bethune for weeks to find his bimbo, to please Wyvern, so that people would vote for Orinda, but messing up a Range Rover, cutting the brake-lines like Wyvern wanted, that was too much. I didn't do it.'

'Yes, you did,' I told him conclusively.

'No, I didn't.'

'What did you do then?'

'I didn't do anything.'

'Your cousin, Basil, knows what you did.'

Usher Rudd cursed Basil with words I'd hardly ever heard even on a racecourse, and somewhere in the tirade came a description of how he'd wriggled under the Range Rover in the black tracksuit he'd worn to the meeting after the dinner in the Sleeping Dragon. The brilliant performance my father had given that evening had convinced Wyvern that he wouldn't get rid of my father without at least injuring him badly. Wyvern had been furious with Usher Rudd that his sabotage had been so useless.

Usher Rudd's rage slowly ran down and he began

first to whine and then deny that he had ever said what Samson and I had both just heard.

Samson phoned the police. Joe Duke was not on duty, but Samson knew all the force individually and put down the receiver, reporting a promise of immediate action.

Usher Rudd shouted, 'I want a lawyer.'

He got his lawyer, passed a night in the cells and on Monday morning collected a slap on the wrist from busy magistrates (for causing a disturbance indoors at the *Hoopwestern Gazette*) who had no real conception of the speed and noise and danger involved.

No actual damage had been done. The newspaper had appeared as usual. Usher Rudd, meek and respectful, walked out free.

I talked to Joe Duke.

I said, 'It was Usher Rudd who stuffed wax in the sump-drain of the Range Rover, and Leonard Kitchens who started the fire. Both of them were put up to it by Alderney Wyvern.'

Joe Duke slowly nodded. 'But they didn't stop your father, did they? And as for you' – he gave a half smile – 'I'll never forget you that night of the fire, sitting there half-naked on the cobbles with that red blanket over your shoulders and no sign of pain, though you'd burns on your hands and feet and you'd smashed down into the square. Don't you ever feel pain?'

'Of course, but there was so much happening – '

'And you're used to falling off horses?'

'Horses fall . . . Anyway, I suppose so. I've hit the ground quite a lot.'

The smile broadened. 'Then why do it?'

'Speed,' I told him. 'Nothing like it.' I paused. 'If you want something badly enough, you can risk your life for it and consider it normal behaviour.'

He pondered. 'If you want Orinda Nagle to be an MP enough, you'll risk . . .'

'Almost anything. I think it was Wyvern who shot at my father.'

'I'm not saying you're wrong. He could have carried a rifle in his golf bag, with one of those covers on it that they use for clubs.'

'Yes.'

'And he'd had to have had murder in his mind to do that.'

'Uh-huh. And when he heard and saw my father's success at that meeting, he judged he needed to get rid of him at once.'

'He was crazy.'

'He still is.'

Joe Duke knew my father was engaged in a power struggle but was dismayed when I explained about Hudson Hurst.

'You don't think,' Joe said, horrified, 'that Wyvern would try *again* to kill your father?'

'Wyvern's stakes are higher now, and my father still stands in his way. If my father is chosen to lead his party, I'm sure he'll be in appalling danger. It frightens me badly, to be honest.'

Joe said thoughtfully, 'You know what ...?'

'What?'

'Just in case we're doing Wyvern a great injustice, thinking it was he that shot at you ... I mean, so far we've only got theory to go on, really. Why don't you and I do an unofficial walk-through ... a reconstruction? I'll use a walking stick for a gun. I'll transport it in a golf bag. And I'll carry it up into the little lounge, and aim it at you while you're crossing the square, like you did that night, and I'll see how difficult it will be to put the walking stick up in the gutter. What do you think?'

'Can't do any harm.'

'We might come across something we haven't thought of. It often works that way with reconstructions.'

'OK.'

'We'll have to do it at night,' Joe said.

'It was after midnight.'

'After midnight, then. I'll be off duty. It will just be the two of us.'

I agreed that we would meet that evening in the

Sleeping Dragon, and that Joe would tell the manager what we were doing.

I went to see Orinda who had finally returned from her weekend and answered the telephone.

Five years had been kind to her. She looked as striking as ever, the green eyes black-lashed, the greasepaint make-up smooth and blended. She was less brittle, less stressed, more fulfilled.

She called me darling with only two or three 'a's. 'Daaarling.'

'Orinda.' I hugged her.

'How you've grown,' she exclaimed. 'I mean, not just upwards, but older.'

She had made us a salad lunch with diet Coke and coffee after.

She knew about the power struggle going on in the party and mentioned that every time there was this sort of leadership contest, the politicians changed the rules.

'They invent whatever procedure they think will give a result that everyone thinks is fair, even if not everyone is happy with the eventual winner. It's now all up to the party's MPs.'

I had forgotten how much Orinda knew about government.

'I suppose Dennis told you how it all works.'

'No, it was Alderney Wyvern.' She frowned. 'I never want to see that man again.'

I said neutrally, 'Did you know that Wyvern now controls Hudson Hurst, like he used to control you and Dennis? Do you realise that if Hurst wins the ballot and becomes Prime Minister, it will be Alderney Wyvern who effectively governs this country?'

Orinda looked horrified but shook her head. 'Your father's more popular in the country.'

'Don't forget *Schadenfreude*.'

Orinda laughed. 'You mean the malicious enjoyment of someone else's misfortune?'

I nodded. 'Half the Cabinet would like to see my father come a cropper after his spectacular way of fighting the fish war.'

'It will be marvellous for this constituency if he wins.' She smiled widely. 'I never thought I would say that, but it's true.'

I told Orinda about the reconstruction that Joe Duke and I had planned.

I asked, 'Do you remember much about that evening?'

'Of course I do. I was *furious* at not being chosen as candidate.'

'How much were you with Alderney Wyvern after the political meeting?'

'I wasn't. I was angry and miserable and drove straight home.'

'Do you know if Alderney Wyvern had his golf clubs with him at the meeting in the hall?'

'What an extraordinary question! He always used to have them in the back of the car.'

Orinda might have hated my father that night, but not enough to do him harm. She had no wickedness in her nature.

I spent a comfortable hour or two longer with her and then drove to Polly's house to wait for my father to telephone from London with the result of the ballot.

He gave me news from his car. 'It was all indecisive,' he reported. 'It was basically a three-way split. All that's certain is that we have to vote again tomorrow.'

'Do explain,' I begged him.

He described a day that had been full of doubt and manoeuvring, but it seemed that what had finally happened was that neither my father nor Hudson Hurst had received enough votes in the first round to secure victory outright. Jill Vinicheck (Education), the third candidate, had received fewest votes and had been eliminated. The next ballot would be a straight fight between Hurst and Juliard, and no one was predicting who would win.

My father sounded tired. He said he and Polly were on their way to join me at the house for a quiet night. He had done all he could behind the scenes to sway the vote his way: now it was up to his colleagues to choose whom they wanted.

I explained about Joe Duke and the reconstruction and, after a brief discussion with Polly by his side, he said they would meet me in the Sleeping Dragon and we would eat together.

Any thought that we might have had about a peaceful evening disappeared between the soup and the apple pie.

While neither Joe Duke nor I had made any particular secret about our plan for the reconstruction, we had not expected the manager of the hotel to broadcast the scenario. He appeared to have told the whole town. The hotel was buzzing, as it had on the night of the dinner, and people came up to my father in droves to shake his hand and wish him well.

Samson Frazer came from the *Hoopwestern Gazette* with his cameraman and gave my horrified father extra details of how Usher Rudd had spent his Sunday.

Usher Rudd himself came – free, unrepentant, bitter-eyed and steaming with malice, glaring at my father and talking into a mobile phone.

When Joe Duke came, he looked at first aghast at the bustle and movement, but my father resignedly told him, as he joined us for coffee, that the hotel had been packed on the night we were reproducing, and the present crowd would make everything seem more real.

Moreover, my father said he would walk with me across the square as he had done before, and although I didn't like the idea, Joe Duke nodded enthusiastically.

Why wait for midnight? people asked. Everyone was ready *now*, and now was eleven-thirty.

Because Joe explained, half of the lights in the square switched off automatically at twelve o'clock, and if the reconstruction was to mean anything, the conditions had to be as near as possible what they had been before.

Joe Duke brought in a bag of golf clubs from his car and showed everyone the long walking stick with the tartan cover that disguised it.

The manager frowned in puzzlement, and I wanted to ask him if he had remembered something significant, but Joe and the crowd swept all before them, anxious to get started. I would ask him later, I thought.

Midnight came. Half the lights in the square faded to darkness. All that were left glowing threw shadows on the cobbles. Over the far side of the square a few lights showed dimly in the party headquarters and the charity shop.

When my father and I walked out into the square, the only lights blazing brightly were those of the Sleeping Dragon at our back.

It was planned that my father and I would walk halfway across the square and wait while Joe aimed his walking stick out of the window and BANG, and then reached or climbed up to put the stick in the gutter. People would hurry from the Sleeping Dragon towards my father, as they had done before.

It all felt alarmingly real to me, but everyone was smiling.

Joe, surrounded by encouraging crowds, turned to go towards the staircase while I and my father walked out across the cobbles. I stopped after a while to look back at the hotel but my father walked on, calling over his shoulder, 'Come on, Ben, we haven't reached the spot yet.'

I looked up at the hotel. Joe's walking stick was pointing out of one of the windows, half hidden by the seemingly perpetual geraniums.

Three thoughts jammed into my consciousness simultaneously.

First, Joe hadn't had time to get up the stairs and walk along to the lounge and hide behind the curtain.

Second, the stick was pointing out of the wrong window.

Third, there was a gleam on the stick and a hole, a black round hole, in the end of it.

It wasn't a stick. It was a gun.

My father was ten yards ahead of me across the square. I sprinted as I had for Orinda and for the technician in the presses, without pause, without thought, with raw intuition, and I jumped in a flying rugger tackle to knock my father down.

The bang was real enough. The bullet was real enough, but the happy crowd which poured out of the hotel still thought it was a game.

The bullet hit me while I was still in the air, jumping

and colliding with my father, and it would have gone into his back if I hadn't been there.

It entered high on my right thigh and travelled down inside my leg to the knee, the kinetic energy bursting apart all muscles and soft tissue in its path.

The force of it whirled me round so that when I crashed to the cobbles I was facing the Sleeping Dragon; half lying, propped on my left elbow, shuddering throughout all my body with my brain disoriented and protesting with universal outrage.

There was enough pain everywhere to satisfy Joe Duke. My eyes watered with it and my skin sweated. I'd been injured now and then in racing falls, and I'd felt shivery and sore the night of the fire, but nothing had even begun to warn me that there was an unimaginable dimension far beyond cuts and breaks.

It didn't really help that I knew the physics of high-velocity bullets and the damage they could do. I'd fired hundreds of them at targets. I shot in a world where all one hit was paper. I didn't know that I'd ever be able to fire a rifle again.

My father was on his knees beside me, his face screwed up with anxiety. My right trouser leg was dark and saturated with blood. The crowd from the Sleeping Dragon were running now, with Polly at their head. I could hear her agonised voice, 'George ... oh, George.'

It was all right, I thought. It wasn't George.

My father held my hand.

Besides the encompassing pain I felt remarkably ill. I wanted to lie down, to stand up, to move somehow, and I couldn't. I wanted someone to come along and shoot me again, but in the head; to give me oblivion, like they did with horses.

Time passed. Nothing got better.

Although ordinary traffic was banned from the square, police cars, ambulances and fire engines weren't. Two police cars and one ambulance arrived, roof lights flashing. People from the police cars went into the hotel. Someone from the ambulance came and, with large scissors, cut open my right trouser leg.

I went on wishing for oblivion.

My leg, exposed to the dim light in the square, looked literally a bloody mess. I gathered that the bullet hadn't severed the femoral artery, because if it had I would have already bled to death. There was, however, somewhere in my mangled muscles, a hard white finger-shaped length of what I understood with shock to be bone. Femur. Uncovered, but also unbroken.

The man from the ambulance hid the devastation with a large padded dressing and went back to the ambulance. He'd gone to summon a doctor, my father said: there were all sorts of rules and regulations about gun-shot wounds.

It didn't cross my mind that I might lose my leg and, in fact, I didn't. What I lost, once everything was stitched and repaired, was the strength to ride half-ton steeplechasers over the black birch. What I lost was speed.

People came out of the hotel and got into the police cars. One of them was Alderney Wyvern, in handcuffs.

When the cars had driven away, Joe Duke walked across the square and sat on his heels to talk to my father and me.

He said to me, 'Can you take in what I'm saying?'

'Yes.'

Joe said, 'When I went up the stairs to position the walking stick, the hotel manager hurried up after me and caught me before I reached the little lounge. He said he didn't know if it was just a coincidence, but not long before, in fact at about eleven o'clock, a man had booked in as a guest at the hotel and he too was carrying a bag of golf clubs. And what was slightly odd about him, the manager said, was that he was wearing *gloves*.'

Joe stood up to stretch his legs for a moment, and then sat back on his heels. 'Are you taking in what I'm saying?' he said.

'Yes,' I groggily replied.

'We heard that cracking bang of the gun going off and the manager used his pass-key to open a bedroom door, and inside we found Alderney Wyvern coming towards the door carrying his bag of golf clubs, but when the manager snatched it from him and emptied them out onto the floor, all that was in it was golf clubs.'

Joe went on, 'He hadn't time to put the rifle up in the gutter, but it was there with him all right. He'd put the gun-butt in the hanging basket with the geraniums, with the barrel pointing skywards, among the chains hanging the basket. I then used the room telephone to bring my colleagues from the police station. While we waited for them to arrive I asked, out of curiosity, how Wyvern had known about the reconstruction. How had he known that he would have a chance to shoot George Juliard?'

Joe smiled lopsidedly. 'Wyvern said Usher Rudd had phoned him and told him.' He stood up again.

My father said, 'How did Wyvern think he would get away with it?'

Joe shrugged. 'He did last time. In the commotion, he simply walked away. If it hadn't been for the hotel manager, he quite likely would have done it again. But it was odd. He seemed just plain tired. There was no fight left in him. He could see he hadn't managed to finish either of you, and he simply gave up. We had no trouble arresting him.'

'And what are you charging him with?' my father asked.

'Attempted murder,' Joe said.

I faintly smiled. 'A 10-lb penalty.'

'Ten years,' Joe said.

*

307

The next Prime Minister held my hand.

I gripped his tight, as if he would give me comfort and security when I needed them badly.

I gripped his hand as if I'd been a little boy.

He just wanted a decent book to read …

Not too much to ask, is it? It was in 1935 when Allen Lane, Managing Director of Bodley Head Publishers, stood on a platform at Exeter railway station looking for something good to read on his journey back to London. His choice was limited to popular magazines and poor-quality paperbacks – the same choice faced every day by the vast majority of readers, few of whom could afford hardbacks. Lane's disappointment and subsequent anger at the range of books generally available led him to found a company – and change the world.

'We believed in the existence in this country of a vast reading public for intelligent books at a low price, and staked everything on it'
Sir Allen Lane, 1902–1970, founder of Penguin Books

The quality paperback had arrived – and not just in bookshops. Lane was adamant that his Penguins should appear in chain stores and tobacconists, and should cost no more than a packet of cigarettes.

Reading habits (and cigarette prices) have changed since 1935, but Penguin still believes in publishing the best books for everybody to enjoy. We still believe that good design costs no more than bad design, and we still believe that quality books published passionately and responsibly make the world a better place.

So wherever you see the little bird – whether it's on a piece of prize-winning literary fiction or a celebrity autobiography, political tour de force or historical masterpiece, a serial-killer thriller, reference book, world classic or a piece of pure escapism – you can bet that it represents the very best that the genre has to offer.

Whatever you like to read – trust Penguin.

read more
www.penguin.co.uk